MW00834712

GIFTED GIRLS SERIES-BOOK ONE

Magical Miri

USA TODAY BESTSELLING AUTHOR

DEBRA KRISTI

Magical Miri (The Gifted Girl Series, Book One)

Copyright © 2020 by Debra Kristi

All rights reserved. Published by Ghost Girl Publishing, LLC.
www.GhostGirlPublishing.com

This is a work of fiction. Names, places, characters, and incidents are either the product of the author's imagination or used fictitiously, and any resemblance to any actual persons, living or dead, organizations, events or locales is entirely coincidental.

Warning: the unauthorized reproduction or distribution of this copyrighted work is illegal. Criminal copyright infringement, including infringement without monetary gain, is investigated by the FBI and is punishable by up to 5 years in prison and a fine of $250,000.

Library of Congress Control Number: 2019921063

Paperback ISBN: 978-1-942191-27-8 / eBook ISBN: 978-1-942191-26-1

Cover design by Fantasy Book Design

Professional editing by Eden Plantz

Magical Miri, 1st ed.

Visit the author: http://www.debrakristi.com/

❀ Created with Vellum

OTHER WORKS BY DEBRA KRISTI:

THE BALANCE BRINGER CHRONICLES
Becoming: The Balance Bringer
Awakening: The Balance Bringer
Empowering: The Balance Bringer
The First Balance Bringer

MOORIGAD DRAGON COLLECTION
Moorigad, Parts One–Three

CURSED ANGEL COLLECTION
Blood Promise: Watchtower 7

THE GIFTED GIRL SERIES
Magical Miri: Gifted Girls Book One
Bewitching Belle: Gifted Girls Book Two
Nowhere Nara: Gifted Girls Book Three
Clever Chloe: Gifted Girls Book Four
Fatal Freya: Gifted Girls Book Five

For Leandra;
Without your extraordinary experiences, Miri's adventures
would not have been nearly as intriguing.

"Be Patient. Like storms, the challenges will pass. Know too, that like the sun, your true soul self is constantly radiating."

—**John Morton**

PREFACE

When I originally dove into the world of the gifted girls, I started with what is now book three in the series. When that story was complete, I realized it wasn't the proper start of the family's journey. Hence, the book Magical Miri developed.

Many of Miri's encounters, as she progresses through her development, were inspired by actual events experienced by someone in my circle of familiarity. Take from that what you will, but whether you believe or not, enjoy Miri's journey.

$\sim$ *Blessed Be* $\sim$

I invite you to visit *The Gifted Girls Series* on Facebook, where they share witchy humor, spell tips, and more.
https://www.facebook.com/GiftedGirlsBookSeries/
Once a month, from January through October 2020, we'll be hosting witchy giveaways!

INTRODUCTION

By Miri

We're halfway through the 1990's, and the grunge look is all the rage. Personally, I love my loose sweaters, T-shirts, and spandex pants, but when I leave the house, I usually opt for jeans. Holy jeans, to be precise. Most everyone I know owns a pager, but not me.

The best jams to get me dancing are performed by Salt-N-Pepa and Janet Jackson. My favorite movie this year has been *Pulp Fiction*, and for my regular viewing pleasure, *The Fresh Prince of Bel-Air* has been replaced by *Friends*.

OJ Simpson has been acquitted of murder, and locally, the crime rate is at an all-time high. The paper reports a homicide rate of something over 410, and the mayor issued a strict curfew for kids my age and younger. Not that it affects me much. I don't tend to be out late.

Anyway, reports say the crime is mostly acquaintance crime—people killing people they know. I've heard it's primarily drug related, but my grandma insists that's a convenient cover and a fair amount of the crimes, i.e. deaths, are related to the magical community. The community our family isn't allowed to associate with and the community my mom actually insists doesn't exist.

Mom and Grandma rarely agree on anything.

CHAPTER ONE

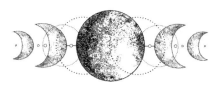

This is my hour of darkness, history homework with a growling stomach. I never cared much for the subject, and remembering all the facts... torture. Why fuss over past events when it is clearly now we should be focused on and doing something about. My opinion on history: what's done is done. Let's move on.

I toss open my book and turn to page 124. Read the first question in the review box.

Crap.

I haven't a clue as to the answer. I bite my lip and twist my dark, spiraled hair around my finger.

"Hey, Miri. When you finish that, would you be willing to do mine?" My sister, Belle, is spread out across the top bunk, flipping through a glamour magazine. Her kinky hair is pulled into twin puffs at the nape of her neck.

We have the lucky pleasure of sharing a room. The situation is rather ironic when you consider the size of the house. It's somewhat huge... and it's Grandma's. My mom, sister, brother, and I all live with Grandma and have helped watch over her ever since Grandpa died. My dad vanished from the picture before my sister was born. Maybe three kids was too much to handle. *Whatever*. We all have each other, and our situation works.

"Definitely not. I don't even want to do mine." I was supposed to finish the assignment over Thanksgiving break, and look at me now... only just starting. I have one day to start and finish. I push the pencil into the paper, and the lead breaks. "Unfortunately, I have to get this done, or my grade will suffer a slow, decaying death."

"Yeah, right." Belle rolls into a sit, drops the magazine in her lap. "You're a solid C student."

The white wood desk at which I work sits at the front of the room, before a rounded wall of windows. The bunk bed is pushed against the wall to my left, placing Belle at the edge of my peripheral vision. I twist in my chair to better see her. "How would you know?"

She shrugs. "I pay attention to *things*."

My head jerks back, and my nose wrinkles, pulling at the edge of my upper lip. "Remind me why you're still in my room?"

The room is tight for one person, much less two people having to share. Old-school style, with a nonoperational fireplace on one wall and a tiny built-in cabinet closet. Attached to our shared bedroom is a small, windowless dressing room used back in the days when women wore large hoop skirts, bustles, and corsets. It's also accessible to the bedroom on the opposite side, but that door is always locked. The dressing room now serves as a closet for me and Belle.

"Very funny." Belle's head wobbles in exaggeration. "You know all too well that Grandma has yet to come through on her promise of clearing out that stuffy, old room on the other side of the closet."

"Right." I turn back toward my awaiting misery, history homework. The rising aroma of Grandma's post-Thanksgiving gumbo makes it that much harder to focus. My stomach complains, and I suck it in tight against my belly button.

On the first floor below us, the front door slams.

"Mom's home," Belle chimes and lies back out across the upper bed.

My muscles tighten, and my stomach churns. I read the first question of my homework again, perusing the chapter in search of the answer.

"Edith?" Grandma calls from the kitchen.

"Yeah, Mom. It's me." The thumps and scuffles of bags being set down and outerwear being shed follow my mom through the first floor, her not-so-quiet footfalls taking her toward the kitchen and Grandma.

The tenor of their voices is soft and calming. The discussion of dinner and edible delights. Memories created over Thanksgiving, only a few days ago. Happy memories lead to dialogue regarding Caleb, the man mom's been seeing. Seeing *a lot* over the last year.

"He makes me happy." Mom's voice rises so that I am able to hear her clearly.

My gaze flickers from my homework to the window and the world beyond, but my attention is glued to what is unfolding on the floor below.

"If I recall, there have been a few men over the years that have managed to make you happy... temporarily." Grandma's response rises in volume to meet Mom's prompt. "Any one of them would have been better suited than this one." The sound of a pot shifting on the range marks a break in her delivery. "All attempted replacements for Isaac, I suppose."

Something slams. My mother's palm against the counter, maybe?

"You need to think of the kids," Grandma adds.

"I am thinking of the kids," Mom shouts. "They need a father."

Belle and I exchange a look of concern. I have picked up on tension between Mom and Grandma ever since Caleb came into the picture, but never before have their discussions escalated in this manner.

I heave a heavy breath and glance from Belle to the pathetic start of my homework. *I totally don't need this today. I need to focus. Need to get my work done.*

Another crash from the kitchen and an exasperated groan from Mom.

"Don't cling to a man simply for the sake of pulling a father figure into the children's lives," Grandma lectures.

I close my book, pull all my homework needs into the cradle of my arms, move away from the desk, and head toward the door.

"Where are you going?" Belle asks.

"I can't concentrate with all this noise." My gaze lifts to the ceiling, as if I could see through the wood to my brother Michael's room on the third floor. "Maybe I can find some quiet in Mike's room. He's not home. He shouldn't mind."

Belle sits upright, and her untouched magazine whirls to an unassisted close. I move, slow and silent, across the room and open the door, step out into the hall. Belle slips quietly from the bed and pushes at my back. I step into the hallway, glance back at her.

"What are you doing?" I whisper, not wanting to be overheard by Mom and Grandma. The last thing I want is to get pulled into their tension.

"I'm coming." She nods toward the staircase to the upper level.

"I was going to wait until after Christmas," Mom says, her

voice carrying easily up the stairs. "But I just don't think I can continue to deal with this, especially through the holiday season."

"What are you talking about?" Grandma says.

My hand reaches out, grabs, and squeezes the railing running the length of the hallway.

"The kids and I are moving out." Mom's statement seeps with finality.

Belle and I freeze. Our breaths held and our feet unmoving. The conflict in the kitchen has also fallen silent. It's as if the entire house has become stuck in time. My gaze blinks to the open stairwell and the space below. The air is thick with Mom and Grandma's emotions. I can almost taste the fear, furor, and frustration.

"What?" Grandma stammers. "Where will you go?"

"We're moving in with Caleb. He can finally start being a proper father to the kids. He's been wanting this for a long time, and so have I." Mom pauses, but nothing in the house steps up to fill the void, so she continues. "Caleb's got a real nice place in the Quarter, near where he works. The change will be good for all of us, you included."

The Quarter? Seriously? Live near the club Caleb manages? My grip upon the railing tightens. That's so far from our school. *What about my friends?*

"We can't leave Grandma." Belle throws her palm over her mouth and stares at me with eyes as wide as the full moon.

Downstairs, the loud thump of Grandma's cane slams to the ground. "You can't live there. You need to be here. The children won't be protected in the Quarter. The others won't accept them. Won't accept their magic." The tension in her voice has me envisioning her stiff body trembling, her frosted curls shaking.

"The others," Mom scoffs. "Queen *Witchywoo* doesn't care

5

for voodoo and hoodoo?" she teases. "We are not a threat to anyone, Mother. Stop with your grandiose fairytales already. The kids have shown no sign of the family magic. Honestly, Mother. You've done nothing but feed us lies their entire lives. There is no magic here."

"You don't believe that. You can't believe that?" Grandma's voice is soft, and I strain to hear her.

"Oh, but I do. I really, really do," Mom says. "And I'm sorry to spring this on you at the holidays, but the kids and I are leaving tonight."

Tonight? No! I shake my head. *No no no no no no.*

"But, Edith..." Grandma stammers. "The crime. The homicide rate. The curfew. It's not safe in the Quarter."

"You know very well that the majority of those crimes are taking place in the impoverished wards, not the tourist-filled French Quarter." Mom starts climbing the stairs, her heels slamming hard against the wood floor.

With a sweeping search of the landing, I take in all our escape options. The bathroom at our right, Mom and Grandma's bedrooms across the hallway, or the stairs to the third floor at our left. No time for any of them. I push Belle back, and we quickly tiptoe toward the bedroom. As quietly as possible, I close the door and step deeper into the room. Mom's footfalls reach the landing and cross the hall. A second later, the door flies open.

"Pack your things." Mom hooks her hands on her hips. Her face is stone, but the earrings dangling in wild fashion are distracting.

Neither Belle nor I move. We stand in silence, staring at her. She's still wearing her work uniform from the casino, complete with name tag pinned to her chest. The short, shaggy layers of her hair are a bit askew and messy.

"I know you heard most, if not all, of what was said, so don't act surprised."

"But. But why, Mom?" I shake my head. "Our school is here. Our friends are here."

Mom's face softens, and she steps forward, places her hand upon my shoulder. "You're both incredibly strong individuals. You'll adjust at a new school."

I have to change schools? My hands ball into bleached-knuckled fists. "But," I whimper. "I'm horrible at making new friends." I realize my school is in the opposite direction of the Quarter, but it's a charter school. I could make it work... somehow.

"You'll do fine," Mom responds with a half-smile, then glances past me to Belle. "So will you, Mirabelle. You're my daughters, and you'll both be great. Now, get packing."

Mom turns to leave the room. Pauses in the doorway and glances back. "Just the essentials. Caleb and I will come back later for the rest."

Grandma moves into view in the hallway beyond.

"Who will care for Grandma?" Belle blurts.

"Tsk, tsk," Mom replies without sparing us a glance. She sweeps past Grandma and disappears into her bedroom at the other end of the hall.

The death of noise swallows the room. No one speaks or makes a sound. I glance from Belle's wide-eyed expression to Grandma's fallen face.

"Wish Michael was here," Belle whispers at my back. "Maybe he could change Mom's mind."

"Mike hates Caleb." My shoulders slump, and my gaze drops to the worn wood floor.

"Maybe Michael will find housing at the college." Grandma sighs and turns from the room.

7

"No," I rebut. I don't want Mike to leave us. Leave me. Not now, when I'm going to be moving into a strange, new place.

"Trust your magic," Grandma says and gimps down the hall.

What magic? I know of no magic.

The sound of a car pulling to a stop slips through the open window. Belle rushes over, edges between the desk and the glass, and pulls back the flimsy, white curtains.

"It's Caleb," she says.

I rush to her side and gaze out the window to the street below. Caleb's beat-up beige vehicle sits against the curb. He gets out of the car, rubs his bald head, and peers up at us. Tilts his sunglasses clear of his gaze. Jabs a pointed finger in our direction. His pale beige plaid shirt sort of matches his car, and he has the top three buttons undone, showing off the gold Benjamin Franklin hundred dollar bill pendant he always wears.

"How did he get here so fast?" I murmur.

"Come on, girls. Let's go home." He beckons us down with a wide-armed swing.

No way. I slam the window shut and pull the curtains closed. I move to the center of the room, stare at my sister, cross my arms. "I'm not going."

CHAPTER TWO

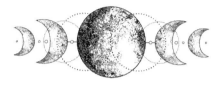

I'm going.

I'm sitting beside my sister in the backseat of Caleb's beat-up beige vehicle, and we're driving to his... our... new home, as a new family. At least, that's what Mom and Caleb say we are doing. Any possessions needed for the next week are either jammed in an old maroon suitcase or stuffed haphazardly into a box, both of which have been packed in the trunk.

Mom promised we would go back to Grandma's for the rest of our stuff later.

I stare out the window, press the tips of my fingers to the glass, and watch the houses of the Garden District fall away, get replaced by the crowded living of the Quarter.

I'm happy for Mom. Happy that she's found some sort of joy. And I don't mind Caleb. Mostly. He's never been unkind to me. It's leaving Grandma... or maybe it's more about *how* we left Grandma... that has my skin burning. That, and leaving what few friends I have, changing schools, settling into a louder, more crowded area, farther away from people I know. Feel comfortable talking to.

The ride is short, and I am quiet the entire time. I can't stop thinking about Grandma, my friends, and Michael. He's not going to be happy with this. He doesn't care much for Caleb, though I'm not sure why. Maybe it's a loyalty thing to a father who left us eons ago.

Even though we drive down streets at the back end of the French Quarter, a fair number of tourists still dot the scenery, punctuating the neighborhood streets with their distinctly not-from-around-here vibe. More so, I think, than they do the Garden District. But we have always lived across a busy street separating us from the main Garden District tourists' walks, so I've never felt on display the way I fear I will feel here.

Caleb pulls to a stop in front of a large building lined with double doors... or single car garage doors that open like double doors. They all have door handles and locks as you would expect any front door to have, but I doubt that was their original intended use. In fact, I suspect all the tiny garages predate modern vehicles and were originally built to hold carriages.

"Hold on." Caleb jumps out of the car. He unlocks and pushes the garage door open like a pair of double doors, exposing a wide-open space, then returns to the car and pulls in. The space is tight; it's a good thing Caleb's car isn't that big.

Inside the new space, there are two doors into the house. One in front of the car and another to the side. Both are only accessed from inside the garage. I didn't notice any doors on the outside of the building, and I wonder if the garage is the only way in or out, but I don't ask. For now, I want to remain quiet, stewing in my cauldron of emotions.

Caleb kills the engine and turns toward the back, draping his arm over the seat. The gold watch on his wrist gleams, as if it is scrubbed to a shine every hour. "Welcome home, girls. I think you're going to like it here."

My lips pucker to the side.

"Come on," Mom says, stepping free of the car. "Let's go see your new bedrooms." She bends over and beams a bright smile at us through the window, then heads to the door at the side of the car.

"Did she say bedrooms? As in plural?" Belle gazes wide-eyed at me.

She did, I realize with a start. "Let's go find out." I step casually from the car, not wanting to seem too eager, even though I've been dreaming of having my own room for years.

Belle hurries after Mom, dashing through the door and up the stairs. Caleb extends his arm, motioning for me to follow her.

"I'll be along in a moment. I'm just going to collect your things and bring them up to your room." He opens the trunk, pulls Mom's suitcases out and sets them to the side.

I glance out the open double doors to the street beyond. A couple of touristy-looking people, and one not so touristy-looking, walk by, staring into the open space of Caleb's garage. I turn and sprint through the open door to the house and up the stairs. The climb dumps me on the main landing with the kitchen in front of me, the living area to the left of me, and a closed door to the right of me. Belle and my mom are nowhere in sight.

"Hello," I call out, taking in the décor. The wood in the kitchen is dated, but the appliances are new, and the furniture in the living area is well used. Between the kitchen and the living space sits a tall shelf with an odd collection of curiosities. I spy a balcony at the far end of the space and can't imagine finding the desire to hang out there with nothing more than cement and tourists as a view.

Hope I can get used to living here.

"Up here! Up here!" Belle's voice sings down the stairs. Mom's laughter follows.

I zip around the landing and climb the next flight of stairs to the third floor. I'm deposited on a small landing with a bathroom in front of me and a bedroom on either side.

"Over here," Belle calls from my left.

I follow her voice to the bedroom at the back of the house. One bed sits in the center of the room. One bed, for one sister. I glance back across the landing to the other room. Another bedroom, much like the one I'm now standing in. Each room is larger than the room Belle and I shared at Grandma's, plus we each get our own. I take in the room, noting the attached bathroom. We also get our own bathroom, sort of. I peek through the doorway. There are two separate toilet and sink areas, with one shared shower space between them.

I can deal with that.

"What do you think?" Mom asks, excitement lighting her eyes.

I bite my lip and turn toward her. Neither Belle nor I speak. I can't shake my concern for Grandma or my worry about Michael. I suspect Belle feels the same.

"Whose stuff should I put where?" Caleb calls from the landing. He's standing at the top of the stairs with two suitcases in hand.

"You want this room?" I ask Belle.

"Sure." She smiles, shrugging her head into her shoulders.

"Got it." Caleb drops a brown suitcase inside the doorway and carries my maroon case across the landing to the other bedroom. "I'll be back with the boxes in a moment." He disappears down the stairs.

"I'll let you girls get settled." Mom hugs us both, in turn, and then follows Caleb from the room. Stops short of the stairs, turns back. "This is going to be a positive change for us. It's time we make our lives our own, on our own, without your grandmother's constant watch and generosity." Mom spins and disappears down the stairs.

Belle and I exchange a wordless stare. Her lips spread into a tight smile, then she retrieves the suitcase from beside the door, drops it on the bed, and pops it open. I take that as my cue, and head across the landing to what will be my room. One bed, two nightstands, one dresser, two short closets, and one small cabinet beneath the only window lighting the place. The window is set high and center. On either side of the window, the roofline cuts across the room at an angle.

I climb onto the cabinet and look out the window. Across the street is a rust-colored building with slender green doors. Standing in front of the building, gazing up at me, is a pale girl with stringy red hair, dressed in all black. She was walking by when I was in the garage.

Weirdo.

Jerking away, I jump off the cabinet and attend to unpacking my stuff.

I shove clothing in drawers without thought, my brain now obsessed with the sight of the girl staring up at me from the street. It was like she was waiting for me. But... who is she and what does she want?

With toiletries bag in hand, I head to the bathroom. The doors between the segmented spaces are open, so I have a view through the shower room, right into Belle's sink area. She has pulled drawers open and is thoughtfully placing makeup, hair combs, and dental needs in different places.

I dump everything in one drawer and slam it shut. Turn and press my weight against the counter.

"This is nice, isn't it?" Belle says. "Having our own area to wash our faces, brush our teeth, and do our makeup."

"Yeah," I concede. "But why do you think Grandma was so worried about us living in the Quarter?"

Belle shrugs.

"She said we wouldn't be safe. That the locals wouldn't accept us."

"I don't know." Belle sets her last item in place and closes the top drawer. "No one is telling me any more than they are telling you."

"There's a girl standing out in the street staring up at my window. I mean, we haven't even been here fifteen minutes, and already the creep factor is slithering in." I cross my arms.

"A creepy stalker? Where?" Belle marches straight into my room. She climbs onto the cabinet and looks out the window. "I don't see anyone."

"Let me see." I climb up beside her, nudging her to the side in order to get a decent view. Belle's right; the girl is gone.

My lips press into a frown.

"I'd rather you girls not do that. The cabinet could tip, and you could get hurt."

We both jolt, spin around. The cabinet wobbles.

"Case in point," Caleb adds with a gesture to the furniture beneath our feet.

"Sorry," we chime in unison and jump to the floor.

He sets a box on the bed. "That's the last of it... for now." He turns his attention to Belle. "I already put your stuff in the other room. "I'm really glad you girls are here." He smiles wide. Neither Belle nor I respond. "Okay, well..." He scratches his bearded jaw. "Have at it." He turns to leave, then pauses in the doorway, glances back. "Your mother has gone to pick up Michael. They shouldn't be long. I'll be downstairs if you need me." He heads back to the lower landing.

"Do you think Michael will come willingly?" Belle asks in a quiet voice.

"I don't know. He's still loyal to our dad, a man I can't even remember. Plus, he's pretty close with Grandma, and not fond of Caleb. Mike's not gonna like it, but will he come?" I shrug. "Guess we'll know soon enough." I drop onto the bed, lay back, and stare at the ceiling. Belle does the same.

Several minutes pass before the silence is broken.

"I know Mom doesn't believe in the magic Grandma is always talking about, but do you think there is a chance that it does exist and simply skipped a generation?" Belle asks.

"You mean Mom. You're wondering if magic skipped over Mom," I clarify.

"Yes. That's what I am asking."

"There is no proof that magic exists." I recall Belle's magazine closing on its own and shake the memory away. The flipping of pages was likely caused by a strong breeze. A breeze I failed to feel. "Maybe Mom is right, and Grandma is a tad crazy," I say.

"I don't think Grandma is crazy," Belle rebuts. "She's never seemed crazy to me." She flips onto her side to face me. "You've never felt anything different or off about yourself?"

I sigh, my shoulders pressing deeper into the comforter beneath me. "I think it's human nature to feel like you're different or made for something more, but that doesn't mean it's so."

"Why not?" Belle challenges.

"Because. It just doesn't." I huff. Cross my arms.

Belle returns her focus to the ceiling, and several more minutes of silence pass between us.

"Do you think we'll like it here?" she asks.

"Don't know," I say to the ceiling. "Let's hope."

"Dinner," Caleb calls up the stairwell.

That was fast.

Belle and I sit up, exchange a glance, and head for the kitchen. Grandma's gumbo had my tummy rumbling with its delicious aromas. We won't be enjoying any of that goodness now, but it doesn't change the fact that I am hungry. Famished.

We find Caleb in the kitchen, standing at the stove. In a large skillet, he has mixed together tomatoes, peppers, onions, garlic, rice, and sausage. Plus, a whole lot of seasoning.

With no official dining table available, I carry my plate of food and a glass of water into the living area where I take a seat on the sofa. Belle opens the doors to the narrow balcony and sets her plate on the tiny bistro table outside.

"Come on," she says. "Join me out here."

I grimace.

"Please?" She blinks rapidly.

With a sigh and over-exaggerated movements of irritation, I move onto the balcony and take a seat beside Belle. I poke at my food, occasionally swallowing mouthfuls to satisfy my hungry belly. I eat my food without giving it attention. Instead, I study the iron work of the bistro table, chairs, and railing, the wood grain of the balcony floor. As well as study the street and nearby buildings. Everything is so much closer here than it is at Grandma's.

Caleb leans into the doorway at our back, plate of food in hand. He rambles on about our presence making the old house feel like a home. About the magic of a family unit making us all stronger. Stronger, because we are together under one roof. I allow his words to wash over me while I study the street and think about the strange girl who was staring at me.

We finish our dinners, scraping our plates clean, and then sit in silence savoring our water. Caleb collects our dirty dishes and returns them to the kitchen. A millisecond later, his car pulls up, stops beside the garage, and Mom jumps out, moving to open the doors.

"Mom's home," Belle whispers the obvious.

Mom unlatches the garage door, and Michael throws open the passenger car door, jumps out. Belle and I both lean forward, but he moves beneath the balcony and out of view.

"Sorry, Mom," he says. "I just can't do this. Not right now. I need time to process everything." He slams the door.

"Come inside first. Talk to Caleb," Mom says.

"That isn't what I need. Don't you get it, Mom? I'm just. I don't." He pauses and I picture his frustration tensing all his neck and shoulder muscles. Belle and I quietly flatten ourselves to the balcony floor and inch forward in an attempt to spy on both my mom and Mike. "I gotta go." He turns and walks up the street and around the corner.

Mom calls after him once, and when he doesn't reply, she doesn't bother calling after him a second time. Belle and I wait in silence until Mom has pulled the car into the garage and closed the doors. With her out of ear shot, we sit up and stare at each other, wide-eyed, then spin on our butts toward the house. Through the glass doors, we watch Mom enter the living space and start crying. Caleb swoops in from the kitchen with a long, strong hug.

I stare at them. Watch the way he soothes her and how upset she is over our brother. My heart hurts, bruised from the experience. Belle's hand drops upon my arm, and I jolt, snapping my head in her direction.

I open my mouth to say something about the surprise, but she cuts me off.

"Poor Michael. Do you think we should go after him?" Her eyebrows pinch together, and she leans closer. My gaze bounces between her and my mom. Caleb leads her back down the stairs, toward the garage.

With the lift of my chin, I motion to Belle, directing her to Mom and Caleb's exit. "Maybe they're going to look for him." I say.

"Then we should definitely go," Belle adds. "Don't you think?" She stands, grabs her water glass, and opens the door to the house.

I follow her, and we both deposit our glasses in the sink and make our way down to the garage. The space remains neatly buttoned up, car present and sitting lukewarm. Mom's voice drifts from the room at the back of the garage. Whatever space lies beyond the closed door at the front of the car, that's where Caleb and my mom have taken refuge.

"Give him time," Caleb says about Mike. "He'll come around, and we'll mold these kids into a proper power family."

What is that supposed to mean? I shiver.

"I don't think they are going to look for Michael." Belle grabs my arm and tugs. "Come on."

I allow her to drag me out onto the sidewalk. We head in the direction Michael went. At the end of the block, we come to a four-lane divided street, across which is the police department.

"I think we just left the Quarter." I scratch the back of my neck.

"Yeah," Belle agrees. "Which way do you think Michael went?"

A great question to which I have no answer. I haven't spent a lot of time in the Quarter. Not really. The prospect always freaked Grandma out. "I don't know. Are there any basketball courts around here?"

"Let's find out." Belle stops a small group of people and asks if they know where the closest basketball court might be. They don't.

"Don't ask obvious tourists," I say and quickly survey the

area. A block away is a bus stop. "This way." I motion for her to follow me. We jet across the street and down the block to the bus stop. Two people linger by the sign, clearly waiting. I ask them if they know where the closest basketball court is, and one of them directs us to the far corner of the park. "At the community center," he says.

The distance is several blocks away, but Belle and I are now determined to find Michael, so we thank the helpful man and make haste through the park.

As hoped, we find Mike actively shooting hoops at the community center. Despite a few other players working on their hoop and swoosh, Mike practices alone and welcomes us into the game. Belle dribbles the ball, passes to me, and I shoot. Miss. Mike laughs and retrieves the ball, then helps me with my throwing form.

A blond guy at the other end of the court looks our way, glances over at me, and smiles. He's clearly been playing for a while. His gray T-shirt is well worn. I blush and bury myself in instructions from Mike.

"Why do you dislike Caleb so much?" I ask. "At least he's continued to hang around and support Mom when our dad simply split."

He knocks the ball from my hold and starts bouncing it between his hands. "It wasn't like that. Dad didn't just leave. And I don't know exactly why I don't like Caleb. Or if it's him I really dislike. Maybe it's the thought of Mom with him. Or the fear he would pull her to the Quarter." He tosses the ball through the hoop with a swoosh. "Which, he now has."

My heart squeezes to a stop. I'm standing limp with my mouth hanging open. I don't know what to address first. His issue with the Quarter or the bit he said about Dad.

My heart says... Dad.

What does Mike know that I don't? If Dad didn't just leave,

what happened, and why haven't Mom or Grandma talked about it in all these years? Why hasn't he visited us, or us him?

What happened to Dad?

I want to grab his shirt, shake him silly, and scream.

I remain still as stone, staring.

"You sound like Grandma with your fear-of-the-Quarter talk," Belle blurts, clarifying where her interests lie. She never knew Dad. He left before she was born, and she couldn't care less about the man.

Michael's lips pull into a silent chuckle. "You got me, baby sister. Our grams certainly has influenced me."

"No doubt." Belle's voice punches the air, and they both break into chuckles.

"But the truth is," he calms, continues. "Police presence is thicker in the Quarter, and police are something people like us should try to avoid."

"People like us?" I blurt. "Why are you afraid of the police? Are you involved in something you shouldn't be?"

He smirks. "Nah. It's just that too many members of the police force are crooked and should be feared, for they would use someone like me, or you..." He swings a finger between Belle and me. "To their unhealthy benefit."

"What is that supposed to mean?" I say. "Why would they be interested in you if you aren't breaking the law?" I narrow my stare upon him and watch for any sign of lies or unlawful involvement.

He presses a flat palm downward, through the open air, signaling me and Belle to lower our voices. He glances around the gym. No one appears to be paying us any attention. He steps closer to us, and we follow suit, closing our ranks.

"Because of our family connection and the fear our blood-line tends to instill in other practitioners." He steps back from our tight-knit circle, bounces the ball once, and then holds it steady in front of his chest.

Belle's intense stare is glued upon Mike, her brow crinkling. Mike is inferring the police are dabbling in the superstitious community. Such a suggestion makes him sound crazier than Grandma. Any interest in the topic evaporates, and I roll my eyes. Mike grins at my reaction and swings his gaze to Belle.

"Whadda ya say we go grab some lemonade and pastries? I'm parched and there's a great place across the street."

It's a clear attempt to deflect and lighten the mood. It works for Belle, because her face lifts and she takes on a joyous glow. But me, I'm still chewing on the information my brother has shared. He believes in the magic of our bloodline. He thinks the cops are crooked, and he's afraid of them using him. And he knows something about Dad's departure. Something I feel I, too, should know.

"Sounds good to me." Belle grabs the basketball from Mike and runs it back to the ball bin at the other end of the court.

"Mike?" I say, finally pushing the word clear of my throat. He turns back to me, a wide smile across his face. "What did you mean when you said Dad didn't just leave?"

His smile falls flat. His gaze narrows. He spares Belle a quick glimpse. She's already dropped the ball in the bin and is dashing toward the water fountain. With a heavy breath releasing from his chest, he steps forward and gently grabs my upper arms.

"I understand why you and Belle feel the way you do where Dad is concerned. She never knew him, and you were too young to remember him. I was just old enough to recall father and son days spent together, as well as some crazy shit that went down that I am still trying to understand. He was forced to leave, Miri. Forced by Mom and circumstance. Mom and Grandma don't talk about him because they don't want any of us asking questions or trying to find him."

He glances toward Belle. She's talking to the blond guy, waving him off, and walking back to us. Mike turns his attention back to me.

"But I'm going to find him, and I'm going to get us some answers."

CHAPTER THREE

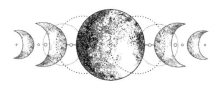

"Mother made him." I shake my head. Using a spoon, I stab at the spices inside the bowl. "I can sorta understand Mike's obsession with Dad. After all, he *is* our Dad. But I can't believe Mike blames Mom for his leaving. We're his children. He wouldn't have left us unless he wanted to. No one can *make* you leave your kids. Right?"

It's Monday evening, and both Mom and Caleb are working late, leaving Belle and me to fend for ourselves. We're in the kitchen cooking dinner.

"I can't believe you're still hung up on that." Belle sighs. Flips the chicken in the pan, searing the second side. "That was over a day ago. Time to move on. Besides, Michael explained the why."

Yeah. Forced into a magical rehab sounds too weird to be real. Plus, that was years *ago. Is it a rehab or a prison?*

I glance toward the stairs, as if expecting to see Mike standing there. He's not. Since moving in on Saturday, Mike has spent his days elsewhere, showing up only at night to sleep.

He got the bedroom on the same level as the kitchen and living area, so as long as we're in the kitchen, he shouldn't be able to sneak in undetected.

"I know he did." I stab at the spices some more. "I'm just having trouble swallowing his explanation. It felt... made up, and too convenient."

"Not to me." Belle grabs the bowl of spices and narrows her gaze upon me, shooting a quick glance at the spoon slammed to the bottom of the bowl. Her message is clear, stop taking my frustration out on the food. I release the bowl, and she sets it on the counter. "You should be focused on other things, given tomorrow and all."

Tomorrow. I sigh. Press my lips together tight.

When Mom ushered us out of Grandma's on Saturday, we left our old school, flat. Never bothering to return after Thanksgiving break. She has allowed us a day to acclimate to the new location, but tomorrow, we start anew at a different high school. One closer to us. One where we don't have any friends or know a living soul.

I can't wait. My lips press into a frown.

Yesterday, I called my two besties from my old school and caught them up on my life. I told them not to expect me back for a while... if ever.

"Oh. Oh." Belle waves her finger in the air, pointing past me to the pot of rice starting to bubble and boil over.

I swing toward the stovetop, grab the pot, and shift it to the next burner. Scalding water splashes from the pot and splatters onto my arm. My skin screams, burns. I gasp. Drop the pot, knocking the edge of the spice bowl in the process. The bowl wobbles, tips off the edge of the counter.

Belle squeaks and reaches for the falling bowl. Her arm isn't long enough, and the bowl slips past her fingers. I cringe, preparing for the inevitable crash, only none comes. I blink and peer toward the floor at our feet. The bowl hovers inches from the ground, floating in mid-air. The mix of spices swirl around and around in a blended line of color and texture.

My stare snaps to Belle. Her eyes are narrowed and her nose twitching. A millisecond later, the bowl smashes to the kitchen tile and breaks, scattering spice all over the kitchen floor.

I yank back, slamming my shoulders and backbone straight. "What was that?"

"What was what?" Belle presses her hands to her chest and stares at the mess upon the floor.

"You know what," I counter. "The bowl and spices pausing mid-fall. That's what."

Belle raises her head and meets my gaze. "Pausing? In the middle of a fall?" Her eyes widen. Jerks a tight shiver. "That's absurd. Just like hoodoo or voodoo or magic. Didn't you say you don't believe in that stuff?" She laughs. "Nah, I saw nothing of the sort." She grabs the broom from beside the kitchen door and begins sweeping at the mess. Steals a mischievous grin in my direction.

My eyes narrow upon her, but I decide not to argue. Not right now. Instead, I grab the dustpan and hold it steady so that she may sweep our spoils into place. I watch her closely, replaying the scene over and over in my head. If I didn't know better, I'd think she had been controlling the elements. But that would be magic. Impossible magic. And despite all the crazy things Grandma says, and Mike's clear belief, magic isn't real.

We mix a new batch of spices and manage to salvage dinner. Taking a seat on the sofa in front of the television, we enjoy the delicious results of our labor. I stab, bite, chew, and think about the falling bowl of spices. Something about the incident reminds me of the magazine flipping unassisted to a close.

Could I have misinterpreted what I saw? I chew on the inside of my lip.

There's a logical explanation. Magic isn't real.

Belle laughs at something on the television, but I can't hold my focus upon the show unfolding. Grandma has always spoken of magic, but Mom swears magic isn't real and that Grandma is full of untrue stories. Which storyteller shares the truth? It's clear which one Mike believes. The one I've never put any stock in.

Belle laughs again, her gaze glued to the television. She reaches for the salt, but before she can grab it, the saltshaker shifts sideways and slips into her hold... as if by magic.

I jerk, intensify my stare.

Belle keeps eating and watching television, as if nothing unusual has taken place. But I saw it, saw her, saw the *magic* at play. The saltshaker slipped sideways, completely unaided, right into my sister's hand.

That *had* to be something.

But what?

My gaze bounces between my sister, the saltshaker, and the bowl of spices.

If a saltshaker moving unassisted and a bowl floating mid-air aren't signs of magic, then I don't know what is. Grandma always insisted we had magic in our veins, and I never believed her. Instead, I believed Mom when she said Grandma was confused. But if Belle *is* performing magic, then that would negate the majority of Mom's arguments. It would also support Mike's belief.

And prove my view wrong.

Furthermore, if what I am seeing in Belle this evening champions their argument, then it would stand to reason that magical blood runs through my veins as well. Which means... I should be able to move saltshakers and bowls.

After we finish our meals and whatever show Belle is watching concludes, we take our dishes to the kitchen, wash them, and leave them out to dry. Belle returns to the television for more evening viewing, and, even though it's only seven o'clock, I excuse myself to my room. The incident with the bowl and the saltshaker keeps pushing to the forefront of my mind, and I'm finding it difficult, at present, to be around Belle. There's a quiver in my stomach and a burning in my chest.

Is magic real? Does Belle have magic?

I stop midway up the stairs and take a seat. Enclosed within the sidewalls of the stairwell, I cannot see what's taking place on the floor below, but I can hear the television show, complete with advertising.

Is magic real?

Belle's soft laughter drifts up to me. I wait and wait, but no hint of Mike comes my way. I have no idea how much time passes, but the sounds of the television show changes from one to another, suggesting I've been sitting on the stairs for thirty minutes, possibly more. My legs bounce, and my fingers fidget. Deciding to crawl into bed early, I climb the rest of the stairs and find mild comfort lying on my bed, staring at the ceiling.

I turn my head and gaze at the few items set upon my dresser. A bottle of perfume, a picture of my family, and a small wooden box holding a handful of jewelry items. If magic is real, *can I conjure some of my own?* I stare at the framed picture of my siblings and me, will it to move. I stare and stare and stare and will and will and will, and nothing happens. Nothing on the dresser or in the room moves. Except for my finger, which starts to point and swirl, as if the motion will provoke a magical response.

The response I receive... nothing. Maybe I'm not concentrating hard enough. I've never tried to perform magic. I don't know what's required. But if Belle is able to make things transpire, then it shouldn't be too difficult. It should be rather natural, I'm guessing.

I fixate on the picture frame, imagine it falling forward onto the dresser's surface. All of my focus and intention rests upon the object. Time and time again, I envision the frame falling flat, face down. I pretend a tiny, invisible hand presses from behind. I think of the action happening again and again and again, until my chest knots and my head pounds.

No magic is conjured. Only a splitting headache... exacerbated by the howling of the wind outside.

I sigh and close my eyes. Maybe the frame is too large of an object for a first attempt. Maybe I should be directing my attention toward something smaller. Something lighter and more easily nudged.

Pushing up to a sitting position, I lean forward and remove a small ring from the wooden box and place it on the dresser. The ring becomes my new subject of attention. Once more, I concentrate on shifting the piece across the furniture's surface, similar to how Belle pulled the saltshaker to her hand. Despite the ring's diminished weight, no amount of focus on my part appears to create any magical force or movement.

My hands slap the bed and I exhale. Recall Belle's shifty finger and twitchy nose. Maybe I should be channeling my inner Samantha Stevens. I try to wiggle my nose like I've seen so many times on Bewitched. The resulting motion is far more rabbit than anything magical.

I want to scream, but I hold the frustrated storm deep within my chest. Instead, I crawl beneath the covers, fluff my pillow, and curl up in bed. If I am unable to conjure true supernatural magic, maybe I can summon the necessary interpersonal-skills magic to help me fit in at the new school tomorrow.

Outside my window sounds the screech of a car coming to a hard stop. Someone gets out, and the car pulls away. A few minutes later, the bang and slam of doors, signaling Mike's arrival home. He's barely begun climbing the first flight of stairs when Caleb's car pulls up against the garage. Mom borrowed the car to get to work, and her shift at the casino ended a while ago. Within moments, Mike and Mom are fighting.

I wanted to talk to Mike, but now Mom will have ruined his mood. I tense, throw the pillow over my head, and press tight in an attempt to block out the sound.

A gust of wind blows my window open with a bang. I startle. Jolt to a sit and pull the covers tight around me. Words dripping with emotion sail through the gale, straight to my ear. Mike is spending time with someone Mom doesn't approve of, and Caleb is her source.

Caleb is a narc.

"My business is my business. Stay out of it," Mike yells.

"As long as you are living under my roof, your business *is* my business," Mom counters.

"This isn't your roof." Mike slams a door, likely locking himself in his room, and the conversation drops.

"You had better straighten up your act." Mom gets in the last jab.

Across the hall... the sounds of Belle's stealthy attempt to sneak into her room undetected by heated individuals.

I lay flat back on my bed with my pillow over my face, as if hiding from my life. I feel small, insignificant, and trapped. I hope tonight is not a sign of what my days are to become.

If I could make magic real, I think I would start by creating a new living situation for myself, Mike, Belle. I'd return to Grandma's house in the Garden District. Put an end to the fighting between Caleb, Mom, and Mike, and live with Grandma, stress free.

Maybe get a pet.

And a boyfriend.

Yeah. I think I'd like a boyfriend.

I smile and slip into the sleep of the night, as one would glide through the waters of a stormy sea. Slumber finds me like a net, bringing with it struggles before the calm. The calm eventually wins, much like a slow death. Oblivion consumes and pulls me deep.

I jolt awake to the relentless badger of my morning alarm.

The day has finally arrived. My first day at a new school. The local public school.

CHAPTER FOUR

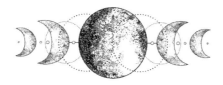

My heart hammers like a mad woodpecker. I hold myself with arms tight and step onto campus. Belle and I check in at the front and then make our way to the main office. After settling everything with administration, I move into the hallway and stare at the slip of paper clenched in my fingers. Such a tiny thing and it holds a major part of my daily life. All the classes I'll be attending for the duration of the school year. That means new teachers, new fellow students, and a complete shift in dynamics. How will this public school differ from the charter school I've been attending?

I glance down at my attire, worn jeans and fitted tee, layered with a comfy plaid shirt. *Should blend in alright.* I turn my gaze to the many girls passing by on either side of me. So far, so good. My newness doesn't stick out like a blinking light on a dark night. My outfit choice appears to pass the grade of the public school's unspoken dress code.

Belle shimmies up beside me. "I'm this way." She throws a pointed thumb toward the hall at our right. "What about you?"

I check my class list against the tiny map in my hand. I point the opposite direction.

"Bummer," Belle says with a touch of disappointment. "Well, catch up with you later." She wanders from sight.

My morning classes are a bore with English, chemistry, art, and geometry. Come lunch time, I have no idea where to find Belle, but the weather is agreeable, and everyone is enjoying their down time at the outdoor lunch tables, so I find a spot by myself and hope I haven't broken any unspoken territory rules. After all, I haven't a clue regarding class or clique location dynamics.

Belle doesn't come and find me, and no one tries to strike a conversation with me, nor I with them. I simply chew and swallow and wonder what my friends at my old school are doing. I should call them. My thoughts shift. How did Belle pause the bowl mid-air, or make the saltshaker move without touching it? Is magic real, and does she possess some of her own? Is it because of magic our father was sent away?

I have so many questions, and I don't know where to turn for answers.

In a mass of darker and darkish skin tones, speckled with the occasional pink, I notice a boy with a paler complexion watching me. I recognize him from the other day at the rec center. He was shooting hoops at the opposite end of the court when Belle and I joined Mike in a little basketball fun. He even spoke to Belle, briefly.

My cheeks warm, and I look away, finish my lunch, and head off to my French class, followed by history.

History class time is dedicated to discussing the War of 1812, and when the bell rings, the teacher yells over the exiting rumble, reminding everyone they need to turn in their field-trip permission slips if they didn't already do so.

"Last chance," he says. "Drop off your permission slip

tomorrow or Thursday. We'll be meeting street-side by the busses Friday morning." On my way out the door, he hands a slip to me and repeats his message regarding the form's return.

I study the permission slip and make my way to P.E. Any field trip has got to be better than sitting in classes all day. Plus, the excursion might help busy my mind, so that I don't obsess over the possibility of Belle conjuring magic every moment of the day. The subject ties my insides into knots and burns my skin. I hate feeling that way, especially about my sister.

I fold the slip and slide it between the pages of my book.

An hour of P.E. is a tad long for me, and I'm thankful when the period ends, marking the end of the school day. I meet up with Belle at the front of the school and together we walk home. We've got about twelve to thirteen blocks to cover, several of which take us right along the edge of the French Quarter.

Due to my grandmother's superstitions, I've never spent much time in the famous district. Now, I'm living on the outskirts of the Quarter and will be walking beside a large section of it every day. It's like my life has flipped to the extreme. From quiet and majestic to bustling and wild. The streets between the school and Caleb's are rich in culture and tourism and home to an entirely different breed of character.

We drop down to Rampart Street and take it all the way to the street where Caleb lives. The walk is along a busy two-lane road, but it's moderate enough and I enjoy taking in the many sites. The bars, the park, the cemetery. More bars... all of which will be overflowing with music, patrons, and jubilation later in the night. A few already are.

Around St. Ann Street, I bump into a girl moving at a quick pace. With a jolt of surprise, she looks up from the pamphlet in her hand.

"Sorry," I mumble, but she only stares back, her eyes

growing ever wider by the moment. She pushes back her draped hood, revealing her pasty skin and dull red hair.

Her upper lip appears to twitch, and her body jerks away from me. I, too, am picking up an unwanted first, or second, impression. For an instant, the image of her face strobes at the back of my mind like an uninvited nightmare, flashing from red to deeply shadowed. I spin away, nudge Belle to move quicker. Half a block away, I glance back. The girl stands at the corner, staring after me. Something about her is familiar.

I suck back a breath and keep moving. When Belle and I reach the next intersection, I chance another peek. The girl is gone, but her absence does nothing to calm my internal sensors. I tell Belle I'm anxious to get home, and I keep pressing until we've made it all the way back to Caleb's place.

That night, after dinner, I grab a moment alone with Mom. I hand her the permission slip. "The school has a field trip planned this week, and I'm a bit behind on getting my paperwork turned in. Could you sign this so that I can give it to the teacher tomorrow?"

My mom takes the slip from me and reads the details in silence. I cross my arms over my chest and wait. Something about her expression sparks a nervous tick at the edge of my eye. Her chest heaves, and she drops her hand... and the slip... to her side, then turns her attention to me.

"I'm sorry hun. I'm not going to sign this. I'd rather you not go on this particular trip." She tilts her head. "Maybe the next one, but not this." She waves the paper at her side.

"What? Why?" My body jolts straight. "What's wrong with this trip? It's not like the buses will be driving long distances. It won't be so far that I couldn't actually walk back here if I needed to."

"Did you look at the destination for this trip?" She shakes the paper between us.

"I did. What of it?" I hook my fists on my hips.

"Battlefields are filled with bad mojo. It's a terrible idea for you to purposely walk into a placed permeated with negative energy."

"You sound like Grandma," I say. "I thought you didn't believe in all that magical stuff?"

"I never said I didn't believe in energy, and that's what we are talking about here. Energy. Lots and lots of bad energy." She folds the permission slip. "As for magic, what I've said is that I don't believe the family line is a bunch of natural-born witches with hereditary magic in the blood."

Mom maybe believes in magic, just not a family line with inherent magic.

"Okay, well, whatever." My shoulders tighten. "Tons of people visit battlefields all the time without any issues, so why should I be any different?"

Mom peers at me, her brow hitched, but she doesn't answer. She takes a deep breath, folds the slip once more, then a second time, and drops it in the trash. "I'm sorry. I won't sign it. I'm sure the school is prepared with arrangements for students unable to go on the trip." She squeezes my shoulder and walks out of the room.

"Seriously?" I call after her.

"Family is precious," she hollers back. "And we don't take stupid chances with our lives and loved ones."

Fumes fill my chest. My muscles tense, and my breath weights. It's only my first week at a new school I never wanted to attend, and already my mom is screwing things up for me. I pluck the slip from the trash and shuffle up to my room.

I flatten the paper out on the surface on my dresser and study all the wrinkles running across the form.

I could forge her name.

Except, the teacher would know it's not her signature. Or...

would he? It's a new school, and all the teachers have yet to meet my mom.

I bite my lip and stare at the signature line. Before I realize what I'm doing, I have a pen in my hand, and I am swirling and curving the letters of my mom's name into place. I step back and admire the art I have created. It's a pretty close replica of her handwriting. Or so I believe.

I go to bed confident that I will be joining the class on the field trip this coming Friday.

Confidence turns to chaos, and I find myself running down a dark, narrow street. I'm aware that I am dreaming, but it does little to calm my response. My mind is racing, my body glistening, and my heart hammering. Paranoia strangles my every breath. I slam against a door set in a sidewall, push it open, slip through, tumble out and over the broken front of a grave. I strangle a scream. I'm lying on the ground in a cemetery, staring up at the houses of the dead in the dark of night. I push myself up and keep racing.

The dream has its claws deep into my psyche. I can't wake, nor shake the uncomfortable images that plague me. I keep running. Running hard. The girl from the walk home is chasing me. But why? Why would they chase me and why do I fear them? They are oddly similar. I realize with a start that the two girls are actually the same.

She changed her hair.

The path narrows, twists into fog. Becomes a haze-filled world with pops and bangs, and uniformed men fighting. Anguish and blood everywhere. Everywhere!

I bolt upright, screaming.

CHAPTER FIVE

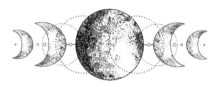

My hand flies to my chest, presses against my skin as if to force my heart to slow. Across the hall, I hear Belle grumble something about it being too early. She's a heavy sleeper. I learned that years ago, in our shared room situation.

Footfalls climb the stairs, and Mike appears in my doorway. "You alright?" he asks.

"Just a nightmare." I breathe, breathe, breathe.

He moves into the room, takes a seat on the bed beside me, and lays his hand upon my blanket-covered leg. "You sure?" he says, and I nod... only, I'm unclear if he's asking whether I'm really okay or if I'm sure I had a bad dream.

"I've had my fair share of bad dreams, but when they are only dreams, you can take control. It is, after all, your dream."

"How do you know when you are dreaming, and how do you take control?" I ask.

"You take control by deciding what you want to have happen and then creating that situation in your mind. You are the creator, controller, of your inner thoughts, dreams included." He straightens his arm before me and tugs at a small rubber-band-type thing he has wrapped around his wrist. "This helps me determine if I am dreaming or if something else is going on." He snaps the band, and it cracks against his skin. "If I suspect I am dreaming, I tug on this, and the tiny shock wakes me up."

"What else would be going on that could be mistaken for a dream?" I stare at his wrist and the band.

"Things," he says with a shrug.

"That's such a blow off." I push back straight against the headboard.

"If you must know... outside of dreaming, maybe I'm hallucinating or witnessing something so insane it's hard to accept as real. Or maybe..." He leans forward and taps his temple. "My mind is being manipulated."

"What?" My head jerks back. "That's crazy."

"Life is crazy." His eyes widen, and he lurches forward with teeth bared and hands flared like claws.

"Stop it." I smack him with my extra pillow, and he breaks into laughter, drops against the bed like I've bested him. "Why are you trying to scare me after my wacked dream?"

He sits up, a sober expression ruling his features. "Sorry. My bad. I didn't mean to upset you. I was only trying to lighten the mood and make sure you're alright."

"I'll be fine, no thanks to you." I shove at his chest.

He stands and steps away from the bed. "If you're sure..."

"Pretty sure." I fold my hands in my lap. "But I want to know why you would be concerned with hallucinations and mind control?"

"Not so much concerned as prepared," he says with a tilt of his head. "I guess the loss of our dad has made me think that way, always preparing for the what-ifs in this world."

My heart squeezes, and for the first time, I realize how

much the loss of our dad has affected my brother. How sad it must be to always worry about when the next bomb will drop.

The thump of the garage door rattles through the front wall of the home. "Caleb's home from the club. I should bug out, in case he decides to come up stairs." He twirls a finger in reference to the room. "You should burn some sage, clear the air, just to be safe." His gaze sweeps around the space, then back to me. He smiles and leaves.

Burn some sage. I didn't pack any of Grandma's sage when we made our quick exit. Never even considered it. I wonder if anyone else did.

"Do you have any?" I whisper, but Mike's already gone.

With the images from the nightmare thick in my mind, and the thoughts of my discussion with Mike weighing heavily upon me, any further sleep is difficult. I glance at the clock on my nightstand. Caleb has been out all night. My alarm is set to go off in an hour and a half, so I decide to shower and prep for day two at the new school.

Day two and day three fall into my history as unremarkable. No sightings of the intriguing blond basketball player from my first day or the day of the move. I flounder with the current lesson plans and find myself somewhat miserable at making new friends. I am the new girl, and most everyone is already committed to a pack. The one notable perk, my history teacher accepts my field trip permission slip with nothing more than a glance at the forged signature.

Come Friday, I join the collective history classes and visit the New Orleans Battlefield. Truth, I'm not interested in the historical site, its significance, or the horrible events that took place at the location. I've never been a fan of history, and I doubt my opinion will ever change.

What I do relish is the time outside of a classroom. The group of students gather along the cannon line and spill out onto the battlefield. I hover at the back of the group and listen to the facts, figuring some, or all, of the information will end up on a test in the near future.

I hone in on words like outnumbered, two months, poorly executed, unnecessary, and treaty. Of course, Andrew Jackson will be on the test. He went on to become president.

"Hey, you're the new girl, right?"

At the question, I glance to my side. Two guys with border-line creepy smiles are glancing over me. I excuse myself and maneuver around the side of the group, moving away from the cannons and deeper onto the battlefield. The further I go, the heavier my feet become. Picking a spot at the edge of the student mass, I square my back, cross my arms, and focus my attention to what the teacher is saying. Or, try to pay attention, anyway.

My vision blurs and clouds of white billow across my sight. My world feels distant, as if I have been plucked from life and dropped into a hazy dream... or nightmare. I'm reminded of my nightmare from a few nights ago. The battling gunfire. I should have gotten myself a wristband like Mike's.

A veil exists between me and the rest of my class, and I can't move, much less pierce through the foggy barrier. Pops and bangs ring in my ears. A multitude of shots being fired. My body shudders, and my heart thunders. My breath is trapped in my chest. I hug myself, squeeze tight. Pinch. Wish to wake up.

A man in an old military uniform steps beside me and fires a rifle. My body cracks with a mini spasm. I blink. Blink hard. Want the fictional vision to vanish.

The man at my side is a nightmare. I can see through him. *He's not real.* I rub my eyes.

Dang overactive imagination.

My center of gravity twists, and my body sways. Overcome

with the desire to fall to the ground, I plant my feet shoulder width apart and shake my head, blink a million and one blinks.

So dizzy. So lightheaded.

I will not pass out, I tell myself. *I won't. I won't. I won't.*

"This way," the teacher says, waving the group to follow him toward the visitor center. The mumbling students move across the edge of the field, and I follow at the back, the distance between me and the moving mob growing larger with each step.

I'm finding it hard to move. As if the ground beneath me is slowly swallowing me. Any sight of my classmates is lost to the visions of ghostly men running, shouting, falling at my sides.

The scream wishing to flee my lungs is strangled deep within me, unable to escape. I am trapped in a hell world that passed into history two hundred years ago. No amount of eye rubbing, blinking, or head shaking makes the experience abate.

Hands, an endless multitude of hands, reach from the ground and grab at my legs and ankles and feet. Their ghostly touch sends shivers across my skin. They tug and hold. Try to keep me on the grass. Attempt to pull me into the dirt.

I press against the friction, pushing forward toward my class.

And yet, the hands drag, drag, drag. I'm walking in quicksand, each step becoming more labored than the last. My chest is squeezing. Closing. I stare at the ground, expecting thick mud, snow even. There is none. The grass is thin and the land beneath, hard and solid. And yet...

I can't move.

I can't breathe.

Wetness pools at my nostrils. I sniffle and wipe at the dampness. Blood streaks across my finger and hand. *Blood.* I wipe again. *More blood. Is my nose bleeding?*

My vision blotches, head swirls. I press the heel of my palm to my temple. Sniffle.

Puffs of gunpowder. Ghostly men shouting, firing. Hands pulling, dragging me into the ground and into their grave. The darkness of the dirt presses upon me, buries me in the pressure of death.

My heart hammers, hammers, threatens to explode. My mind bursts, pain, then black.

The world sleeps.

And I fall.

CHAPTER SIX

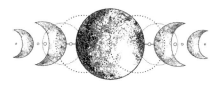

"There you go, hun. Keep it held, nice and steady."

My lips press into a half-frown, and I hold the cold pack against my forehead. The school nurse is nice enough, but I have been embarrassed beyond my tolerance level for the day. Possibly, for the month. Year, even. First, for the bloody nose and passing out, and then, by the firm talking-to received from both my teacher and the principal. The truth of my forgery has been uncovered, and now I sit in the nurse's office awaiting the arrival of my mom.

I close my eyes and try to keep soothing thoughts at the forefront of my mind. Only, everything is battle action. Gun and cannon fire. Men fighting. Men dying. Why was I the only one to witness these things? Why am I still seeing these things in my mind, reliving the events over and over?

Could be stress over Mom and the move. Or... is there something else? A reason for Mom's concern about me visiting the battlefield. An ugly, bad mojo.

"Miriam."

I am soo busted.

My mom's call comes from the outer office. A moment later, she swings into the small nurse's space. Mom clearly came straight from work. Her casino uniform is partially hidden beneath her jacket. She rakes her hands through her short bob.

"Do you have any idea how it makes me look when the school calls to tell me you've had an incident during a class trip I never approved?" She stands in front of me with hands fisted firm on her hips. Her brow is pressed and her gaze narrowed. "Do you comprehend the severity of the situation?"

I pull into myself, my head attempting to collapse into a nonexistent space. My gaze drops to my knees.

"You placed the school in a horrible position of possible liability." She breathes deep and glares at me. I remain quiet. "I spoke to the principal and your teacher. You have detention everyday next week."

Yep. That's what I was told before my mom arrived. Great start at a new school.

"In addition," she says. "You will be doing Belle's chores as well as your own all next week."

My gaze snaps up, and my mouth pops open. "But Mom…"

She wags her finger in the air. "You have no ground on which to stand. You will accept your punishment with grace and make sure to never commit any such foolish act in the future."

I inhale deep, pulling my lips into a tight line. Temperature rises, in my blood and in my skin. The throb at my temple increases in pulse and pressure. My anger is directed at her, even though I know I have no one to blame but myself. I was told not to go. Told I couldn't go. And I ignored her, defied her, forged her signature, and went anyway.

"Get your things," she says. "I'm taking you home."

I slide out of the chair, grab my flannel shirt, slip it on over my T-shirt, and follow my mom to the car. On our walk from the office to the parking lot, we pass the blond-haired, basket-ball-playing boy from the beginning of the week. The sport has treated him well. His muscular arms stretch the fabric of his short sleeves. The boy and I exchange lingering glances. School isn't yet out, and I'm walking two paces behind my fuming mom. It probably couldn't be clearer that my situation is hella ugly.

We ride, the entire trip home, in silence.

Mom pulls the car into the garage and shuts off the engine. She bites the inside of her lip and stares through the windshield to the garage wall. Her mind appears to be wards away.

"Can we talk about what I experienced?" I ask.

"You can explain to me why you forged my signature on the permission slip."

"Because I wanted to go," I say. "I didn't want to be that one kid left in class when everyone else was outside for the day. But that doesn't matter now." I shake my head. "I saw things I can't explain."

"What do you mean it doesn't matter?" She twists in her seat to face me. "Of course, it matters. You can't go around signing other people's names to things whenever it fits your needs."

"But, I saw things, Mom. Crazy, strange things."

"Serves you right, after what you did." She yanks the keys from the ignition and steps out of the car. "I expect you to go straight to your room. I'll check on you shortly." She slams the car door. "And close the garage door, will you?" She disappears into the room at the back of the garage. The room might have once been a supply room or something, but it was since converted to a bedroom and bath, with access to a small back patio space.

With Mom and Caleb making their room down here, it's

difficult for anyone to come and go without one of them knowing.

I get out of the car and stomp up to my room. Slam the door. Drop onto the bed. Mom has never been the most agreeable person, but I thought she would at least listen to what I had to say.

That night, I make dinner, wipe down the kitchen, take out the trash, and wash the dishes. All under my mom's watchful eye. Belle paints her nails, gossips over the phone, and watches television. I catch her watching me and cringing at my circumstances, but we don't speak of it. Caleb pokes at me, making comments, and asking questions about my day.

"Guess you learned your lesson the hard way," he says. "It creates bad karma disobeying your mom the way you did."

For the most part, I ignore him. Refuse to be needled into a reaction. And any responses I do make are blunt.

"Your mom and I are working to make this a strong family," he says. "In order for that to happen, we each have to do our part, and your part includes staying in line."

I keep my head down and roll my eyes, continue scrubbing the dirty dishes. Mike missed dinner, and my misery, as he has stayed out late *again*. Everyone else, whether meaning to or not, has left me feeling itchy in my skin. When the dishes are set aside and drying, I choose to escape any more *family* time. Saying no more than ten words to my sister the entire evening, and eager to slip away from Mom's fumes of irritation, I head to my room early.

In my room, with the lights off, I sit on the bed, staring out the window, and contemplate my day. It's been hours, and yet my stomach remains tight, and my head woozy. How could I have been the one and only lucky student to pick up on ghosts from the past?

Why me?

My skin prickles and I shiver... have the oddest sense of being watched. Of course, that's a silly notion. I'm alone in the room.

I'm being silly and obsessive.

I blame Belle and the things I saw her do, or *thought* I saw her do.

Magic isn't real.

That *has* to be the truth. Because, if it's not, then that would mean Grandma isn't crazy and Mom has led me to believe a lie with her carefully crafted words.

Belle did not do magic, and I did not see ghosts. I just stressed because of everything that has happened this last week.

Could also be low blood sugar.

Sometime around nine o'clock, Mom pops her head in the door. "Just a reminder. You're grounded for a week. That means, when I am at work or out running errands over the weekend, you are not to leave the house." She turns to leave but spins around. "That goes for television and phone calls too. None of that."

I sigh, and crawl into bed. I don't dignify my mom with a response. Instead, I frown into my pillow. Then follow her rules all day Saturday. I had planned to call my friends from my old school, but Mom removed that option. Hope they don't forget about me before I get my phone privileges back.

Come Sunday, when Mom and Caleb are at work, I break the rules and go for a walk. Make my way into the Quarter... alone.

CHAPTER SEVEN

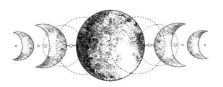

Sunday midmorning, Belle was picked up by a friend. They had plans for lunch and a movie, maybe some shopping. That was over an hour ago, and I wasn't allowed to join them because... grounded. Which means, no fun. Only work and boredom.

When Mom and Caleb head off to work, Mom reminds me that I am not to watch television, use the phone, or leave the house.

The only chance at something interesting is Mike. Only, he is extra lazy and won't get out of bed.

So far, Sunday is beyond boring.

I try to wake Mike, and he pushes me away. With a groan, he complains of being tired and hungover.

"Drinking?" I ask.

"No." His response is curt and irritated.

"Smoking? Drugs?" I push.

"No and no." He yanks his covers over his head. "It's not that kind of a hangover. Now go away."

What other kind of hangover options are there?

It's after that conversation, and my failed attempts to get him up, that I decide to leave, explore the French Quarter. I zigzag through the streets. Down a block, over a block, down another block, and over again. I've never been alone in the French Quarter, and walking the streets by myself takes on a different vibe than when visiting with my mom or Caleb. Some of the streets are busy with life, work, and tourists. Others, discomforting in their silence. The sidewalks are still damp from the earlier hose-down, leaving the smell of concrete to linger in the air. That, plus stale alcohol and vomit.

On the fifth block, I spy a girl following me. I recognize her. She's the one that stood outside my window on Saturday, the night Mom moved us into Caleb's. I also bumped into her on Tuesday, during my walk home from school. Like before, she is dressed in all black. I glance over my shoulder and spy her walking along the street behind me. I turn the corner. She turns the same corner. My heart quickens, as does my pace.

Is she following me?

Why is she following me?

My chest grows tight.

What am I afraid of? She's only a girl.

I dodge between a group of people and glance at my back. She's gone. I breathe deep and slush the weight off my shoulders. Catch the eye of an officer. He appraises me with an odd look on his face. It makes my skin itch, and I recall Mike's words about the cops wanting to use our kind to their advantage. I cross the street.

"You're a witch."

I startle. Stop in my tracks. Pull my purse to my chest like a shield. The girl stands on the sidewalk in front of me, her accusation appearing to be directed at me... but it can't be. It doesn't make sense. She doesn't know me, and I am not a witch.

I take in the people moving on either side of us. They move

49

past with expressions of complete unawareness. She is not accusing them. No. Definitely not.

I glance behind me. There is no one. Only me.

My attention pins on her, then averts to the side, where I direct my forward motion. Past her, on the sidewalk.

She steps into my path. "You shouldn't be here, witch. The Quarter is no place for one such as you."

"I don't know who you think I am," I say. "But I am not a witch." Even as I am speaking the words, my mind is obsessing over my trip to the battlefield. The hands pulling me into the ground, and the ghostly figures of soldiers fighting.

Seeing ghosts does not make me a witch.

Her gaze narrows to dark slits. "Is it me or yourself whom you are attempting to fool?"

"I assure you; I have no idea what you are talking about." I move to step past her, but she shifts to her side, blocking my passing, once more.

"If you do not know yourself, then I think it's time for a little self-discovery." She grabs my arm and yanks me toward a discreet doorway at our side. The door is pushed open wide, allowing a view of a dark and beguiling store. Many curious items, not uncommon in New Orleans, decorate the many surfaces. Candles burn in wall sconces and a large candelabra sits in the middle of the shop, with a flame flickering high, reaching for the ceiling.

"What are you doing?" I yank my arm and try to extract myself from her grip. She's strong and her hold is firm. My purse dangles at my side, threatening to slip off my arm. "Let go of me."

She spins and stares at me. "If you are a witch and are unaware, don't you want to know?"

Her words strike a chord within me. My struggle calms, and she pulls me through the door into the shop.

Shelves and counters brim with tiny coffins, creepy dolls, shrunken heads, vampire lesson boxes, blood bags, bottled spirits, gargoyles, holy water, umbrellas, sunglasses, books, and more. My gaze bounces from spot to spot. At the back of the shop, a sign warns of dangers beyond.

The girl drags me to the burning candelabra at the center of the store. "If you aren't a witch, then you should be able to hold the center candle." She motions to the large white pillar set in the holder. "Go on. Grab the candle," She prompts.

My hands tingle, and I stare at the candle. It's flickering flame. I want to grab it, prove her wrong, and be done with this entire awkward situation. And yet, my fingers twitch at my side, refusing to move.

"What are you waiting for?" She angles into me. "If you are no witch, then this should be easy for you."

My hand extends, reaching for the candle, but snaps into my chest. "It's just a candle. Why wouldn't I be able to hold it?" I ask.

A wicked smile spreads across her lips, and she leans into her hip. "You're scared, aren't you?"

"No, I'm not." I cross my arms. Glance toward the door. I shouldn't be indulging her. *I should leave.* A guy dressed in all black slips in beside the doorway and presses his weight into the frame. He watches me, a twisted grin upon his face.

"The candle is blessed against a witch's touch. If you aren't a witch, touching it won't be an issue. But, if you are a witch... well then." Her cheeks dimple.

I heave a heavy breath and glance toward the guy standing at the door. *What have I gotten myself into?* I swing my attention back to the candle. *Just touch it and get this over with.*

I reach a tentative finger toward the flickering pillar. My forward motion stops an inch before the candle. The girl's silent laughter squeezes my insides. I fingertip-touch the candle.

My muscles scream, and my finger, curled within my fist, yanks firm to my chest.

The girl's boisterous laughter bounces off the walls of the cramped shop. "What a day of discovery this must be for you? You, thinking yourself nothing, and discovering you are a witch. And not just any witch. A witch not welcome in the Quarter."

Her smile widens, and her fangs descend.

CHAPTER EIGHT

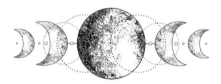

"I've made no such discovery," I snap and take a step back. The girl is clearly bonkers. It's probably because of freaks like her that Grandma didn't want us visiting the French Quarter. Some people get far too immersed in their make-believe.

"No? Then why did you yank away from the candle so quick?" She smirks, fangs hidden. The guy in the doorway now sports a hint-of-fang grin.

Crazy-like attracts crazy-like.

"Instinct." My shoulders straighten. "Pure reaction to your heavy attempt to scare me. First with your ludicrous story and behavior, and now with your toothy leer."

Her mouth falls flat. "Don't like my teeth? Then you should leave the Quarter."

"I have as much right to the Quarter as you do." I straighten my shoulders. Clasp my hands. "I am not some banded witch, as you make me sound."

"You still don't believe you're a witch?" Her gaze narrows to slits.

"Of course not. Witches and magic are not any more real than vampires." My chin jerks forward, motioning to her monster play.

If I had stayed with Grandma, listened to and believed in her colorful stories, would she have eventually made me equally as enthusiastic about witchcraft as this black-clad girl is about vampirism? I don't know... maybe. I swallow hard. Guess it *is* a good thing we moved out last week.

And yet... *why do I feel like I am trying to convince myself?*

An image of Belle blooms in my mind. I shake it away.

The vamp girl's hand shoots forward, lightning fast, and grabs my elbow, yanks me toward the back of the store and the sign warning of danger.

"What are you doing?" I resist her drag, but she is stronger than me.

"Not a witch?" She tosses me a sideways glare.

"No," I say. "I'm not. I'm just a high school student."

She laughs, as does the guy near the shop door. She pulls me out the back exit, swings us around, and drags me through the next opening. A long, narrow hallway, with little room to maneuver, much less struggle. The space is flooded in red light. Dark red light.

At the end of the hallway, we turn a corner and step into a dingy tavern. Neon beer signs decorate the walls, and flashing colored lights spin in the two far corners. The bar stretches across one side of the room, a row of pleather stools pushed up against its side. On the opposite side of the room, a red-curtain-backed stage. Unattended instruments stand in wait for a musician to strike up a tune.

The girl directs us to the stairs in the corner. A worn-wood climb to an open-railed landing. Releasing her hold, she pushes me up the first couple of steps. "If you honestly believe you are not a witch, test your theory up there." She directs me up the stairs with a swinging point of the finger and a head nod.

"This is ridiculous," I say and descend the steps climbed. "I'm leaving."

She steps in front of me, blocking my exit.

"Get out of the way." My hands ball into tight fists.

"Make me." Her hands drop onto her hips, and her head tips into her shoulders. A giant of a bald man steps up behind her, crosses his steroid-bulked, tattooed arms, and stares at me. I take another descending step, and the intensity of his glare burns through me. Thick red, like blood, washes behind my eyes, and my heart pauses. The pain of his glare alone, pushes me toward the second level.

What will he do to me if I try to leave?

My insides quiver. I swallow the lump in my throat... turn and climb the stairs.

The upper landing turns into an open hallway, one side overlooking the lower level of the bar and the other side, a wall set with doors into another room. I glance over the railing at my left. The establishment appears to be more of a night spot than one patronized during the day. Only a few people linger in the open space. The crazy vampire wannabe and her big bald bouncer keep an intense watch upon me, urging me onward.

I turn away from the railing and step through one of the doorways into the next room. It's dark. Too dark. And it takes my eyes a moment to adjust. My breaths are shallow, and my heart throbs with the severity of an organ ready to burst.

How is it possible to be this dark in here? It's as if a thick, black cloud is swallowing any glimmer of light or reflection.

Freaky. But I am not scared.

I hug myself, rub my arms, and allow my vision to adapt. Which it quickly does. Turns out, I left one somewhat empty bar downstairs for a creepier, more crowded one on the second level. Clearly, this is where their customers prefer to hang out, but why are they all standing around in the dark?

Everything is decorated in reds and blacks, which explains some of the light absorption. Some. Still, my skin tingles, and shivers race up my spine. The air weighs upon me with oppression, smelling of death and dying.

Several people turn toward me and smile, a fangy, evil grin.

My heart jumps into my throat. I want to disappear. Bolt from the establishment, the street, the French Quarter.

And yet, my feet aren't ready to move. Something within me is clamoring with curiosity. The room is filled with people pretending to be vampires. I've heard of such things but never expected to witness a gathering of this magnitude. Vampire mimics, *vampics*. Could this many people have nothing better to do than play vampire all day long?

Men and women sitting at the bar and standing around the outskirts have all now twisted to gaze at me, their faces bright with interest... hunger. My chest squeezes to a painful shudder, and my feet unglue. I turn to leave, bump into a body. My exit is blocked. Wannabe vamps have closed ranks around me. They move forward, pushing me deeper into the room.

I want to scream, but who would hear me? Plus, my voice is flattened by metal weights lodged within my throat, sinking ever downward toward my gut.

I step back and back and collide with a tall man standing against the bar. His face lowers into the curve of my neck, and he inhales deep, breathing in the scent of me. His arms move to encircle me. My body erupts in trembles. I jolt and push away. Thrust into more hungry grins.

My heart pounds with the strength of a battering ram. I press my flattened palm to my chest in hopes to calm my chaos. Possibly clear my mind for proper thought.

Greedy hands nab at me. Noses press to my skin, sniffing,

inhaling. I yelp and yell, push and shove, against an army of strength and want. People reaching and grabbing. Grins widening, teeth gleaming, laughter booming.

"She smells of power," one says.

"A rich, bold aroma," says another.

My body is bounced between them, vampic after vampic showing their teeth and commenting on the scent of my blood. My fingers wrestle with the latch on my purse. It gives and I search blindly for the item I want. Things are shifting and falling in the way. My hand yanks free with the tiny can of pepper spray in my grasp.

"Get back," I yell, brandishing the small weapon. Someone moves and I spray. There's a hiss, and the pepper spray is snatched from my grasp. My breath catches. Body grows numb.

Hands twine through my hair and yank my head back. I stumble. Heat, sharp as a blade, cuts across the space behind my ear, and a wet chill races down the back of my neck. The person holding me licks the wetness away.

"Perfection," they whisper, accompanied by a subtle moan.

I scream. The air distorts, reverberates. Around me, howls rise... and the hand upon my hair releases.

Pulling my purse into my chest, I push the horde away. Bulldoze a path from the room. The environment prickles with heat and electricity and channels a wind moving with the force of a bullet train. Bodies stagger, fall from my path, pushed by forces unseen.

And I run.

Run with sights set on each new exit as it comes, forcing myself past every interjecting obstacle. I rush from the room, the hallway, the stairs, the lower-level bar, the stretched red-lit entry. I knock the crazy girl off her feet... she's laughing and dabbing blood from her ears... and I keep going. Refuse to look back.

Stay in motion, until...

I itch to know I'm not being followed. I chance a glance. Slam into a body at my front. My momentum knocks me forward and sideways. Arms clamp around me, holding me steady.

"Wowa!"

My gaze swivels forward, and I come face to face with the blond guy from school. His expression is wide with surprise, but his smile is warm and comforting.

"Devil on your tail?" he asks.

CHAPTER NINE

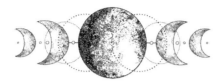

"Um." I'm in the arms of the good-looking senior, and I don't even know his name. I press my hand to his chest to help steady my footing, straighten, and take a step back. "I'm sorry. I didn't mean to plow into you like that."

A flush creeps over my skin, and my chin dips into my neck.

"I don't mind." His eyes are bright and his smile, wide... authentic.

My fingers fidget, and I find myself glancing back once, twice.

"Hey." He inclines his head to catch my gaze. "Something really got you spooked, didn't it?" His brow wrinkles. "How about we move out of the shadows?"

I nod. "Yeah. I'd like that." I gaze down at my purse and notice that it's still unlatched. I close and secure it.

He wraps his arm around me and guides us away from the far-reaching gloom of the vampy bar. My heart is thrumming at an unprecedented rate, and I'm not sure if the excitement is remnants of my freaky experience or related to his close proximity.

"I've seen you around school," he says. "You're new, right?" I nod, glance back toward the vamp shop and bar. "Well, I'm Phillip, and you can calm down because I am not going to let anything happen to you on my watch."

A smile cracks my lips. "I'm Miri," I say.

"Nice to meet you, Miri." He presents his hand, and I shake it. "Want to tell me what spooked you?"

"You," a female voice yells.

I swing toward the shout, expecting to see the vampic. It's not her. No one from the shop or the bar appears to have followed me. Instead, an older woman stands at the door of a nearby voodoo shop. Her eyes are ablaze, and her face is beet red. She shouts an endless parade of words, none of which I recognize. She yells in a different language where every word sounds angry and accusatory.

"Do you know that lady?" Phillip asks.

I shake my head and stare at her. First the girl on the street, then the cursed candle, followed by the crowd of vampic freaks in the bar, and now this... voodoo lady shouting at me on the street. Maybe I should have stayed home, like I was supposed to. I rub at the back of my neck. Find a cut... the cut received in the bar a short while ago.

A spike of pain rattles through me, causing Phillip to glance over me, but his gaze quickly returns to the lady standing in front of the voodoo shop. He steps forward, positioning himself between me and the shouting lady. "Listen lady," he says. "You had better calm down and shut up. This girl doesn't know who you are or what you are going on about. She doesn't deserve your abuse."

The woman silences for a moment, appearing to consider

him and his words. Her gaze flickers to me, and the sound of livid foreign words spew forth once more.

My body tenses, and my nostrils flare.

"Let's just get out of here," Phillip says, directing me across the street.

My teeth grind. I could leave. Allow Phillip to lead me wherever he feels I'll be safe. But I'm tired of these people in the Quarter pushing me around. Who are these people, to think they are all vampires and voodoo practitioners? I push around Phillip and head toward the shouting lady standing in the doorway of the voodoo shop.

She gasps. Her hands fly to her chest, and her eyes pop wide. Five more unrecognizable words fly from her lips and she turns, runs up the street.

"That was weird." I watch her disappear around the nearest corner.

"What did you do to her?" Phillip asks.

"I didn't do anything. Didn't even speak. It's like the sight of me scared her away." I frown.

"That *is* weird. But this is the French Quarter. It's full of weird." He cracks a grin and I laugh.

"You're telling me. My last hour has been packed full of out-of-this-world weird. I think I've exceeded my limit for the day." I take a deep, calming breath.

"I hope I don't fall into that bucket of weird," he says.

"No." I shake my head. "Running into you might be the only bright spot in an otherwise messed up day." I rub at the cut on the back of my neck. Flinch.

"In that case, maybe you'll let me take a look at what's bothering you there?" He motions to the back of my neck.

"It's nothing." I flatten my hair into place over the cut. My hair touches the slight open sliver, and I flinch... again.

"Clearly, it's not nothing. Come on." He takes my hand and leads me across the street and into a restaurant. Without pause, he pulls me through to the restroom at the back. Directs me inside. He pulls several paper towels from the dispenser, wets them in the sink, and turns to face me. "Come on. Show me."

I heave a frown and glance down at the wet paper towels held in his hand. "What makes you think you'll need that?"

He points to my hand. The hand I used to rub the back of my neck. I flair my fingers and turn my hand to better see. A blot of blood is smeared across two of my fingers.

"Wow." I raise my hand to eye level, then let it drop. "Seriously keen observation skills."

He shrugs. "Your flinch caused me to look a tad closer than normal. Now, why don't you let me help you.

"Fine." I hold my hair up and turn so that he may see the back of my neck.

"Hmm." He dabs at the cut.

"What?" I ask and start to turn. He grabs my shoulder, stopping me from moving.

"The cut is thin but looks deep. How did you get this?" He switches damp towels.

"Backed up against something. It was an accident." I rub my hands on my legs.

Phillip doesn't respond, and I get the sense he doesn't believe my answer. Rightfully so.

A heavy bang sounds on the door. "The restrooms are not for recreational purposes. What are you doing in there, Phil?

Phillip pushes open the door, revealing a guy in a waiter's uniform. He smiles; then his forehead crumples. Phillip and I are clearly not in the position the guy expected to find us in.

"Could you bring me the first-aid kit?" Phillip say. "Miri, here, managed to get a nasty cut on the back of her neck."

The guy's gaze swings to me, and he waves. "Hi Miri. On

62

it." He disappears from the doorway.

"What exactly did you accidently back into that caused this clean, yet deep, cut?" Phillip asks.

"Um…" I don't have a good answer for that. Do I tell him I suspect the damage was done by the fingernail of a freaky vampic?

The bathroom door flies open, and the waiter leans in. "Here you go." He hands Phillip the first-aid kit. "I have customers waiting at table seven, so I gotta go." He turns his attention to me. "Hope you feel better, Miri." He disappears and the door slowly pulls to a close.

Phillip tears open tiny packages and rubs ointment onto the cut using a Q-tip. He completes the process with a Band-Aid set securely in place. He closes the kit, secures the latch.

"Thanks," I say, turning to face him.

"Anytime." He pauses for a brief moment. "Be gentle with that area, keep it clean, and you should be good as new in a matter of days."

"Sure." My fingers twine together. Fidget. I glance around the bathroom. "So, what's the deal?" I throw my hands out to the side. "You know the waiter. You're totally at ease rushing us into the bathroom, borrowing the first-aid kit."

"I work here. Part-time."

"Oh. That makes sense." My muscles relax, and my hands drop at my side. A long, pulse-pausing moment drags out between us. "Okay then, thanks again." I reach for the door.

Phillip's hand drops over mine. "Can I walk you somewhere? Home perhaps?" His hand flares out to infer forward motion.

With his forward gesture, my thoughts swing back to the vampy girl, the freaks in the bar, and the screaming lady in the street.

"Do you think she had me confused with someone else?" I

ask, releasing my hold upon the doorknob and nodding in acceptance of Phillip's offer.

"Who?" He pushes open the bathroom door and motions toward the front of the restaurant, leans around the corner and sets the first-aid kit on an empty counter.

"The woman in the street who was yelling at me," I say.

Phillip shrugs a shoulder and leads us out the front door. "Who can say? Anything is possible, including a full diagnosis of crazy." He smiles and I giggle. "Where to?"

I have no plans to head home yet. Not with Phillip tagging at my side.

"You pick. I don't want to go home yet," I blurt.

"Um. Alright." He jams his hands into his pockets and rocks up on the balls of his feet. "Would you be interested in grabbing some beignets at Café Du Monde?"

"Only if you twist my arm," I quip.

"Consider your arm twisted." He imitates the twisting of my arm. We head toward the river's edge and Café Du Monde.

We wait in line for the famous café in awkward silence. Stealing glances every few seconds or minutes. He's dressed casually enough, jeans, V-neck T-shirt, high-top tennis shoes, and a flannel shirt tied around his waist. Still... *hot*.

"Who was that guy I saw you with at the Community Center?" he asks.

I blink, my mind blank for a moment. Then it dawns on me, he's asking about that first day of my life change. The day Belle and I went looking for Mike and found him shooting baskets. "That was my brother," I say. "He's a first-year college student."

He nods, the hint of a smile twitching the end of his lips.

"He attends the University of New Orleans. Ever since he enrolled, my mom has been busting her butt to pay the tuition."

"Doesn't your dad help with the tuition?" He asks, his gaze questioning and curious.

"Table for two?" the hostess asks. We nod and she tells us to wait one moment.

"My dad left years ago," I say matter-of-factly.

"Oh. I'm sorry." His gaze shifts to the side. I've seen it enough times in the past. People ask about my father, and are then embarrassed to have asked based on the answer provided.

"Don't be. I don't even remember him. "I straighten my shoulders. "Besides, if he were still around, I probably wouldn't be standing here right now with you."

"How so?" His gaze snaps back to me. His brows are raised.

"I just moved into the Quarter because my mom moved us all in with her boyfriend. If my father had stuck around, there probably wouldn't have been a boyfriend or a move to said boyfriend's house."

"Ahh." He nods his head slowly. "So, I should thank your father and your mother's boyfriend for this encounter."

I cough a laugh.

"This way." The hostess leads us to a table in the middle of the crowded space.

We take a seat and order immediately. I glance around at all the people stuffed into the cafe. So many lives traveling their own paths. How many of them are into voodoo or vampires? I shuffle my silverware and napkin. Take a sip of my water.

"The girl you were with that day at the Community Center, was she your sister then?" he asks, continuing our conversation from when we stood in line.

"Yep. That was Belle. Her name is actually Mirabelle, but everyone calls her Belle for short." I torque my head to the side. "I thought you would have known that already. I saw you talking to her at the center." I bite my lip. I'm talking too much. I'm a vomit of words. Am I nervous in his company or frayed from the day? Maybe both.

"Oh, yeah. We spoke, but I didn't ask her about you or

anything. She asked me if I knew where the restrooms were, and I asked her if she was new to the area. That's about it," he says.

Sounds about right. Belle told me their exchange wasn't more than a few words.

We drop back into a pit of silence, and I stare at his hands. There is a darkness trapped within the creases and cracks of his skin. Grease, maybe?

The hostess returns with our order. Two plates of beignets and no coffee. We're sticking with water.

"The other day, when I passed you in the hallway, before the bell rang, you looked..." He shakes his head, lifts his hands. "I don't know. Upset, maybe. I assumed that was your mom walking out ahead of you, when I saw you leaving school early. Was everything okay?" He bites into his beignet and white powder drifts all over his pant leg.

"Everything was fine." Not wanting to discuss the day of the field trip, my response is short and decisive. I take a bite of my own beignet. My taste buds become submerged in perfection. I wipe my napkin across my mouth, not wanting to fashion snowy lips in front of Phillip.

"You got a little..." Phillip points to the edge of my mouth. "Do you mind?"

My eyes widen and I nod, giving him the go-ahead. With a gentle finger, he curves around the edge of my lips, removing any lingering powdered sugar. He licks his finger.

"I'm glad you ran into me." He smiles at me, and my insides warm.

"I'm glad too," I say and our conversation flows naturally into nonthreatening topics. There is no discussion of vampics or angry voodoo ladies. It's all classes at school and plans after school. Phillip doesn't see himself going the full college route. Maybe a two year and then on to something else. Funny, even with Mike already at the university, I hadn't given much thought to life after high school. I have time, though. It's only my sophomore year. Phillip graduates at the end of this year, so thoughts of the future are a tad more predominant in his mind.

We finish our beignets and brush away the powdered evidence as best we can. From the café, we walk around Jackson Square, his hand slipping close to mine, every now and again. We pause and wrap our hands around the surrounding gate, stare at the statue and at St. Louis Cathedral.

Phillip leans into my ear. "Did you know that it's rumored the original engineer of the cathedral is buried somewhere on that site?" He gestures to the cathedral.

"Really? I pull my head back. "Does he haunt it?" A grin inches across my lips, and I suppress a laugh.

Phillip jerks with a quick chuckle. Smiles.

If I was able to see the ghosts at the battlefield, would I be able to see them here, at the cathedral?

The battlefield. The field trip to the battlefield. The field trip I wasn't supposed to be a part of.

"I should probably get home." My gaze tears from his steel blue eyes and drops to my feet. This day has been a mixture of frightening and fabulous, and I don't want it to end, but I also don't want to be on the wrong side of Mom's wrath if she discovers I broke her rule.

"I'll walk you. Where to?"

We leave the square behind and head northwest, straight through the Quarter to the far edge. Come to a pause in front of Caleb's garage door.

"Thanks," I say.

Phillip takes my hands in his. "Maybe, someday, you'll tell me what had you so freaked out earlier today."

My heart jumps into my throat at the mention of earlier. "Maybe," I say.

"I can wait. I'm not going anywhere." He gazes deep into my eyes.

"Miri!" My name calls from the balcony above. "You are *soo* busted."

CHAPTER TEN

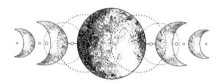

Belle stands on the balcony above, gazing down at us. My lips pucker into a tight line, hiding my smile. I tilt my head back and wave.

"Mom called. You're lucky I covered for you. I told her you were trapped in the bathroom." She smirks.

Great.

I force a return grin, then turn to Phillip. "Thanks for the adventure and the walk home." I step toward the garage door, stretching the handhold between us. "I had fun."

"Yeah, so did I." His smile is slight and warm. "Maybe we can do it again sometime." He allows his fingers to linger and slip from mine. We stand in silence, staring at each other, the moments passing between us.

From beyond the garage door comes a thump, thump, thump, thump. The door opens, and Belle steps forward. "You coming in or what?"

"One sec." I glance from her back to Phillip. "See you around?"

"Definitely." He doesn't move to leave but watches me, waits for me to make the first exit.

With a meek smile I slip into the garage, and Belle closes the door behind me.

"How long have you been out?" Belle asks.

"Not long," I say and follow her up the stairs.

"Mom will be pissed if she finds out." She glances at her watch. "She's probably already on her way home, so you'd better change unless you want to explain the white powder all over your outfit."

I glance down at my attire. Despite my efforts to clean up after our visit to Café Du Monde, I managed to bring home a significant amount of evidence.

"Good point." I rush up the stairs to my room.

I toss my purse onto the bed and change into something comfy for the night, dropping my day clothes in the hamper. *I'll deal with them later.* I start for the stairs, and before I leave the room, I get the notion to check my purse. I pop it open and rummage through the contents. The pepper spray is gone, as expected. It had been yanked from my grasp at the bar. But other things are also missing. Things that likely fell from the bag when I was frantically searching for the pepper spray. Most of the stuff can be replaced. Lip gloss, a hair clip. But it's my old school ID that I had rubber banded together with my new, temporary ID that gives me pause.

I drop to a sit on the bed. *My ID. My school ID.* Did I lose it at the bar filled with vampic freaks? What if they find it? They'll know my name. Maybe even know how and where to find me. I press my palms to my chest. It's tight. So suffocatingly tight.

What if... what if Mom finds out?

"Hey," Belle says from the doorway. "It's your turn to make dinner."

My eyes close and my hands drop to the surface of the bed. I exhale. Stand. Spin around. "I know. Every night this week is my turn to make dinner." I march past Belle, down the stairs, and into the kitchen.

~

T he next day at school, Phillip is waiting for me when I am released from detention.

"Saw you sitting in the glass bowl after the dismissal bell," he says, in reference to the classroom used for detention. "Thought I'd hang out and wait. Want to grab a burger? I know a great place not far from here?"

"Burgers?" I cling to my book bag and glance toward the main exit. Mom's demands would have me heading straight home to do homework and chores. But, she should be a work right now. So should Caleb. I turn my gaze back to Phillip, consider the alternative.

"Yeah. Burgers. You know, fat, juicy meat patties, set between toasted bread buns, and smothered in all kinds of deli-cious goodness. Ketchup, pickles, tomatoes." He pauses, glances over me. "They also have salads if you like to pretend you don't eat meat." His smile is rather Cheshire cat, as if daring me to eat a solid, full-of-carbs meal in front of him.

"Okay. I'm in,' I say and follow him off campus. We head toward the river, along the eastern edge of the Quarter.

"You're going to love this place. I guarantee it." We slip through a door into a well-packed burger joint and bar. "Just wait until it's dinner time. There will be a line out the door and down the street. This is one of the best times to come, before the after-work crowd shows up. And after the school-released crowd has departed."

Attending school so close to the Quarter is different from

my school on the other side of the Garden District in ways I had not imagined. So many businesses cram the streets, in easy walking distance of the school campus.

I smile and peruse the menu. Decide on a cheese and mushroom burger with a side of fries and a Coke. My order appears to please him. I've now proven myself as something more than a panic-salad-ordering kind of girl. Even if I do enjoy a good salad every now and again.

I tell him about Belle's talent in the kitchen and how she loves to create heavy Cajun meals. He tells me he lives alone with his dad, who is very much a meat and potatoes kind of guy. They don't do fancy meals at his place.

"He works a lot, which means he isn't home so much. I kind of raised myself." Phillip's shoulders rise and fall with a hint of pride.

"My mom works a lot too. She's always picking up extra shifts where she can, in hopes of making a little extra cash." I dip a french fry into the ketchup.

"Yeah. It's like my dad is married to the job. I need to make an appointment if I want to see him." Phillip takes a sip of his drink.

"What's he do?" I ask.

"He works for the city." He shoves several fries in his mouth, chews, and swallows them down. "Do you play basket-ball often?" he asks, in a clear subject change. I allow it. I'm not keen on discussing my mom either.

"Me?" I feign surprise and press my hand to my chest. "Only when I play with my brother. He used to play *a lot*. Now he only plays once in a while."

"Maybe you'll play a little dribble ball with me sometime?"

I giggle. "What? So you can embarrass me?"

"Of course not. I would never." He frowns, but the curve of his lips is quickly flipped upward into a smile.

Time with Phillip eases my mind for a short while, but the case of my missing school ID continues to weigh on my thoughts. I watch Phillip's lips while he talks and continue to capture a glimpse of the clock on the wall, making sure to note the time. How long can I stay before Mom becomes wise to my actions? And how can I search for my school ID without her finding out? Or me getting bounced around by more vampics?

"You seem pretty distracted," Phillip says. "Is everything alright?" He leans into the table, reducing the space between us.

"Yeah, yeah," I placate. "I just lost my school ID, is all. It's only the second week, and I can't find it."

He leans back in his seat. "It was the temporary one, right? Doesn't matter." He shrugs and settles into his seat. "You'll be getting the official one soon. That will solve the issue of your lost school ID."

"I guess you're right." I bite my nails. If that were the only concern regarding my ID, his advice would be solid. But I am less concerned about the absence of my ID than I am about the hands within which it may now be held.

I need to find it.

I'll go look for it tonight, after Mom and Caleb are asleep.

I smile at Phillip and take a sip of my soda. Ask him about the grease trapped in the crevices of his skin. His face lights up, and he tells me he has an old motorcycle he works on in his spare time. He hopes to have it running sometime soon. "When I do," he says. "How about you and I go on a small adventure."

Even though we've only just met, his suggestion makes me smile. I keep a close eye on the time, and at five minutes short of an hour, I excuse myself, informing Phillip that I have to get home. He jumps to his feet, pays the bill, and walks with me. It's a walk I wish to drag out and make last as long as possible, but I can't, or I may get caught. Still, I savor the moments as much as possible.

Phillip doesn't try to hold my hand, but his body often slips close enough that his heat wafts over my skin. It's a delicious sensation. He pauses in front of Caleb's garage door and stares at me. For a moment, I think he means to kiss me.

I yearn to kiss him, back. But what if I do? What if I kiss him and things go sideways? Do I care? Care about any fallout?

I roll forward on my feet, my lips inching closer to his.

A bang sounds behind me. I jump, spin around.

"Oh hey, sorry." Mike waves, covers his mouth, flushes with color, and turns away, walks up the street.

Right. Perfect timing. Maybe it means something.

"Thanks for another great time," I say. "See you tomorrow."

"Looking forward to it." He shoves his hands in his pockets and takes a crooked step backward.

I slip into the house and run straight to my room, climb to the window and spy Phillip halfway down the street. I watch him until he walks out of view.

I move through the rest of the day in a rush. I do my homework and the laundry. Make dinner and clean the kitchen. Go to bed and wait for the house to fall silent. The minutes and hours pass with the speed of a thick honey drip.

It's after ten before the house becomes still. With as much stealth as I can muster, I get dressed, grab my hoodie, and sneak down the stairs. Next to the kitchen, I pause beside a narrow shelf cluttered with touristy items. A long wooden stake catches my eye. I grab it and shove it into my bag.

If wannabe vamps aren't afraid of pepper spray, maybe the thought of a stake to the heart will slow their aggression.

I spin and head for the stairs toward the garage. Behind me, a door opens. A heavy foot drops upon the top step.

I gasp and freeze.

CHAPTER ELEVEN

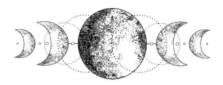

I'*ve been caught.*

Maybe, if I don't move, the shadows will hide me, and I won't be seen.

"What are you doing?" Mike's voice is a firm whisper.

I spin around to face him. He's sporting a similar attire to mine, dark jeans and a dark hoodie. "I could ask you the same."

"I'm several years your senior. The rules that apply to you don't apply to me. There's a citywide curfew for kids your age." He crosses his arms. "Whatever you're planning to do is dangerous. You could end up drawing the attention of curfew enforcement. In other words, cops. And trust me, Miri, you don't want to end up on their radar."

He glances over me, and I don't say a word. Instead, I'm thinking about the warning he gave me about cops using our family as pawns in some attempt to control or guide the witch community.

"Why are you sneaking out, anyway? You've got school tomorrow." He takes a step closer.

"So do you, and yet, here we are." I swing my arms in the air between us in reference to our standoff.

"Fair point." He moves past me and descends the stairs to the garage with slow, silent steps. I follow. "You meeting that boy I saw you with?" I don't answer. "Whatever you do, be smart and don't wander down any dark alleys alone. You hear me? And stay clear of the cops."

"I hear you."

I follow his lead through the garage. He eases the door open, closing it with barely a click behind me. "This is our secret. I don't want to hear any news of this evening repeated to me from Mom." He extends his pinky, and we pinky promise, like we used to do when we were younger.

"You feeling confident Caleb won't check on you? Find you missing?" he asks, and we start walking down the block.

"You're concerned about Caleb and not Mom?" I jab.

"Mom values her sleep too much. We both know that," he says, acknowledging the fact that Mom sleeps like a stone. The house could crumble around her, and she wouldn't stir.

"Guess you're right, but Caleb checking in on me in the middle of the night, that's just creep-*ish*, don't you think?" I shove my hands deep into the pockets of my hoodie.

"From our perspective, totally. But Caleb has some perverse idea that he can step into Dad's shoes and start living the part of our father." Mike shoves his hands into his pockets, matching my stance. "I'm not going to be so quick to let that happen."

At the corner, he reminds me, once more, to be careful. Then we part ways. It's late, but it's not that dark. Not once I move into the thrum of the Quarter. Lights are bright and music is pumping on all sides of the street. There's laughter and cat calls, yelps and screams. I slip my hoodie into place, hiding my face, and keep my head down. Move through the thrum of people, holding my unzipped bag at my waist, with my hand slipped within, holding firmly to the wooden stake.

Why would Caleb have such a thing? I hadn't realized he was a fan of vampire macabre.

Following the same path I had taken the day before, I weave through the streets until I find myself standing beside the small shop the vamp girl had dragged me into. The store with the candle. The candle still sits within the candelabra, burning strong.

I glance toward the voodoo shop. The doorway is empty and the angry lady who yelled at me is not in sight. It's a tiny relief in a night that has my teeth clenched. Following the loud rumble of dark music, I make my way toward the bar where I suspect I lost my school ID.

If I didn't lose it there, then I really have no idea where to begin looking.

At night, the shadows courting the long, narrow passageway and bar feel similar to black holes waiting to swallow me. The overhead red lights drench everything in a bloody bath effect. Within the tight walk, people socialize, some dance, many reveal fake fangs and pretend to bite others. A few are in full make-out mode. My skin warms, sending blood rushing to my cheeks. I raise my hand flat to block any lovers from view and push myself forward. Onward to the club.

The vibe is dark, though nothing as dark as what I felt the other day. Inside the club, people are laughing and appear to be having a good time. None of them seem to notice me. They are too busy fulfilling their carnal desires. Mouths lip-locked, hands on flesh, teeth—fake vamp teeth—sinking into bare necks.

I shiver. Rub my arms. Make my way to the bar.

"Are you lost?" The bartender angles into the bar, his gaze

narrowing. "You don't look like the type we normally attract at this establishment."

A nervous smile tugs at my lips. I lean forward, clutching the bar's edge, and bounce on the balls of my feet. Give the place a quick scan and then return my attention to the bartender. "I lost something in here yesterday. I was hoping someone found it?"

"Aww. So, you're the one." All hints of friendliness slip from the bartender's face. He straightens and raises his head toward the second level. "What you're looking for is up there."

Great.

I turn my gaze to the people on the dance floor. No band occupies the stage. The music is pumped in by way of speakers anchored in the four far corners of the room. And the sound is loud. Cranked up to deafening level. I doubt anyone would hear me scream, should I do so from the smaller bar upstairs.

Not that I think anyone here would come running to my rescue anyway. I am not a care on any of their lists.

My attention is drawn like a magnet to a couple plastered against the far wall. A slight woman has a not-so-small man pressed firmly against the brick. Her hands, pinning his arms flat and still. From his neck, she laps at a dark substance oozed over him. The house special, I assume. A thick drink made to resemble blood in their patrons' roleplay scenarios. I can't decipher if the man's expression is one of excitement or fear. Maybe a little of both.

Gross.

My nose wrinkles, and I quickly turn back to the bar. Stare at the surface and remind myself that I find nothing about this place or its customers even the slightest bit interesting. I suck back a deep breath, then release. Turn my gaze upon the bartender.

"Thanks. You've been a ton of help." I allow sarcasm to seep heavily into my tone.

With a sigh, I turn my back to the bar, and gaze up to the second landing. Strobe lights flash through the wall of open doors. I can't decide if the light show makes the upper level appear more exciting and livelier, or disorienting for unsuspecting stragglers.

At the base of the stairs, stands the large bald man from the day before. His legs are planted shoulder length apart, and his arms are crossed. He's being selective as to who he allows up the stairs verses who he turns away, giving the upper level a kind of VIP status.

I glance back at the bartender. He's gone. Turn my gaze toward the exit. Fight the desire to turn and run. Or... if the girl was right about her accusations yesterday... jump on a broom and fly away. Except...

I really need to find my school ID.

I weave through the patrons, with slow, reluctant steps, making my way toward the bald man guarding the stairs.

A smirk creases his left cheek. "I had a feeling you might grace us with another visit." He raises his chin. "What you seek is upstairs. Good luck retrieving it." His tone teases, and he steps to the side, allowing me passage.

I shiver, hug myself, and hesitate. Stare at the bar beside me, then the landing above. What am I doing here? This is stupid, coming to a bar like this one, late at night, *alone.* I glance over at the large guy standing beside the stairwell. He cocks a brow and tilts his head, telling me to get moving... make a decision, up or out.

I chew on my lower lip and start climbing, clutch the stake in my purse. Follow the flashing red light.

Seventeen steps to the upper level. Four steps across the landing. I move toward the first open door into the second-story bar. Crimson and black flash opposite a stream of light. Light bloodied by dark décor and a mass of dark bodies drinking and dancing and getting familiar. I step into the doorway.

The lights go out. Everything drops to pitch black.

A hand wraps around my wrist. The wrist of the hand shoved inside of my purse, holding the stake.

I yelp and my hand flexes, releasing my grip upon my safety precaution.

Out of the darkness, bodies and hands converge on me. They swarm. Pick and press. Pull me into the depths of the enclosed room. A room now holding a strong smell of nickel.

I wrench free of the wrist hold. "Do you mind?" I jerk, scoot, and push. "Aren't you taking this whole wannabe-vampire thing a bit too seriously? You don't need to do this. I just want to find something I may have left here the other day." Someone grabs my upper arm, and I slap their hand away. "Did anyone happen to see or pick up a small pink wallet?"

A sharp nail cuts my skin at the base of my neck, extracting blood.

"Ouch." I spin around. Slap my palm over the cut. "What are you doing? What are you all doing?"

"Beautiful," someone murmurs.

Another cut, this time, a long slice across the top of my hand. "Intoxicating," says another.

Slit. Slash, across my other hand—top, palm, wrist.

"A profusion of power."

A knife-edge nick along my collar bone.

I squeal, want to yank the stake free of my purse, but the push of my palms hold several people at bay and I'm afraid to drop a hand, allowing another face to leer closer.

"Let us have you. Delight in you," they whisper. Their hands grab at me, pull at me, and their tongues lap at my wounds.

I scream and push and yell, then scream some more. "Stop it. Stop it now." Why did I come here alone? Such a stupid, reckless thing to do. I should have confided in Mike, asked him to come with me.

I'm pressed between bodies, unable to move or thrash free. I pull inward, shriek, and drop to a ball on the ground.

"Please. Please leave me be," I whimper. "All I want is my wallet."

Somebody laughs, igniting the entire group to roll with laughter.

"Your wallet?" Someone says from the back. "You may have your pretty pink wallet... for a small price."

"What?" I hug my knees. "I don't have much money." Tears well at the corner of my eyes.

My words extract more chuckles from the crowd. Between the cackles, the sound of my name, shouted from the bar below. It must be my imagination, because no one knows I'm here. I shake my head, attempt to clear the hallucinations nipping at my mind.

A bark of deep, dark laughter rolls through the room. "It's not your money we wish in exchange for that which you seek. It's the power strumming through your blood." Bodies shift and a leering grin appears before me. I gasp. "That's right." He presses closer. "We want your blood. Sips and cups and pools of your blood."

The crowd pushes in around him, their eyes glimmering with greed and their teeth bared, showing set after set of fangs. Hands, a multitude of hands, clamp onto me and I scream. A deep, all the way from my core screech. The lights blink and return to a frenzy strobe, as they had been when I first ascended the stairs. Red, black, flash. Red, black, flash.

A smack, stamp, stomp thunders from beyond the walls of the room. A second later, a thunder of dark, oppressive fusion booms through the bar below, and the building thrums with verve.

In the return of manic light, I catch sight of a face looking all too familiar. If I didn't know better, I'd think it was Caleb I'd seen. But it couldn't have been Caleb. He was sleeping when I left the house... wasn't he? And if it were Caleb, he would step in and help me... wouldn't he?

The moment is brief, the sight of the man and his features. In this lighting and my state, he could be anyone, but in that instant, he reminds me of my mom's boyfriend. He stares at me with an appalled expression, conflicted with misery. He's there, and then he is gone, turned away from the mass pressing in upon me.

A hand clasps over my shoulder. I twitch, tug away, slip my hand into my open purse and pull free the stake. "Get away," I say, holding the wooden weapon against my chest, pointed outward.

"You can't impale us all, little witch."

The mob throbs and pounces. The stake is knocked from my hold, kicked into the moving mass of feet. I throw my hands over my head and attempt to disappear. My head and hands burn, warmth slithers over me, and an orange glow burns through my eyelids.

I scream, they howl. Drown me in the sea of hands, bodies, and fangs.

CHAPTER TWELVE

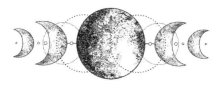

"What's going on?"

The yell comes from the doorway. The light burst to full illumination, minimizing the effects of the harsh strobe. Hisses and growls follow a wave of disruption through the crowd where people are being shoved aside. A hand reaches through the press of bodies and takes hold of mine, yanks.

"Come on," Phillip says.

My heart leaps into my throat and, with a gasp, I gaze up into his tight pressed face. His attention darts to our clasped hands for a brief moment, then back to my face. He readjusts his hold in a manner that suggests there's something uncomfortable about my touch. Can he feel the burn of my skin? The burn I took for psychological. Without a word, I allow him to pull me into a stand, and guide me in a slip through the throng of bodies.

"You had better stop harassing this girl. I called the cops and the fire department before I stepped foot inside the door,"

Phillip says. "You should also thin out this crowd, or the Fire Marshall will get involved."

He pulls me into his side and maneuvers us onto the landing and down the stairs, neither one of us saying a word. The bald, burly guy at the base of the stairs moves to the side with nothing more than a raised brow and a smirk. Phillip keeps his arm securely wrapped around me and ushers us straight out of the bar and into the street beyond. Free of the blood-hungry crowd, he pulls us to a stop and turns to face me. Releases his grip upon me.

I shiver and fix my jacket, making sure any new nicks upon my body are covered. It's bad enough he found me curled in a ball on the floor. Phillip doesn't need to know I managed to get vamp-nail scratched a half dozen times.

He raises his fisted hands at his side, gives them a quick shake, then slaps his hands together, and presses them into his forehead. "What were you doing going into a place like that..." He jabs a point toward the bar. "Especially alone, and at night?"

"I'm sorry, I didn't realize I needed to answer to you." My nerves kick out a wide-eyed snide remark.

"Miri." His shoulders and face drop. "That was some serious stuff in there."

I shake my head, drop my chin. "Sorry. I was in there the other day... during daylight hours, of course," I quickly add, and glance back at the narrow entrance to the bar. "At the time, I dropped my wallet and didn't realize it. I was only trying to get it back. It has my school ID." My hands twist together, wiggling and wringing.

"This is where you lost your school ID? Why didn't you say something to me earlier? I would have helped you." He sighs and drops his hands against his thighs with a soft pat. His black pants and a white shirt carry a heavy aroma of greasy food. I'm guessing he just got off work.

"I'm sorry I didn't say anything." I drop my gaze to my feet, shove the ball of my foot into the ground and twist. "I guess. Well. We haven't known each other that long, and I have trust issues." Folding my hands in front of me, I peer into his eyes and frown.

He responds with a crooked frown of his own. "I'll give you that one. We haven't known each other long at all. But it's now my goal to gain your trust and know you for an outrageously long time."

A barely there smile tugs at the edge of my lip. The idea of him working to earn my trust is an entertaining and enjoyable thought. We'll see if I continue to like him well enough to keep him around.

"Promise me you'll be smart, and safe, and not go back in there again? At least, not alone and never at night."

I hug myself. "I'm not a child."

"I know that." His voice strains. "It's just..." His gaze darts toward the bar. "Of all the bars in the Quarter, I trust that one the least. It isn't safe. The patrons are shady."

"Shady?" My head jerks back. "Freaky and creepy is more like it. Besides, what were you doing in there?"

"I saw you enter, and I got worried, so... I followed." He shoves his hands in his pockets and narrows his gaze. "Was I wrong to come?"

My eyes widen, and I don't know what to say. I'm glad he came. I really am. That was a scary incident that I don't care to ever again experience. But do I tell him that? Expose my mistake and weakness?

A group of tourists walk by, and we fall silent, waiting for the people to move out of ear shot. Although the street where we stand isn't flooded with people like Bourbon Street, it's well enough traveled that there is little privacy to be had. There's a fair selection of bars, restaurants, and shops.

"You just happened to be hanging out near the creepy and disturbing bar?" I cross my arms, choosing to act tough in an attempt to cover my desire to shake and cry.

"No." He jerks. Shakes his head. "It wasn't like that at all. I was at work." He throws a casual point to the restaurant across the street from the bar. The one where he patched the cut on the back of my neck. "I was bussing the table at the window and happened to look out at the street right when you stepped into the narrow passage leading to the bar."

My muscles relax. He does smell like greasy foods. Probably spending too much time in the kitchen. "You just walked out on your job and came looking for me?"

"Sort of." He shifts his weight. "My shift was almost over anyway. I dropped the dirty dishes in the back and told the manager I was taking off for the night. I came, found you, and now, here we are."

"Here we are." I flex my hands down the front of my body.

"Can I walk you home?" He shifts an inch closer. "It's after curfew. We can't be too careful."

Right. The curfew set in place because of the out-of-control homicide rate. The acquaintance murders Grandma said were partly related to the witch community. Something those freaks in the bar happen to think I am a part of.

I suck back a deep breath and let it out slowly. Glance back at the vampy bar. "I still need to retrieve my wallet."

"Forget about that right now. I can get it for you tomorrow... if you're okay with that?" He scratches at his collar bone.

"Um..." My gaze swings back and forth between him and the bar. A few sinister characters have gathered at the entrance and now watch us. "You'll do that how?" I ask.

"Come on." He takes my arm and turns me up the street, starts walking, putting much needed distance between us and the gathered vampics. "On occasion, my boss has sent me on errands to the bar. I haven't liked it, but I've done it enough that they know me in there. Tolerate me, out of respect for my boss. If that respect is what helped me get you out of there tonight without any serious issue, then I'm glad for all those uncomfortable assignments. The awkward relationship finally came in handy."

"Yes, it apparently did." I nod.

"Hey, would you mind?" His hand slips around mine, finishing his question through demonstration. I glance down at our now intertwined hands and smile. In lieu of a vocal response, I tighten my grip, tug him a tad closer. After dealing with a swarm of freaks wanting to drink my blood, my skin tingles with comfort having Phillip at my side. We walk the rest of the way to Caleb's house hand in hand.

"You want to hear something strange," I say as we turn a corner and head up the street on which Caleb's house is located.

"Stranger than you walking into that bar tonight?" He throws me a sideways glance and smug grin. We've moved into an area that consists primarily of residences, making for a quieter, more intimate stroll.

"Maybe." I shrug my shoulders and try not to smile too wide. I fail. "It's just, when all those people were swarming in the bar, at one point, I thought I saw my mom's boyfriend."

"And it would be strange for him to go to a bar like that one?" Phillip asks.

"Honestly, I don't really know," I say. "He does work at a club, just not that one. But that wasn't the strangest part. The strangest part was the way he looked at me and did nothing to help."

"And this guy, your mom's boyfriend, he's generally good to you?"

"Well, yeah." I shrug. "He's never been not good to me." I take a beat, recall what I saw, and frown. "I was probably confused. It couldn't have been him."

"Are you sure?" Phillip presses. "If he *was* there and he *let* them attack you like that..."

We slow to a stop in front of Caleb's place, and I turn to face him. "I'm sure it's all fine. You don't need to worry. It doesn't make sense for him to have been there. Tonight is his night off, and he passed out early."

"Are you sure?" He takes several locks of my wavy, dark hair into the fold of his hold and allows them to fall loosely from his hand. "I don't want anyone to hurt a single hair on your head."

Heat radiates through my chest. I bite my lip and glance over my shoulder to the quiet balcony set above the garage. The house is silent, dark.

"Fairly sure." My face lifts and butterflies dance in my belly. "I should probably go. We have school in the morning."

"Miri?" His palm melds to the curve of my jaw, his thumb rubbing a gentle stroke. His gaze is soft, yet intense, glued upon me.

"Yes?" My eyes blink wide, and my lips part.

"I don't want..." His gaze drops to my lips, and his breath slows. My heart kicks into a race. The silence existing between us is thick with anticipation. A building, billowing want. He steps closer. My breath snags in my throat.

With slow, deliberate measure, his lips press to mine and swallow any doubts or inhibition I harbor regarding him or us. He holds my face in his hands, and it might as well be my heart he cradles. Who knew a single kiss could so easily destroy any resistance within me? I savor the flavor of him, and my arms find their way around to his back, pulling him closer.

The moment may be short, but it is precious, beautiful, changing. He shifts back, presses his forehead to mine, our noses touching. He closes his eyes and breathes slow and steady. His fingers weave through the hair at my temples.

"I think you may have successfully trapped me in your magical snare." His thumb runs a path down the side of my face.

"There's nothing magical about me," I say, breathe shallow.

"I beg to differ." He presses his lips to my forehead.

The night grows still around us, and we slip into a perfect peace.

Until... a cat yawls.

A laugh hitches in my throat. "Guess that's my cue." I bite the inside of my lip and take a step toward the garage door, letting our hold stretch the space between us.

"Sleep well," he says.

I nod and allow joy to permeate my features. I open the garage door as quietly as possible.

"See you at school tomorrow." Our fingers reluctantly separate.

"Tomorrow," I say and step over the threshold.

"Miri?" Phillip says. I glance back at him. "Thank you for allowing me to walk you home."

I smile so wide I fear my face might crack. "You can walk me home every day if you want."

"I may take you up on that." He shoves his hands into his pockets and rolls up on the pads of his feet, drops back flat-footed on the street.

I take my leave, start to close the door, and a black cat attempts to slip through the opening behind me. I block the critter's passage with my foot.

"Nope," I say. "Wrong house, buddy." I push him back, silently close the door, and sneak into the house.

With breath held, I tiptoe to the door at the back of the garage and crack it open a sliver. Wide enough to peek inside without exposing myself to the room beyond. Mom is sprawled across one side of the bed, and the other side is oddly unoccupied. My chest tightens, and I ease the door closed, head upstairs.

If Caleb's not in bed, where could he be? Is there a chance he was the man I saw? My lips twist to the side. He could be in the bathroom. I pause midway up the first flight of stairs and listen, wait. I don't detect any noises. No flushes. No running water faucets. I finish the climb to the next level.

A quick and quiet peek informs me that Mike is not yet home. I sigh. Wonder where he went and what he's up to at such a late hour. He's not yet old enough to legally drink, not that such a fact would stop him from hanging out in the midst of the bar scene or prevent him from getting served at several Quarter establishments.

I've heard the stories where *drinking* age is less a requirement and more of a suggestion.

I tiptoe up the remaining stairs to my room. The creak of a bedspring comes from Belle's room, causing me to be extra careful. Slipping free of my jacket, jeans, and shoes, I take a few moments in the bathroom to clean my cuts before sliding beneath my covers for the night. I lay my head upon the pillow and gaze at the moonlight spilling in through the window. My thoughts are of Phillip—a never-ending, scrolling dream scene about my blond-haired, light-skinned temptation.

I float into the world of dreams, leaving reality behind, tethered in the room where I have fallen asleep.

Phillip and I walk, hand in hand, down a deserted street. The moon is full and bright, and his mouth is an inviting perfection. I can't stop stealing glimpses of his delicious lips and delightful eyes. My emotions are a chaotic mess, plaguing me with an overactive heart, warming blood, dry throat, and clammy hands. I lick my lips, swallow, and trip over my internal sensations... and my feet.

I smack the ground and Phillip is gone, our dream moment evaporating. The floor beneath me becomes dark and slick. Nothing like the concrete of the street. My hands slip and slide beneath my shivering weight. I've fallen from the bliss of the night's walk home, into the terror of the vampics in the bar. The air nips at my skin and goosebumps cover me.

I'm curling, curling tight into a ball, as the red light blinks, blinks, blinks. I want to escape. Press my eyes shut and wish hard. The voices of vampics whisper at my ear and crowd my mind. Their teeth are bare, and blood drips... drips everywhere. My fingers claw at the linoleum, digging and digging and digging. Digging an exit, a me-sized hole. Wood and vinyl give way to earth, and chunks of both natural and man-made materials topple aside, revealing a person-sized rabbit hole.

Heart hammering at a frantic pitch, I climb into the opening I've created and pull my way along. My breaths drag hard and labored. My fingers cramp and sting. The surrounding walls are rigid, shifting from floorboard to concrete to dirt. The passage is dark and dank.

I can't imagine Alice Liddell willingly climbing into any dark, earthen hole. *Why am I?*

As if on cue, hisses and growls at my rear remind me of why I am urged forward.

I pull, drag, thrust, moving deeper and deeper into a tight hole leading nowhere. My skin is damp with perspiration, and my stomach has turned to stone. The tiny tunnel is crumbling, collapsing on either side of me.

No, no, no, no. My palms press against the dirt walls, attempt to hold them firm.

The tight space caves in.

I scream, chest crashing in on itself. *Tight. So tight.*

Will this nightmare end with my death?

My fingers claw at the dirt, using my nails like trowels to cut through the soil. My cuticles tear and nails crack, break. I yelp and fight the tremors threatening to rock my limbs.

It would be so easy... so darn easy... to give up and let death consume me. But I won't be that girl.

I yell and thrash and pound. The land beneath my hands gives and falls away, creating a gap to the outside world. Gasping for the night's air, I heave myself forward through the gap, free of the tight, earthen space. Scooch out and drop down to the packed and ungiving ground.

I breathe deep.

Breathe, breathe, breathe.

Calm my erratic heart and blink wide.

I'm laying at the base of a wall vault inside one of New Orleans' cities of the dead. I shiver, jerk, quickly pull myself from the ground. How did I get here? Or better question... why did I end up here?

A soft, indiscernible voice whispers on the breeze. I wrap my arms around me and hunch my shoulders.

I feel as if... as if something... some part of me, some piece of me I should recognize, has pulled me here.

The tomb from which I have emerged is broken wide, the name once displayed across the front, now lays upon the ground in a multitude of concrete pieces. I stare at the littered pieces, spy a capital C. It means nothing to me. The vault beneath the one from which I crawled hosts the name Johnathan... I think. The letters are worn with time, making a reliable read of the first name difficult and the last name, impossible.

Who is Johnathan, or C, to me?

"Miri." My name whispers at my back.

I gasp. Spin around.

The night is dark and a mist rises, swirls upon the ground, but no one is near. My breath strangles in my throat, fights to escape.

"You could have taken them all. Destroyed them beyond recognition," the voice says, and an image of the creeps in the bar, slumping lifeless upon the ground, flashes across my mind. My body tenses and pulls in upon itself. "The power is yours for the taking." The voice is raspy. A chilled wind at my ear.

I step back. Hold myself against the shudders. I do not know this voice, and yet I feel as if I should. I should know it and fear it.

An icy grip drops upon my shoulders. "Take it," she howls.

I gasp and my hands fly to my throat.

I vault awake, find myself in my bed, gulping for air. My breath is sour, and my fingers, cold as ice. My hands drop to my chest and press against my heart. I wheeze with labored intake of oxygen.

"Unusually dark and dangerous night?" Belle asks from our joint bathroom.

CHAPTER THIRTEEN

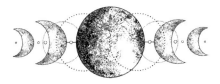

I press the palms of my hands into my temples. "Bad dream," I say in response to Belle's inquiry.

She doesn't need to know that I snuck out or was escorted home by Phillip. She doesn't need to know the crazy thing I did or what my actions led to. I don't want that to be the example I set. I was impulsive and reckless, and such actions shouldn't be repeated.

I slide out of bed, wander to the sink, turn the water on full, and close the door between the two sides of the joint bathroom, blocking my sister from view. I quickly get ready, making sure to dress in something that covers my multiple new scratches. I then head down to the kitchen for a small bite before school. Breakfast consists of dry toast and a glass of orange juice.

I lean against the kitchen doorframe and stare at Michael's closed bedroom door. The space beyond the barrier is rather quiet. I wonder if he's still sleeping... if he was out late... where he went that was so secretive.

Now that I think about it, he's been somewhat secretive for a while. Long before we were forced to move in with Caleb. If it's not drugs or drinking, but it produces a hangover, what is it he is doing?

A thump comes from his room. A moment later, the door creaks open. Michael appears in the doorway, wearing nothing more than his underwear and a white tee. He looks like he's been recently raised from the dead. The whites of his eyes are crowded with red lines, and black shadows droop in heavy bags.

I swallow my toast. "Are you doing drugs?" I blurt.

His head jerks back. "What?"

"You heard me. Have you been sneaking out to get high?" I set my glass of orange juice on the counter and pin all my attention on Mike. Step in front of him. He may have told me he wasn't doing drugs, but his body seems to be expressing a different story.

"I already told you, I'm not doing drugs. Now, if you will excuse me..." He shoves past me. "I need to visit the toilet." He slips into the bathroom.

"Someone doing drugs would have to visit the toilet as soon as they regained consciousness," I say through the closed door.

"So would any normal person," he counters.

I cup my hands to my mouth and press them against the door. "If you aren't doing drugs, then what is wrong with you? Where did you go last night? What did you do that has you looking like a hell-bound candidate?"

The toilet flushes. The sink water runs, shuts off. The door swings open. "Keep your voice down." He moves past me, back toward his bedroom. "I'm not asking questions of you. Why are you asking them of me?"

"I'm not the one looking in need of an intervention." I follow closely at his back.

"Listen, Miri." He turns to face me. "My business is my

business and no one else's. You shouldn't be asking questions. In fact, you should stay as far away as possible."

My nose crinkles. If he thinks there is a single chance in all the world that I won't press after his last words, then he doesn't know me at all.

"What are you guys talking about?"

Mike and I both spin to face Belle, she stands on the bottom step. She's ready for school, with books in hand.

"Nothing," Mike and I say in unison. He thrusts his bedroom door closed, cutting off our access to him, and I spin toward the kitchen. Remove the bottle of orange juice from the fridge, pour myself a glass, and swig the liquid down.

"Did I interrupt something?" Belle leans back against the counter behind me.

"Not at all."

Mike's words play back in my mind. *"...you should stay as far away as possible."* I grab my backpack from the spot where I dumped it on the floor. "He was tired and grumpy and bugged that I tried talking to him." I move toward the stairs. "I'm going to head out. I'd like to get to school a bit early this morning. Meet you there?" I thrust a thumb over my shoulder, pointing toward the stairs to the garage.

Belle's gaze narrows, and she leans heavily into her elbow. "What are you guys up to?"

"Nothing." I straighten and shake my head. "What is there to be up to?" I add air quotations to my pronunciation of up to. "See you at school."

I take the stairs to the garage at a quick jog, open the door at the base, and slip around the car toward the double exterior doors. The door at the back of the space opens, and Mom steps out, straightening her skirt.

"Morning," I say and push at my exit, my mind still obsessing over Mike's last words.

Mom's head jerks up and she startles. Smiles. Carefully closes the door to the room she shares with Caleb. "Caleb's still sleeping," she whispers.

Caleb is still sleeping. I thought he had gone to bed early. Why would he need to slumber for so many hours? Because, he, too, snuck out in the middle of the night, I answer my own thought. My lips pull to the side, and I nod at my mom.

"You've been working a lot more lately." I raise my chin in reference to her work attire.

"Been picking up extra shifts at the casino," she says. "This place isn't paid off like your Grandma's old house is. There are more bills to be paid, living here."

I frown. "Got it." That's pretty much how I presented it to Phillip. Mom is working overtime for the extra cash. With a nod of acceptance, I step through the open doorway onto the street.

"Have a good day, hon," Mom's says. I two finger salute her and close the barrier between us. Head to school.

The walk to school can take twenty minutes on a normal day. Those minutes are plenty to contemplate Caleb and the possibility that he *was* the one I spied at the vampic-infested club. After all, he wasn't in his bed when I returned home.

The walk is also long enough to ponder my brother's situation and his words to me. Never have I seen him look as bad as he does this morning. What has he gotten involved in? And what did he mean when he made it sound like I, specifically, need to stay away? I need to know. With clenched fists and set jaw, I decide to follow him when he goes out tonight. Answers will be gathered, and hopefully I'll also get to the bottom of what he's doing.

I get to school early, and I hang out in a quiet corner until the bell rings. I didn't really need to arrive early for any particular purpose. I was simply looking for an easy way to avoid a Q

& A from Belle. If I were to start talking to her about Mike, not only would I be breaking my promise, I'd be opening myself up for a parade of inquisitions. None of which is anything I want to deal with.

At lunch, Phillip finds me. We sit together and enjoy our boring bagged lunches.

"How are you feeling today?" He asks and takes a bite of his cold pizza.

"I'm alright. Had a wicked nightmare, though." I pick and pull tiny pieces from my bread. The images of the dream remain fresh in my mind. Dragging myself through the interior of a grave, falling through the broken crypt onto the ground, and finding myself lying at the foot of a vault, inside one of New Orleans' cities of the dead. I shiver.

"I don't doubt it," he says and offers me a sip of his soda. I accept. "After what you experienced last night, I'd have been surprised if you didn't have a nightmare. Might have actually been concerned." He shoulder-bumps me. "Concerned what a peaceful night's sleep said about your personality, to be indifferent to such fear and panic, after such a crazy experience."

"I wasn't afraid," I say, fully aware that those words are a hot lie, and he knows as much. My mind bounces from the vampy bar of freaks to the cemetery from my dreams to the ghost soldiers I experienced on the battlefield.

"Sure you weren't." He leans into me, drops his face against my shoulder and neck. Breathes.

"What do you think happens to us after we die?" I chew on my food and stare at the school courtyard, not really seeing anything.

"After we die?" Phillip jerks back a tad. "Gosh, I don't know. I mean..." He readjusts in his seat beside me. "Everything around us is energy, right? All our bits and pieces are made of energy. Energy taking a physical form. And energy is a constant. Never dying, simply changing." He heaves a breath. "So, it would stand to reason that, when we die, our energy merely changes form into something else."

I twist in my seat to face him.

"Whether that energy is able to recall what it was previously or not, I can't really say." He frowns and nods once slowly.

"But you've thought about it, right?' I ask.

"Well, sure. Who can live in this city of ghosts and not ever consider life beyond?" He raises his hands to the side of his face and wiggles his fingers. Makes a fake ghost sound.

With a playful swing, I knock one of his hands down.

"What? You don't like my ghost impression?" He lunges forward and captures me in his embrace. Draws me close, studies my facial features. "Want to hang out after school? I don't have to work today, so my schedule is wide open." He pulls back, and a hopeful smile pulls at the edge of his lips.

I bite my lip. I want to spend more time with Phillip. I'd love to do so right now. Ditch school and go, but I can't. That would be completely irresponsible. Of course, that isn't what he asked me to do. Only, what he has asked complicates the plans I've already made to get to the bottom of one or more family secrets. What is Mike messed up in?

Plus, I have detention, and then I'm on restriction. Home and chores. No television. No phone calls. No hanging out. *Zero fun allowed.*

"I'd love to, but I can't," I say.

"Oh." He nods, lowers his head. "Okay."

"It's just..." I stammer and avert my gaze. Press my hand to my warming cheeks. "I have detention every day this week, and after that, I'm supposed to head straight home. If I do manage to get free of the house, I've already made plans to follow my brother tonight."

"Follow?" Phillip asks. "As in, some sort of covert mission?"

A smile cracks my facade. "When you say it that way, it sounds silly."

"Isn't it, though?" Phillip sets his lunch aside and turns his full attention to me. "You're talking about your brother."

"I know, but I'm worried about him. Something isn't right, and he won't talk to me." I gaze at my lap.

"And you think spying on him will help somehow?"

"I'm hopeful." I bite the inside of my lip.

"You're a strange girl, Miri, but that's one of the things I like about you. We have yet to experience a dull moment." He grins. "I will join you on your spy mission."

"Oh." My back straightens, and my head shakes "You don't need to. I don't want to cause you any trouble."

"It's no trouble. In fact, it could be kind of fun. A day and night of mystery." His brows rise and eyes widen.

"But if Mike discovers us, he could get mad."

"Probably." Phillip shrugs. "Not sure how I would feel if I discovered family following me, but that's just one more reason why I should accompany you."

"One *more* reason?" I lean back and stare at him. "What's the other reason?"

"With the talent you appear to have for finding trouble, someone should be close at your side to help you stay in line or get out safely." A satisfied smile presses deep into his face.

"Very funny." I deliver a light punch to his shoulder.

His mouth pops open, and he grabs the afflicted arm. Rubs. "You been working out?" he teases.

"Miri, can I talk to you?" Belle steps up in front of us.

I startle. Turn away from Phillip and face my sister. "Yeah, sure. What's up?"

She glances at Phillip and back to me. "You know you can trust me, right?"

My head jerks back. I've never not trusted Belle. I've been jealous of her, irritated by her, but never have I felt betrayed. "Of course," I say.

"Then, will you please talk to me about last night?" Her voice is laced with a hint of frustration.

"Last night?" The topic I don't care to discuss. In this case, it's less about trust and more about not wanting to get her involved or make her privy to my horrid mistakes. My eyes crinkle, and I glance at Phillip.

He jerks, crushes his bagged lunch into a ball, and stands to go. "Catch up with you later," he says and walks away.

"There's something weird going on with you and Michael, and I'm left in the nosebleed section, far from the activity. I'm not crazy about that."

"Seriously?" I pull back and stare at her. "There is nothing going on that you need to worry about not being a part of. If there was something worth sharing, I would let you know... because you're my sister and I trust you." My smile is weak but honest. The things I withhold are not worth sharing. Not right now.

The bell rings.

"I'm going to be spending some time with Phillip after school," I say. "I won't get home until later. Please cover for me?" She frowns but nods. I head for the classrooms.

"You kind of like him, don't you?" she calls after me.

A warm, uncontrollable smile curls across my lips. I glance back at Belle but don't say anything. I make my way to class.

CHAPTER FOURTEEN

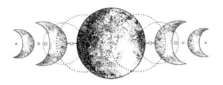

After detention is over, I meet Phillip in the school pickup area, and we head toward the edge of the Quarter.

"How do you propose we do this?" He asks. "I don't expect your brother is patiently waiting at the house for us to arrive and follow him."

"Smart aleck. Of course, he isn't." My hold upon my backpack tightens. "His last class over at the university gets out in about thirty to forty minutes." *I think.* "He'll get a ride home, like he usually does, then change his clothes before heading out on his regular 'secret' mission. I'm guessing he wants to appear far less university student wherever it is he goes."

We walk along the quieter, less traveled streets, as much as possible. When we arrive at the Louis Armstrong Park, we cross the busy traffic and drop into the Quarter. In order to avoid running into Belle and her inquisitive nature, I steer Phillip down one of the earlier streets and approach Caleb's house from a different direction.

"Do you want to wait inside or be spy-like and lurk around

someplace on the street?" Phillip asks. Caleb's house is within a block's distance, and we have hit the deadline on determining a course of action.

I make my way to the intersection where the home is located and study the streets in all four directions. There is a bar on one of the corners, but neither Phillip nor myself would blend in with the crowd. Up the street, a half a block past Caleb's, there is a small parking lot, but it doesn't offer good visibility of the garage front where my brother will likely get dropped off.

I turn down the street and point to a spot not far past the bar. "Why don't we hang out there? You can stand between me and the house, thereby blocking me from Mike's view, should he happen to look."

Phillip turns his attention to the place I have pointed out.

"Mike has only seen you that once, and I doubt he would recognize you. What do you think?"

"Might work," Phillip says and starts crossing the street. "Guess we'll have some time to kill, so what do you want to talk about?"

I skip to his side, and we move down the street, take up a position beside some stairs no longer leading to anything. I lean against the brick of the short climb, and Phillip stands in front of me, placing himself between me and the stakeout location. "Why don't you tell me about the motorcycle you are restoring," I say.

"It's my dad's old bike," he says. "A 1970 Triumph Bonneville. He told me he would give it to me if I could get it running... which I will. It used to be a sweet ride and will be again someday."

"That's not even twenty years old yet," I say, glancing past him to the street at the front of Caleb's house. "Why doesn't it run anymore? Did something happen to it?"

He smiles at me like I am a child. "Mechanical engines need to be cared for, loved, and exercised. When they are left to sit, things stop working. Fluids dry up, seals crack and break, things corrode. The older a piece of machinery becomes, the more difficult it can be to find replacement parts. That's basically where I'm at now... cleaning and replacing her many pieces."

I nod, and he tells me all about the bike and the ride he plans to treat me to, when he gets the bike running. "Maybe we can take a short trip over the summer," he says. "That's if your mother will allow you to go."

I listen and keep a watchful eye on the house. Cars drive by, but none stop. I don't want to admit it yet, but I doubt my mother would allow me to take an overnight trip with a boy. Mom was pretty young when she got pregnant with Mike, and as far back as I can remember, she has been adamant about behaving when it comes to the opposite sex. I guess she doesn't want any of us kids to start a family as early as she did.

A car pulls to a stop in front of Caleb's garage, and my brother hops out. He exchanges quick words with the driver and then dashes into the house. The car drives away.

"He's here," I say.

Phillip spins around and takes a seat beside me on the brick. "How long do you suppose we have to wait until phase two of Operation Brother-Tracker begins?"

My face hardens, and I frown at his jab. I understand that he doesn't grasp the importance of following my brother, but he didn't need to come, not if he was planning on making fun of me along the way.

"Okay." He throws his hands up at his side. "I see I've hit a nerve. My apologies. I didn't mean to upset you. I'm merely having fun with the situation. I'll stop if you find it upsetting."

"I'll get over it," I say and shift in my seat. "You don't know my siblings or my family dynamics, so I understand why you wouldn't experience the sense of urgency that I do in this situation."

"True. I don't know your siblings," he says. "But if you are concerned, then I am concerned." He grabs my hand and holds it firmly in his grasp. Our touch creates a buzz of warm tingles throughout my system.

"It's nice not to feel alone in all of this," I say.

"Alone in what way?" he asks. "In a secretly-following-your-brother kind of way?"

"Well, yeah. That. But it's also nice to have someone to talk about the everyday life stuff. Someone who isn't all mentally twisted by my family stuff and is someone I might be able to relate to, somewhat." I stare at my hands, twisting in my lap.

"Hey, I'm here for you. I'll gladly volunteer to be your partner in stalker crime." He drops his open hand over mine. "You're not the only one who feels in need of someone to talk to."

"Do you feel like you don't belong? Like you are an imposter in your own life, and you are just waiting for someone to notice and call you on it?" I ask.

"All the time." He nods. "It's probably one of our natural human flaws, to always doubt ourselves. Feel left out of the crowd."

"You think so?"

"Fairly sure," he adds.

I release a small breath and twist my hand beneath his, weaving my fingers with his. "Then we can feel on the outside of it all together. I'll be your backup and you be mine."

"It's a deal." He squeezes our hold to a snug embrace. We turn our gaze back to the house, and the garage door my brother is expected to emerge from sometime soon.

We don't need to wait more than twenty minutes before

Mike reappears, dressed down in basketball attire. He heads up the street and turns at the corner in the direction of the park and recreation center.

"Here we go," Phillip says. We step away from the support wall and follow my brother at a distance. Mike is dressed for sports play, and he is heading the proper direction for such fun. He almost has me convinced I got everything wrong. Almost. But when he should turn north to head toward the rec center, he doesn't. He scans the area, as if he expects to be followed, and when he doesn't see whatever it is he's watching out for, he keeps moving straight. He walks another block and then turns back into the Quarter, travels down the darker, lesser-visited streets.

It will be harder to go unnoticed on quieter streets, and so Phillip and I slow our pace, hoping to remain unnoticed. We go undetected for two or three blocks along the new route. Then someone calls Mike's name.

My hand flies to my lips and I freeze. The call came from somewhere near where Phillip and I are standing. My brother turns. Phillip grabs my hand and yanks me up several stairs into the shadows of a recessed door. He presses me to the wall, shields me from sight.

"Who's that?" Phillip asks of the person hailing my brother.

"I don't know." I turn my head, press to the side, and try to see onto the street. My brother and his new acquaintance are walking our direction. I jerk back into the shadows. My entire body is swirling with anxiety and excitement. My hands are shaking.

"Miri," Phillip whispers.

"Yeah?" I don't look. My head remains turned to the side, waiting and watching for Mike to pass.

Phillip says my name again and turns my head to face him. "Everything is going to be fine."

I blink. How can everything be alright when Mike is walking our way and we have barely a space in which to hide?

"It will," he says and leans closer. His breath washes over me, and his lips meld to mine, his hands cupping my face, with a soft, delicate touch.

My heart slams into overdrive. His kiss is an electrical fire. An instant awakening of my soul. My muscles soften, turn to putty, and the shadows around us erupt into the brilliance of a color-bursting nebula exploding with stars. Anxiety melts away, into the ground, and all that is left is the featherlight drift of a cloud.

I am that cloud, and I am floating away.

Our lips separate, and I suck back a haggard breath. Shake my head in an attempt to drag myself to my senses, anchor myself to the real world once more.

"Told you everything would be alright," he says.

I glance at the street. It's clear. I lean forward and peek around the corner of the door recess, glance both directions. The street is clear. I pull back to my spot against the wall and sigh.

"He didn't discover us," Phillip says.

"No. He didn't." I bite my lip and replay the kiss. The amazing, relationship-changing kiss. My gaze finds Phillip's lower lip. I can't look away. His kiss spun me into another world. An impossible, most miraculous world, and I became completely unaware of anything happening here, in the now. "He didn't catch us, but we lost him in the process," I say.

"He couldn't have gone far. We'll catch up to him soon enough," he says. "Shall we assess the terrain and reacquire the target?" He winks.

More fun at my expense. I frown, but it doesn't touch my heart. I'm flying after our exchange in the shadow-filled doorway. If he wants to play spy and use silly spy words, I'll play along.

"Yes. Let's." I grab his hand and lead him down the steps to the sidewalk. "Last seen, the target was headed north. We'll scan to the north and north east."

"Target, huh?" Phillip's smile widens, and he nods, drags me forward.

A twinge of guilt stabs at my thoughts. Here we are, sneaking through the streets, attempting to follow my brother to places unknown. And we do this because I want to know. Know what my brother is up to. What does that controlling action say about me as a person? As the person I am destined to become?

"Phillip?" I speed-walk with short, quick steps at his side. "Where do you see yourself in ten or fifteen years?"

"That is the question of the year, isn't it?" he says. "I need to have a plan for next year, and I'm still wavering on what I should do."

"Will you jump on your newly repaired motorcycle and hit the road, leaving this place in your rearview?" I ask, thinking about the many times I considered what life would be like far from my family history and roots.

"Doubt it," he quips. "I mean, sure, I want to take a road trip, but I would come back. This is my city, and this is where I want to be, helping my fellow citizens."

"Helping, huh?" That's a pretty cool goal. Maybe I should consider how I could give of myself and help others. "You've been pretty amazing at helping me... coming to my rescue. Will you be a knight for hire?"

He chuckles. "I don't know. Maybe a paramedic or a fireman..."

"Or a policeman," I add.

"Maybe." His response sounds less than enthusiastic, and I

guess I can't blame him. The police have a negative stigma surrounding them.

We search for almost an hour, sweeping the streets and outlining spaces. We cover the street north of us and check intersecting streets, several blocks to the south. There's no sign of Mike.

"It's been too long," I say. "If we haven't found him by now, we aren't going to find him this evening."

"I'm sorry," Phillip says, bowing his head. "I know this was important to you. Sorry I messed it up."

I stop walking, spin, and stare at him. "You didn't mess anything up. You kept us from getting caught."

"I could have handled it in a different way so that we didn't lose sight of your brother," he says.

Someone walks our way, and I pull Phillip against the wall of the building at our side, allowing them to pass us with ease. "I don't regret your choice. Not for an instant." I caress his cheek, press up onto my toes, and kiss him.

"Miri?"

My body calcifies. My heart slams to a stop. I jerk away from Phillip and spin toward Caleb.

"Caleb?" My voice spikes. "What are you doing here?"

"I think the more appropriate question is, what are you doing here?" Caleb's scrutinizing gaze rakes over Phillip and me. "Who is this boy you're getting chummy with?" He accentuates the word 'boy.'

I clench Phillip's hand tight. "This *boy* is Phillip, a friend from school."

"Nice to meet you, sir." Phillip thrusts his free hand forward.

Caleb glances at Phillip's hand but doesn't take it. "A rather close friend?" He crosses his arms. "I hope you don't go around kissing all your friends?"

My mouth drops open.

Phillip's free hand drops to his side. "Miri has never been anything other than proper, sir. You should be proud."

"Is that so, Miri?" Caleb turns his glare upon me. "If that is true, then why are you here, in this neighborhood?"

"Sir?" Phillip asks and scratches his jaw line.

"This street is known to house a less than desirable crowd." Caleb swings his gaze back to Phillip.

By less than desirable, Caleb means suspicious or shady individuals. A tag that could refer to anything from drugs to violence to dark magical practices.

"I..." I can't manage to come up with an excuse fast enough to fill the void slipping from my lips.

"Completely my fault," Phillip interjects.

"Really? What kind of boy are you that you would walk my daughter through an area such as this?" Caleb pins his glare upon Phillip.

"I'm not your daughter." My shoulders pull straight and tight.

"You might be... someday." Caleb tilts his head and narrows his gaze. I gasp. "You know what your mother and I hope for us, as a family." My nose wrinkles.

"I didn't know," Phillip says. "We were merely exploring the Quarter, given the area is new to Miri. I was trying to impress her and didn't know about the negative element." Phillip drops his head and shakes. "It was foolish of me. I'm sorry, sir. Please forgive me."

"It's alright," I say to Phillip.

"No, it's not, Miri." Caleb glances between us. "Yes. You're right, Phillip. What you did was very foolish. You should know better, given your father is on the force." He shakes his head in clear disapproval.

"You know my father?" Phillip asks.

"I know of your father," Caleb responds. "And I'm not comfortable with Miri spending time in such irresponsible company or with the kin of law enforcement." He pronounces the words law enforcement with a hint of loathing.

I start to speak and Caleb flashes a sharp finger in my face.

"I think it's time the two of you part ways." His penetrating glare shifts from Phillip to me. "And you get straight home. You understand me?"

"Home? Now?" My head jerks back. I want to argue with Caleb, tell him he's being unreasonable. Especially in light of the fact that he, too, is wandering through an undesirable area. But such an argument would likely make my situation worse. Caleb is no stranger to confrontation, and he has proven himself, on more than one occasion, well-versed in the art of word wars. My lips pull into a tight line.

"Yes. Home. Now," Caleb demands. "It's my understanding you are restricted from any outside activities this week. So, whatever it is you are doing now, it's in clear violation. I'll be calling the house in twenty minutes, and you had better be there to pick up the phone." His glare tightens. He doesn't need to finish the threat. I know I'll be in some sort of nasty trouble if I don't follow his rule.

Mom has already let my punishment for forging the field trip permission slip slide a tiny bit. If I'm not home to answer the phone, not only will that penance watch probably return, but something new and socially unacceptable will be added. Like, being grounded for a month.

"I'd take you home myself, but I still have some business to attend to," Caleb says.

I bite the edge of my lip to avoid making a scrutinizing face. *Still has business to attend to. In this neighborhood.* The hairs on the back of my neck prickle. The impression of having seen him in the vampic bar the other night is still fresh in my memory.

"I'll see Miri home safely," Phillip says. "That is, if that's alright with you, sir."

Caleb's shoulders tense and then relax. If his stare could burn, Phillip and I wouldn't be more than ashes right now. "I'm not crazy about it," he says. He steps closer and drops his fists to his hips. "Just this once. You take her straight home. You understand, boy?"

"Yes, sir. Straight home." Phillip shakes his head.

"Better get moving." Caleb tilts his head. "I'll be calling the house in twenty."

I grab Phillip's hand and drag him away from Caleb in the direction of the house.

CHAPTER FIFTEEN

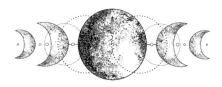

My feet move fast, as if I can't put my mom's boyfriend deep in my past fast enough. At the corner, I glance back and catch Caleb standing right where we left him. His stare upon us is intense. We round the corner, cutting our travels from his view.

"I'm sorry about that," I say to Phillip, weaving my fingers with his.

"You have nothing to be sorry for." Phillip squeezes my hand. Drags me to a stop. "I know what he said, but I don't want to stop seeing you."

"Caleb isn't my dad." I clench my jaw. "He doesn't get to dictate who I do and don't see. I'll clear this up with my mom. Everything will be alright."

I tug at his hold and jolt us into motion once more. I don't want to deal with any fallout as a result of missing Caleb's call. My heart pumps heavy, and my blood rushes. I need to get home before the phone rings.

In less than fifteen minutes, we are standing in front of my new place of residence.

"Still want to hang around this town and protect the people?" I turn to face him.

"Yep. I remain unmoved." He takes my free hand in his own.

"Even people like him?" I jab my thumb in the direction we came from, in reference to Caleb.

"All people deserve equal help and protection," he says,

"If you say so." I scuff my toe upon the ground. Glancing down with the motion, then back up to meet Phillip's gaze.

"Guess this is goodbye... for now," he says.

"Yeah, but I'll see you tomorrow at school." My lips lift in a weak smile. This day would have gone so much better, if only Caleb hadn't shown up. And if we hadn't lost Mike. Two too many *ifs*.

"I look forward to it." He leans his forehead against mine, and his breath is warm against my skin. "Promise me you'll call if you need me for any reason."

"I don't have..." I start to tell him I don't have his number, but before I can expel the words, he pulls a pen from his pocket and writes his phone number on the inside of my wrist. I stare at the digits, etching them into my memory. He just raised the level of our newfound relationship. I'm trapped in a whirlwind that is all him, and I don't want to get free. I bite the inside of my lip and attempt to keep my smile from engulfing my face.

His finger traces a lengthy cut beside his scrolled ink information. He flips my hand and studies the similar scratch across the top of my hand. "What happened?"

I blink. *Think of an excuse. Think of an excuse.* "A cat scratched me," I say with a shrug.

"I didn't know you had a cat." He rubs the top of my hand with his thumb.

"There's a lot about me you don't know," I retort.

"Another thing I need to remedy," He says. "Add that to my list with 'gain your trust.'"

"You're doing pretty great with the trust thing. I expect you to do rather will with the info gathering task too." A car backfires and I jump. Glance toward the door. "I should probably get inside," I say with a point over my shoulder.

"Be careful tonight." Phillip's lips glide across my cheek, teasing me. My hair follicles tingle, and goosebumps bloom across my arms. "I got the sense I really upset your mom's boyfriend."

"It wasn't you." I wrap my hand around the curve of his neck. "Following Mike was my idea. This afternoon is all on me."

"I would do it again in a nanosecond if it meant spending the day with you." His mouth skims over mine and melds to my lips. His essence breezes through my soul, caresses and warms my heart.

I could spend the entire night standing on the sidewalk kissing Phillip, but Caleb will be calling soon and I need to be in the house, ready to pick up the phone. I say my goodbyes, and I head inside, plop onto the sofa beside my sister. Her schoolbook is open, and she has papers spread out all over the coffee table. She is deep in homework mode.

Algebra. Not my best subject. Besides, I can't focus. I have Phillip on the brain. I may have only just met him, but I am in deep. It happened as fast as stepping off a cliff. I am trapped in the desire for him, and I can't wiggle free.

Mom comes up from her bedroom and into the kitchen. I join her, help prepare dinner.

"You promised we'd collect the rest of our stuff from Grandma's house. When is that going to happen?" I ask, wanting for more wardrobe options than I currently have available.

"Soon enough. How about this weekend? We can pick up a tree while we're out." I press my lips together, trying not to frown. Christmas has always been at Grandma's. Celebrating it at Caleb's just feels wrong. And crowded.

I peer around the kitchen threshold into the family room. Space is tight. Christmas here will be cramped.

"What about Grandma and the holiday?" The idea of her spending it alone causes my heart to sink.

"We'll have to see." Mom stirs the rice in the pot of boiling water. "Your Grandma and I have a few things to work out before we can sit down and enjoy time together." She switches her attention to the fry pan, shifting the contents of beans and peppers.

"You mean on the subjects of Caleb and magic?" I position myself in front of the rice, taking charge of its preparation.

"Caleb is a non-topic." Mom grabs the butter from the refrigerator.

Because he's the forever one for you? I want to ask, but I don't, lacking the courage to go down that path. Does she get as excited about time spent with Caleb as I do about Phillip? Caleb, the guy who has always been nice to me, but lately has been freaking me a bit out. "Despite everything that has happened, she's still your mother."

Mom huffs... ignites the heat beneath a second fry pan and drops the butter within, wipes it around, making sure to cover the entire surface.

"If you want Grandma to soften her stance on Caleb, shouldn't you do the same with regards to magic?" I ask. "After all, Grandma has always felt strongly on that subject. She has never made that a secret. Is it so hard to simply let her believe what she wishes?"

"It's not that simple." Mom cracks three eggs on the side of the pan, drops them in and fries them, keeping the yolks intact.

"If it were only about your Grandma believing, that would be one thing. But she keeps trying to press those beliefs upon you kids and that's unacceptable. It's hard enough fitting into this world without harboring crazy ideas."

"Is the belief in magic such a bad thing?" Belle leans around the corner, into the kitchen.

"It depends on the degree of belief. Simply believing in magic is one thing." Mom's answer is sharp and quick. "But nothing good can come from your Grandma's level of commitment. Her absolute certainty that her bloodline is magically infused with greatness."

"So, those weren't just words you threw at Grandma the night we left?" Belle leans against the door frame. "You honestly don't believe in magic?"

"Define magic." Mom flips the eggs, one by one.

"You know what I mean." Belle crosses her arms.

"Not in the kind of magic your Grandma advocates. An in-your-face, instant change kind of magic." She grabs a few bowls from the cabinet and scoops into each bowl some rice, followed by the bean mix, topping her creation with a fried egg. She passes one bowl to me and another to Belle. We move to the balcony to enjoy our meal.

"I think the reason you have never witnessed magic is because you refuse to believe in its existence." Belle sets her bowl on the table, takes a seat.

"Maybe," Mom counters. "But I didn't always feel this way. I gave her magic plenty of years to make itself known. Grow into something magnificent."

I frown at my food. Is there any merit to Belle's words? Did I spy her doing the impossible because some part of me wants to believe? But then found myself unable to do anything remotely as interesting because I can't seem to make myself believe I'm capable of such feats?

We all settle in to eat and the phone rings. Mom slips back into the house, answers, talks to Caleb. He doesn't ask to speak to me.

It took me about approximately fifteen minutes to walk home, five minutes or so to say goodbye to Phillip, and about twenty-five minutes to help Mom cook dinner. Caleb did not call when he said he would, unless my math is far worse than I thought it was. I'm pretty sure that's not the case. He scared me into rushing straight back.

After dinner, Belle and I help Mom wash the dishes and clean the kitchen. I have one short lesson to complete for homework, which I do rather quickly. Belle finished her homework before dinner. With work done and the kitchen cleaned, I pack my backpack for the next day and excuse myself in favor of my room.

I haven't yet made it up the stairs when a procession of doors opening and closing announces Caleb's arrival. Attempting to avoid confrontation, I slink up the stairs, pause mid-climb, and listen to Mom's greeting.

Mom and Caleb kiss and converse, but he doesn't mention seeing me earlier in the day. I press against the wall and wait. Wait and wait. They settle on the sofa to watch television. The sounds drifting my way indicate a comfortable couple enjoying downtime together. Smooches and whispers. Caleb says many things, and none of them are about me or Phillip.

When Caleb discovered me with Phillip, he acted upset. Made demands and threats. Been a total jerk. Now, he's close-lipped on the topic. Why would he now avoid tattling on me to my mom? When she is the only one who has clear authority over me? Since moving in with him, I've found it difficult to understand his behavior. Both in word and action.

I sit and listen until Mom and Caleb take their conversation downstairs to their bedroom. Only then do I finish the climb to my own room. My face presses with the stress of my Caleb contemplation, and I slip into my pajamas.

"Spying on Mom and Caleb?" Belle stands in the glow of the adjoining bathroom.

I opt for a shrug, versus a verbal answer, and slip into bed.

Her eyes narrow. "Let me know if you hear or see anything off about him."

My back straightens. "What do you mean by 'off'?"

"You know, odd and out of character."

I blink. I don't believe I know what is *in* character for him.

"What are you suggesting?" My fingers crush the bedsheets, wadding them into my grasp.

"Nothing really," she says. "I just find myself trusting him less now that we live under his roof. He seems different." She steps back to her side of the bathroom. "Goodnight." She closes the door to a mere open crack.

"Goodnight," I whisper after her and drop flat against my bed. I'm ready to leave this day, and the interaction with Caleb, behind... start fresh in the morning.

Dreams are quick to take over. Consume me. Morph into nightmares. The solace I sought is swapped for a cramped, dark space. Surrounding walls of cold cement. I'm trapped within a sliver of a tomb. One of New Orleans' many wall vaults.

I scream.

Another nightmare. Another grave. What is it with me and death?

"Fear not, child. This is merely a resting place." A ghostly whisper sends chills across my spine. "Come find me. Take me from this place. Be my vessel."

Vessel? As in allow myself to be possessed? I scream. Scream for Belle, for Mom.

I beat at the hard walls surrounding me, the rough texture scratching at my skin. I beat and I scream, and yet I am not released from the illusion. *"Be my vessel."* The words whisper through me. *"Be my vessel, and become stronger than you ever imagined."* My screams turn to tears. Tears that continue to roll with the nightmare and the ghostly prompting... Until I awake, face puffy and red.

I need to escape. Get out from beneath Caleb's roof. I want the safety of Phillip.

CHAPTER SIXTEEN

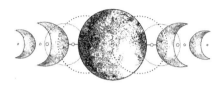

I dress in a hurry, bind my hair back, and rush for the door, eager to get to school and find Phillip.

"Miri." Mom stops me before I can slip out the door.

I turn to face her and plaster a smile on my face. We're standing in the garage with Caleb's parked car resting between us.

"Is it true you have a new boyfriend?" She leans against her bedroom door.

"I wouldn't go as far as to call him 'my boyfriend.' Nothing has been made official." I readjust the weight of my backpack.

"But you are seeing someone?" She probes.

"I am. But Caleb said..." I start to unload the concerns Caleb has thrust upon me about any further dates with Phillip, but Mom raises her hand, halting my words.

"Caleb knows about your new boyfriend?" she blurts. "Why am I the last to know?"

"He's not my boyfriend," I say.

Mom shakes her head, waves her hand. "Well, never you mind about Caleb. We'll set things straight." She glances through the open door at her back. "I would like to meet this young man of yours. Would you invite him over for dinner this Friday?"

"Like... to meet the family and stuff?" My eyes widen. "I don't know, Mom. That seems like a lot to ask of a baby-new relationship."

"Just do it, darling. As your mother, I have a right to meet him, and I would prefer to do so as soon as possible." She thrusts her hand onto her hip and narrows her gaze.

"Yes, ma'am. This Friday. I'll ask." I nod, twist my hand on the door handle. "But if Caleb didn't tell you, how did you know?"

"People talk," she says. "And you live in a house with two siblings that are clearly better informed than I am."

I frown. "You have been working a lot."

"That's unavoidable I am afraid. "And it doesn't help the current strain between me and Michael. Something I aim to fix. Family is too important to let things continue this way."

"I'm sure you'll figure it out. I have faith in you." I give her a thumbs up and then slip out the door onto the street. Make my way to school. Think about my parting words to my mother. *Do I have faith everything will find its way to a healthy balance? I'm not a hundred percent sure.*

I get halfway down the block when Belle races to catch up with me. "Why are you in such a hurry?"

"I'm not really in a hurry," I say. "Just somewhat anxious to get to school"

"And see Phillip?" she adds.

"No." My voice spikes, shoulders stiffen... then relax. "Maybe a little."

"I knew it!" The bounce in her step is so pronounced she all but jumps at her declaration. "That boy has you all tied up in knots like cord magic... a long, ongoing spell with a thousand and five castings."

"I wouldn't go that far, but yeah... He does scramble my thoughts a tad." My lips lift at the thought of Phillip.

"A tad?" Belle laughs. "Boys are a menace to the higher brain function."

"What are you saying?" I glance sideways at her. "Haven't you ever had a strong crush on a boy?"

Belle shrugs. "Nope."

"Really?" When I was her age, I think I'd already had several short-lived crushes. How has Belle escaped the follies of the heart?

"Do you remember that girl Tiana, back at our old school?" She says.

I blink. Think back. Nod. Tiana had beautiful midnight skin, with dark eyes to match, and her hair was always elaborately braided. She was super sweet but could also have the personality of a bulldog. I held an intense admiration for her.

"I was totally into her," Belle says. "Doubt I'll ever see her again now." She bows her head.

"Really?" I pause in my forward steps. "How come I never knew you were into girls?"

She shrugs. "It's not like I was advertising. I chose not to talk about it at home, and you never asked. So... you were never enlightened."

I bite my lip. *I need to be a better sister.* This information is something I should have known. "Find anyone interesting at this school?"

"Not really. But I'm rather picky," she says.

We laugh, drop into a quiet chatter.

"Did you tell Mom about Phillip?" I ask.

"Sorry." She grimaces. "I may have inadvertently let it slip that you had boys on the brain. Or one boy, in particular."

I nod. My mini mystery solved.

Once on school campus, I wait for Phillip near his locker. He arrives with ten minutes to spare before the bell rings. When he sees me, a face-wide smile spreads across his lips. He sets his stuff in his open locker and turns to me. Hands me my missing wallet and school ID.

"You are amazing!" I clutch my returned property to my chest.

"Usually, I go for super amazing, but I'll accept amazing since it's coming from you." He grins. I fake a laugh and play-fully slap his arm.

"How did you retrieve it so easily?"

"Did I say it was easy?"

"It wasn't?" My eyes widen with concern.

"Nah." He shakes his head. "It was super easy. I used my dad's name and presto... your missing items were returned."

"Your dad, the cop?"

"Yeah, that one." He glances around us, as if nervous someone might overhear our conversation. "So..." He wraps his arms around me, pulling me close. "How was your night?"

It's a clear change of subject that I allow without argument. If he doesn't want to talk about his dad, or his dad being a cop, I can respect that. Maybe he's worried about how he will be perceived should others find out what his dad does. After all, Mike basically said the cops were dirty. Of course, he couldn't possibly have meant all of them... could he? Regardless, if that's the public's opinion of the cops, then policemen, in general, aren't likely well received.

"It was alright. Caleb didn't say anything to my mom. At least, not while I was listening. But something she said to me this morning makes me think you and I were discussed later in the night. Something to which my sister has confessed." I frown. Perk up a millisecond later. "Thankfully, I got the vibe my mom doesn't have the same feelings regarding us as Caleb does."

"Thank goodness for minor miracles." He leans against his locker, pulling me with him in the shift.

"My mom wants to meet you. Can you stand to be around Caleb for an evening?" I ask.

"For you... of course," he says.

"She'd like you to come over for dinner this Friday." I bat my eyes.

Phillip's face drops. "I'm supposed to work this Friday." His face torques with thought. "Let me see if I can trade shifts with one of the others. I don't want to disappoint your mom."

"Who is going to want to take a Friday night shift?" My lips dip.

"Someone with a Saturday night shift." His eyes twinkle, and he leans forward, kisses me. My heart jumps, and I happily reciprocate.

The bell rings.

"Can I walk you to class?" he asks.

"That will make you late for your class," I say.

"Nah. I can make it. You have yet to see all my moves," he teases. "I am capable of lightning fast movements when necessary."

"Of course, you are." I grin. Allow him to walk me to class. We walk the school corridors, and I dwell on the thought of Caleb and what his behavior will be at the upcoming dinner. Assuming Phillip is able to trade shifts with someone.

The thought of Caleb sends a shiver through my system. Caleb caught us in our attempt to spy on Mike. Caleb was walking through an area of the Quarter he told us is unsavory and should be avoided. And yet, he was there. And I'm still unsure if it was his face I spied at the vampic bar. It sure did look like him.

I stop several feet from my classroom and turn to face Phillip. "Have you ever noticed Caleb hanging around that freaky vampire bar?"

"I don't work there, you know that, right?" His brows arch. "I work across the street. If I am doing my job correctly... which I usually try to do... I'm not keeping tabs on everyone who comes and goes at the bar across the way."

"I know." My shoulders slump. "I just thought..."

"I haven't noticed him, Miri. But that doesn't mean he hasn't been there a few times, or a lot of times. I'll make a point of paying closer attention, if you'd like. Let you know if I see anything where he is concerned."

"Thank you," I say.

"You're welcome." He kisses my forehead. "Now I've got to run. Catch ya later." He jogs off in the direction of his first class for the day.

Even though he needs to work later that evening, he waits for me to be paroled from detention. He's leaning against the side wall, a basketball held to his side, when I exit the classroom.

"Up for a few baskets?" He grins like a cat who knows the kill is all but made.

Our time together is short—thirty to forty minutes at best —but we laugh and dribble and block. Of course, he beats me. Not that anyone is keeping score. And the time for him to head off to work, and me back to Caleb's, rushes upon us all too fast.

The next forty-eight or so hours rush by in a blur with plenty of schoolwork to keep me occupied. The teachers are piling things on last minute, in order to wrap classes before the approaching holiday break. Phillip has to work on Wednesday but not on Thursday. He doesn't notice Caleb visiting the vampic bar, and I'm not surprised. Caleb was home both nights, as if he was purposely hanging around the house to keep an eye on me.

Seems like a rather boring pursuit for Caleb, and it's probably my overactive imagination that has jumped that idea to the front of my mind. He likely has more important things to do than watch me do my homework. Like, work on his relationship with my mom. He helped her with dinner both nights and made lots of notes in his journal. The purpose of the journal, I have yet to discover.

Phillip was able to trade shifts with one of his coworkers, so he can come to dinner... and a possible family interrogation... this Friday evening... tonight.

When school gets out on Friday, and I complete my last day of detention, I head straight to Caleb's. I'm not yet comfortable calling the place home. When I get to the house, the kitchen counter is cluttered with ingredients for the night's meal, the furniture in the family room has been shoved to the sides, and a folding table and chairs set up for a more formal meal. Perched on the sofa are several open and overflowing packages of holiday decorations.

"Good. You're home." Mom greets me at the top of the stairs and slips my backpack from my shoulder, sets it aside.

"Finally." Belle rolls her head back. "I was beginning to think you were never going to get here."

I glance between Belle, my mom, and the evidence of activity spilling out all over the room.

"I thought you girls might like to liven the place up for the season." Mom motions to the boxes.

I move into the room. Sift through the collection of trimmings. Everything is vibrant, bursting with color. A far cry from Grandma's solstice décor... muted colors, snow, and ice.

"Sure," I say, not wanting to put a damper on the festivities before the evening begins. Especially with Phillip arriving in a couple of hours. I pull a strand of green garland free and twine it between my hands... study the room, determine a decorating strategy. Belle hands me the tape and then grabs a few items from the first box, starts placing them around the room.

At some point during the preparation period, Belle switches places with Mom in the kitchen. Mom sets the table, fusing over the straightness of the tablecloth, and Belle's meal creation serenades us with the clangs of kitchenware.

The doorbell rings.

"That must be Phillip," I say, glancing at the clock. "I'll get it."

Mom grumbles about Michael not yet being home. She finds it concerning. I agree that his absence, although not surprising, is curious, but I am not at all concerned. On my way to the stairs, I make a quick stop at the kitchen to check on the readiness of the meal.

I stop cold.

Belle hums a catchy tune and is busy stirring a large pot. Spices float, dance in the air, and drop into brewing dishes, matching the beats in Belle's music.

At my appearance, she jerks, and the floating spices disappear into the preparing meal. "It will be ready shortly," she says over her shoulder.

I blink. Shake my head. This last week, I allowed the thoughts of Belle using magic to evaporate from my mind, but I cannot easily explain away the craziness I just witnessed.

The doorbell rings again. I shiver. Rush down the stairs to greet Phillip. I open the door to find him holding three floral bouquets.

"For you, your mom, your sister," he says, pointing to each individual flower bundle.

"You're too sweet." I deposit a kiss on his cheek. "Between

my mom and Caleb, this evening is likely to edge toward torture."

"I highly doubt that." He follows me up the stairs to the main level, and I introduce him to everyone. Belle pops out of the kitchen, and he hands my mom and Belle both their respective flowers.

"These are beautiful." Mom sniffs the bouquet. "Terribly thoughtful of you, Phillip. Thank you."

Belle thanks him, as well, and my mother collects all the flowers, slips them into vases with water. Sets them down in the center of the table.

Caleb emerges from the stairwell. "Nice to meet you, young man." He crosses the room, his arm extended. He clasps Phillip's hand in a firm shake. "Sorry Miri's older brother couldn't make it. I don't know what is going on with that kid these days."

"It's fine, sir." Phillip's smile wavers with an edge of nerves. "I'm sure meeting some high schooler isn't high on his to-do list."

"Some high schooler that appears to hold Miri's attention," Caleb adds. "So... Phillip... what are your intentions with regards to our Miri here?"

Phillip glances at me, and the edge of my lip lifts. Caleb is treating Phillip like this is his first time to set eyes upon him. *I don't understand.* I scratch the back of my neck. Caleb's gaze snaps onto me, his glare brimming with warnings. I bite my lip and inwardly promise to avoid the subject while in the company of family.

"Completely honorable, sir," Phillip says. "I find Miri a delight to spend time with. She's smart and funny and simply a joy to be around."

Caleb presses his lips into a tight line and nods, motions us toward the table. "Can I get you a beer?" he asks Phillip. My eyes widen, and Mom pops clear of the kitchen.

"Caleb!" she says.

Phillip clears his throat, flashes me a nervous glance.

Is this a test?

"I don't drink alcohol, sir," Phillip says and takes a seat at the table.

"Good for you, Phillip," Mom says and turns her attention to me. "I better not hear of you drinking, young lady." I shake my head, take a seat next to Phillip.

"Yummies for your-all tummies." Belle sets the main dish in the center of the table. "Hope you like your food spicy." She grins at Phillip.

"How can I live in this town and not enjoy spicy food?" he counters. Belle's smile widens, and she plops into her seat.

"Does that mean you enjoy the other things this town is known for?" she asks.

"Such as?" he asks.

"You know." She throws her hand into the air at her side. "Ghosts, vampires, magic, and voodoo, to name a few."

"All superstitions start with some thread of truth, do they not?" He piles the food onto his plate, and Belle sneers, as if she has discovered some sort of challenge in Phillip. "By the way, your place is truly festive, and this meal looks amazing."

"Thank you," Mom says. "The girls decorated a bit before you arrived. As for the meal... I cook pretty well, but the amazing aspect really comes from my youngest, Belle. She is quite the wiz in the kitchen."

"I'm not sure that is the right word for what she does in the kitchen," I blurt, and everyone stares at me.

"What is that supposed to mean?" Belle says.

I swallow hard. "I mean to say..." I straighten my shoulders. "Your way with food preparations is somewhat magical."

Belle raises a brow.

"It is, isn't it," Mom says.

"Oh wait." Belle bolts from her seat and rushes into the kitchen. Returns with a full pitcher of water. Sets it on the table. "This may be necessary to douse a few fires," she teases.

My gaze bounces from the water pitcher to the food to Phillip.

"Fire to the taste buds?" Caleb asks. "I accept the challenge." He digs into the food and shovels a large helping onto his plate.

Phillip drops a large portion on his plate and takes a bite. His eyes bulge, cheeks puff, and face flushes. His hands jump into action fanning his mouth and tongue.

"Somebody call the fire department," he says through gasps. "This accelerant is igniting." He grabs his glass of water and gulps it down in one long, continues motion.

"Someone can't handle their spice." Belle bursts into laughter.

I pour more water into Phillip's glass and hand him a piece of bread. "This will help. Possibly more so than the water."

Phillip takes a bite and chews. Nods his head in thanks.

"Surprised you can't handle the heat," Caleb says. "Given the roof you live under."

"Caleb, stop." Mom moves Caleb into silence with a wave of her hand.

He shrugs. "I'm just saying. Cop's kid and all."

"Oh, I didn't know your father was a police officer," Mom says. "You must be very proud."

Phillip glances around the table before opening his mouth to speak. "I guess so. He's my dad, so I guess I don't think about it much. He's not a cop when he comes home."

"That's a healthy way to look at it," Mom says. "He's your

father, first and foremost." She reaches across the table and pats his hand.

The evening continues with the enjoyment of savory food and inquisitive conversation, disguised as pleasantries. Dinner is followed by dessert and hot coco. Caleb jokes with Phillip, never once mentioning having seen us in the Quarter the other day.

In the eight o'clock hour, Phillip excuses himself, and I walk him to the door. Caleb follows us down the stairs and turns toward his room at the back. Halfway across the space, he pauses, turns back. "I expect you'll be making yourself scarce around here?" he says to Phillip.

"Mom does not have the same idea as you do about Phillip," I snap. "And she is my parent. Not you."

Caleb's gaze narrows to a slit, and his nose wrinkles. He stares at us for a moment or two and then turns into his room, looks back. "She is not as familiar with the dynamics in the city as I am. We don't need to suffer the connection to a cop. Especially a dirty one." Caleb closes the door, ending the conversation.

"I get the feeling he doesn't much care for me," Phillip says.

"Never you mind about him. Like I told you before, he's not my father." I take his hands in mine and squeeze. "It means a lot to me that you came. Especially in light of..." I tilt my head toward the back room to infer Caleb.

"Anytime." Phillip extricates his hand from my hold and caresses my jawline. "I enjoyed getting to know your family a bit."

"And they didn't scare you away?"

"Not at all. If a bar full of crazed vampires-in-training didn't scare me, how could you honestly think your family would get under my skin?" He asks. "But, you know, Caleb may have a point about the cop thing. It's probably not healthy for your reputation to be seen with me."

"You are not your father," I counter. "And you shouldn't be judged as if you were. Besides..." I wave my hand through the air. "My reputation is already clouded by my family connections, so I doubt spending time together could worsen things for me."

"How has your family affected your reputation?" he asks.

"It's a silly thing that goes back centuries." I grab his hand and rub his fingers. I don't want to tell him about the whole witch belief surrounding my family, but now that I've opened the conversation, I have to tell him something. "If you haven't noticed, the people of the Quarter have a long memory, and they dislike my family because of one of my ancestors. I guess she was well-known but wasn't well-liked."

"Family can sometimes be a difficult test to our character," Phillip says with a downward-turned grin.

"Exactly. And because of the discrimination I suffer in the face of my family, I will not discriminate against you for basically the same. I don't care if your dad is a cop."

"You're an extraordinary person, Miri." He squeezes my hand.

I shrug. "So... does that mean there's a chance I might see you over the weekend?" I bat my eyes.

He huffs a chuckle. "You can plan on it." He glances down. Shifts his weight. "I'm close to getting my dad's old bike running. Maybe I'll be able to take you for that ride soon." He gazes into my eyes. "You know, that one I promised you."

"I remember. Maybe we can escape the crazy of my family for the better part of a day," I say.

"Your family isn't all that crazy. I'd say they're pretty normal for these parts." He leans closer, and his breath washes over me.

"You're just being kind." I raise my face toward his.

"Maybe I am, and maybe I'm not. But from what I've seen, superstitions and overprotection come with the territory." He tilts his head, presses forward, locks his lips with mine. With the connection, everything else is forgotten. There is only a rush of warmth and belonging. My body linked with Phillip's.

Someone clears their throat.

Our body's jerk apart. I blink, turn my gaze up to Mike.

CHAPTER SEVENTEEN

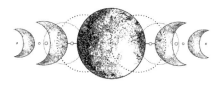

Phillip's arms drop to his side, and he steps back, allowing space to sliver in between us. He shoves his hand toward my brother Mike. "Nice to meet you," he says.

"You missed dinner," I add. "Caleb seems to be rather heated over that fact." I shove my hands into my pockets and shift my weight. Study Mike's appearance. His face is drawn, his eyes deeply shadowed and cracked with red.

"I couldn't care less what Caleb thinks or doesn't think." Mike's gaze travels over Phillip, from head to foot.

"You should care," I say. "If only a tiny bit. We do live under his roof."

"Such conditions are not permanent." Mike raises his head in a quick nod to Phillip. "Is this guy treating you well?" he asks of me.

"He's been great." I link my arm with Phillip's. "You don't need to worry about him. I swear it."

"Is that true?" Mike leans toward Phillip, lowering his head to meet Phillip's stare. On any normal day, Mike can be intimidating with his athletic build and height. Today, in his condition, he's downright scary.

Phillip straightens and leans back. "I really care about Miri. I would never do anything to hurt her, physically or mentally."

Mike pulls away and smiles. Relaxes. "I'm just having fun with you, kid. If Miri likes you, then I'm sure you're great. But do try to keep her from doing anything stupid."

Something stupid like you, apparently? My head jerks, and my nose wrinkles.

"Of. Course." Phillip's gaze shifts to me, and his brows presses with a hint of confusion. I bite my lip and shake my head.

I've never seen my brother like this. He swore to me that he isn't doing drugs, but his appearance would suggest otherwise.

"Well." Phillip scuffs his foot against the pavement. "I should probably get home." He swings toward me. Grabs my hand and lifts to his lips. "See you later." He places a gentle kiss upon my skin. His gaze upon me lingers for a half a second. Then, with a brief peek at Mike, he turns and walks down the street, glancing back once before turning the corner.

"For your sake, I hope he really is a good guy and has nothing but the best of intentions where you are concerned," Mike says at my back. "A girl like you can't be too careful." He turns toward the house.

I grab his arm. "What does that mean... *a girl like me?*"

Mike flinches, turns back, and peels my hold from his arm. His stare burns through me for the eternity of a half a minute before he responds. "I merely meant a girl whose family comes with roots seeped deep in local history and lore." He crosses his arms. "As I've told you several times before."

"Family line, maybe, but what lore are you talking about?" I match his crossed arms and stern expression.

"Have you not listened to the wealth of information our grandmother has bestowed upon us all these years?"

"Mom says Grandma is delusional," I rebut, still resistant to walking down the crazy road where magic and witchcraft are real.

"As any nonbeliever would insist." Mike dips his head and narrows his gaze.

"Are you saying you're a believer?" Mike glances away, across the street. "A believer in what, exactly. Witches and magic?" I ask.

His stare snaps back to me. "Open your eyes, Miri. Magic is all around us in this town. How can you not see that?"

My head jerks back, and I recall the floating spices in the kitchen when Belle was cooking dinner this evening. I stare at Michael and his gaunt face, tired eyes. "Is magic responsible for the horrid condition of your body?"

"Why would you think such a thing?"

"I'm worried about you. You look tired and strung out," I say. "I don't want anything to happen to you. You're my brother, and I love you."

"You don't need to worry about me," he snaps. "I am a big boy, and I can handle myself." He turns toward the garage door.

"But Michael." I grab at his arm. He yanks away.

"Stay out of it, Miri." He lifts his chin toward something across the street. "You should worry about yourself with people like that lurking so close to where we sleep.

I swivel in the direction he acknowledges. All I spy are people lingering outside of the corner bar across the street. "What are you talking about?"

"Don't look." He jerks me forward and leans close. "Beside the front door, in close company is one of the Quarter's voodoo priestesses and a local Bokor. Both are bad news, and both

137

appear to be keeping an eye on us. Stay clear of them, Miri. Do you understand me?"

My mouth pops open and I nod, glance across the street once more.

Mike spins back to the house, and marches through the garage. I hesitate, then dash after him. Catch up to him just as he throws open the door to the stairs. Caleb is standing there, waiting.

I gasp. Take a step back.

Mike sighs and drops his head. "Of course, you were listening." Mike's voice seethes between his clenched teeth.

"I may be irritated that you couldn't bring yourself to be on time for dinner, but do you think me so underhanded as to spy on your conversation?" Caleb says, stepping into the garage space. "I couldn't care less what the two of you were talking about. I was merely coming down to my room when I happened to run into you." His shoulders rise and fall. His gaze narrows upon Mike.

Michael raises his head, the muscles in his arms and shoulders stiffening.

"Right." Caleb swings his gaze onto me, then back to Mike. "You need to start showing your mother more respect. Next time she requests you be home at a particular time, do so." He turns away, walks to his bedroom, closing the door between us.

Mike glares at the closed door through which Caleb disappeared. The shadows upon his haggard face are intensified by the inflection of his mood. The thumps of Mom and Belle moving around upstairs carries through the ceiling, down to us. Mike turns away from Caleb's departure and begins his climb toward the main level. Once more, I grab his arm, pulling him to a stop.

"Are you dabbling in magic?" I ask. "Is that what is taking such a toll on your body?" I motion to his stature.

"Listen," he says. "I'm going to bed. I recommend you refrain from talking about any of this around Mom. She doesn't get it and has a difficult, if impossible, time accepting."

"But Mike..."

"Make time to visit Grandma." He plucks his wrist from my hold and ascends the stairs two at a time. Heads straight for his room without a word to Mom or Belle.

I remain on the steps, staring into the empty space where he stood moments ago. My restless fingers wiggle and twist. *Wish Grandma was here.* She'd probably have some sort of understanding of whatever it is Mike is involved in. They always had a close relationship.

What lore was Mike talking about? What more does Grandma know that I have yet to learn?

I return upstairs and help Belle and Mom tidy up. We put away the folding table and chairs and clean up any remaining mess in the kitchen. I head to bed before ten o'clock, drained from an evening of family rebuff and inquisition.

Tomorrow, we'll shop for a Christmas tree and visit Grandma to collect more of our personal belongings. My body buzzes, eager to pluck answers from her in response to the various questions Mike has spawned within me.

I hope I can manage a few minutes alone with Grandma... somehow keep Mom busy elsewhere in the house.

I fall into bed, my mind busy creating a list of topics to discuss with Grandma in the morning. Within minutes, the mental list is lost in a haze of dreams and nightmares. I'm hugged to Phillip's body, riding on the back of his motorcycle. I'm wandering the streets of the Quarter, his hand held in mine. Finally, I find myself wandering the streets alone... beneath the night sky.

I make my way toward the cemetery. Someone walks behind me, but I refuse to glance back. Or... at least... know better than to do so. They don't wish to be seen by me, only heard.

"Our last encounter frightened you, so, this time around, I chose a nighttime stroll in its stead," the voice whispers. It's the same voice from my previous nightmare. The voice that requested I lend it my body as its vessel.

I don't want to be a vessel for anyone. Only for my own mind and soul. I will not share.

"Who are you?" I demand.

"I am your reason for being," it says. "Without me, there would be no you."

The voice of a long-gone ancestor? Can it be true?

"You had your time. This life is mine. Leave me alone," I say and toss in my bed. Press my pillow over my head. *Go. Go away*, I scream in my head.

"You are all my children," the voice says. "The children of my children... the children through many generations. Like me, you are stubborn and willful, but you always come to realize the truth and power... eventually. When that day comes, you will be mine."

CHAPTER EIGHTEEN

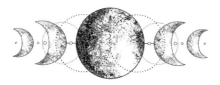

You are all my children. The words whisper through my mind and tangle my nerves into knots. I definitely need to talk to my grandma and find out what she knows about our ancestry. I'm counting the minutes until we head to her house.

At midmorning, Mom ushers Belle and me out the door. We find an acceptable Christmas tree at the first holiday lot we visit. I don't have much of an opinion on what we get. Flocked. Not flocked. Fat, skinny. I don't care. After all, the thing will be set up at Caleb's house, not Grandma's, and that fact is making it difficult for me to get into the holiday spirit. Mom picks something green that smells heavily of pine. Since space isn't ample in the living area, the tree she decides upon is neither wide nor tall.

Belle makes an effort to be helpful in the tree sorting process, but I'm present in body only. I have zero yeas or nays to give. In an attempt to raise our spirits and put smiles on everyone's faces, Mom gets us peppermint cocos from the makeshift goodie stand in the corner of the tree lot.

I press a forced smile to my lips to appease her before downing my coco. Mom arranges for the tree to be picked up later by Caleb, and we head over to Grandma's to collect a few more personal possessions. When Mom pulls to a stop in front of the house, Grandma steps onto the porch and waves a joyful greeting.

Belle bolts from the car and rushes toward the front door, throws her arms around Grandma in a big hug. I'm right behind my little sister. As soon as Belle steps away, I follow suit and embrace Grandma like I haven't seen her in years.

"I'm sorry we left you," I whisper.

"It's not your fault, dear. Do not fret about things over which you have no control." She rubs my back, kisses the top of my head, and releases me. "Every bird must eventually learn to fly from its nest."

That's one way of viewing the situation. I reply with an unsure, crooked grin. Grandma pats my back and turns her attention to my mom.

"Edith." Grandma greets her with a slight tilt of the head. "I trust you are doing well."

"We are. I hope you are getting along fine." Mom says.

"Oh... I get by." Grandma turns toward the door and meanders inside. The rest of us follow. "I made sugar cookies. Can I interest any of you?"

"Give me. Give me," Belle says with animated hand motions and makes a beeline for the kitchen.

I take in the clear absence of holiday decorations. Every year during this season, the house has always been covered in a silver and white solstice décor. Grandma notices my visual search and wraps her arm around me. Hugs me to her side.

"It's not the decorations that make the season, but the spirit," she says.

"Will you put any up?" I ask of the annual ornaments.

"I shall. I have yet to ask Nero to help me get the boxes down."

Nero is one of the neighbors. If we were still living in the house, Grandma would not need to ask for outside help. My gut drops.

"We are on a bit of a tight schedule," Mom lies. "I'm going to grab a few empty boxes from the storage room so that we can get busy packing." Mom walks away, climbs the stairs.

Belle returns to the living room with a tall glass of milk in one hand and two cookies in the other. "These are amazing." She takes another bite of her treat. "Someday, you'll have to tell me what your secret ingredient is," she says through a mouthful of food.

"Of course," Grandma replies. "But something tells me you are on track to become rather amazing in the kitchen."

"I hope so," Belle says.

"Girls," Mom calls down the stairwell. "I put a few boxes in your old room. Why don't you come up and get started."

"Coming." Belle marches up the stairs. "Time to get busy in the grind," she mumbles and takes another bite of the cookie. "You coming?" she asks.

"I'll be there in a minute. I want to get a drink of water first."

Belle disappears onto the second level of the house, and I head toward the kitchen. The space is inviting with the smells of fresh baked cookies. Grandma follows me.

"I am getting the sense you would like to talk to me." She weaves her fingers together. Without a word, I pull a glass from the cabinet and fill it with water from the tap. "Am I wrong?" she asks.

I glance in the direction of Mom's old bedroom, as if I could see through all the walls standing between us to know what she is doing.

"Your mother is currently engaged and outside of earshot." Grandma pulls a chair out from the dining table and motions for me to have a seat.

I stare at the chair and sigh. "As always, Grandma, your senses are dead on." I move toward the table and take a seat. She settles into the chair beside me. Nervous and unsure where to begin, I sip water from my glass. She patiently waits.

I place my glass on the table and twist to face her. "What do you know about our family history?"

"Has something happened?" Her gaze narrows upon me, and she leans forward.

"Living in the Quarter has definitely been interesting... and the new home arrangements, challenging. There have been things that leave me... wondering." I recall the vamp girl who watched me from the street, dragged me into the strange shop, and eventually pushed me into a room filled with vampics interested in my blood. I then focus my thoughts upon the voice. "But the thing that has rattled me the most has been the barrage of nightmares. Dreams of graves and cemeteries and disembodied voices."

Grandma sits straight, turns her gaze toward the window. "Magic runs in your veins. That can bring many things. From wonder and amazement, to fear and terror. I tried to protect you girls from the negative effects, but that is hard to do when you no longer live under my roof."

I follow her gaze out the window and see nothing other than the house across the street. "So... all that stuff you always talked about. You're saying it's true and not a personally created fantasy?"

She closes her eyes and drops her head ever slightly in confirmation.

"Are you saying that you are so powerful that you were able to shield me from such nightmares when I was here?"

"No." She shakes her head. "It is the house that shields. It is a safe haven for our family. Its bones are permeated in strong protective magic as old as its construction." She turns to face me. "You are a descendant of one of the area's most powerful witches. She warded this home when she lived here long ago."

"Powerful witch? Like Marie Laveau?" I ask.

Grandma smiles. "Everyone knows about Marie Laveau. She spread her name and influence wide. Our ancestor preferred to keep her status concealed. She may have avoided the written threads of history, but the founding families remember. They are aware of the magical strength she possessed and passed on to her descendants. To me... and to you. That is the reason you may run into unpleasant and unwelcoming reactions for the locals within the French Quarter."

"Our ancestor was a powerful witch?" My head jerks back. "And she lived here..." I toss my hand out, motioning to the house. "In a big house set at the edge of the Garden District?"

"Well. Not always, but she managed to marry well," Grandma says. "In an era when it was not socially acceptable for the races to blend, her lover overlooked what was expected of him and made her his bride. Their home was in the French Quarter for many years, but a tragic fire destroyed that house. I suspect the fire wasn't on the up and up, because, when they had this house built, she weaved protection magic into its very foundation and every fiber of its construction."

"That's intense." I bite my lip and glance around. "In the nightmares I've been having, there is a voice beckoning me. I think she wants to possess me."

Grandma's hand drops over mine. "As powerful as she was, I have no doubt she continues to be powerful on the other side. You must resist her."

"I'm trying, but she's so strong." My voice sounds like a whine and I hate it.

"I know, honey." She pats my hand. "Maybe I can help you. I could make you a talisman for the day, or..." She glances to the kitchen, and her face puffs with thought. "Maybe get you something for the night, as well."

"Really? You could do that?" I say. "That would be great."

"Of course, dear. Anything for my grandkids." She rises from her chair and walks into the kitchen and grabs something from the back counter. Returns to the table with an apple. Hands it to me.

"Um. Thanks." I set it on the table. "I'm not really hungry right now."

"You take it. Use it." She wraps my hand around the apple.

"Use it how?" My stare bounces from her to the apple now wrapped in both of our hands.

"Use three of the seeds from this apple to protect you from the dream invader," she says.

"And how does that work?"

"Put three of the seeds in a small linen bag and safety pin them inside your pillow. After seven days, the magic should have done the deed. Toss the seeds out the front door." She splays her hand as if she has just flung the seeds herself.

"That sounds more like silly wise tales than magic." I frown and drop my gaze to the apple.

"Why don't you try it before you condemn it?" She pats my hand and releases.

"Miri?"

Grandma and I spin toward the staircase. Mom descends, stops on the last step. "Belle and I are about ready to go. Are you going to pack anything?"

"Sorry." I bite my lip.

"You were the one that asked me about coming here to get some of your stuff." Her brows press into her forehead.

"Right." I nod, turn to Grandma. "Sorry, Grandma. I need

to go pack a few things." I stand, push the chair into place against the table. "I've really enjoyed our conversation."

"Of course, dear. Anytime." She pats my hand.

I race up the stairs to my old room. At my back, strike the sounds of Mom scolding Grandma about discussing magic with me, like it was a solid subject worthy of consideration.

The rest of the day falls into a blur of packing and unpacking. Packing boxes with stuff. Packing boxes into the car. When we return to Caleb's, unpacking boxes from the car and unpacking stuff from the boxes into our respective rooms. It's all rather tedious and boring. Caleb brings home the tree, and Mom decorates it with Belle's help. I bow out of the task. The only Saturday highlight, a thirty-minute call with Phillip. I invite him to join me for breakfast at the house on Sunday. He agrees.

Come Sunday, Mom has to work early and Caleb sleeps in, having come home extremely late Saturday night... or early Sunday morning, depending on how you want to read the clock. Mike is in his room, also dead to the world. Neither Belle nor I have a clue what hour he got home the night before.

That leaves Belle and me pretty much on our own for breakfast prep. We dice onions and peppers. Mince garlic, slice sausage, and shred cheese. In the hour before Phillip's arrival, we toss together all the ingredients for mouthwatering breakfast soufflé and pop it in the oven to cook.

"How have you been adjusting to life at Caleb's?" I ask Belle.

"It's been an adjustment, as I'm sure you know. But I am managing." She leans against the kitchen counter and stares at the oven.

"How have you been sleeping?" I lean against the counter across the room from her.

"Fine, I guess. Nothing unusual to report." Her lips quirk, turn down. "Why? Have you been having issues?"

I chew on the inside of my lip. I could open up to my sister and tell her the truth, but I'm not sure how she will respond. I don't want any awkwardness to exist between us when Phillip arrives.

"Nah," I say. "It's different, but alright... I guess."

Belle raises her head, suggesting she doesn't fully accept my response. She opens the oven and sprinkles a few spices on the baking dish. Fifteen minutes later, the oven beeps, followed by the ring of the doorbell. For Phillip's arrival, the home is ripe with the pleasant aroma of eggs, sausage, and cornbread. Belle pulls the meal from the oven and spins it around, spreading the fragrance. I usher Phillip upstairs, and we all sit down to a deliciously filling meal.

"This is seriously flavorful," Phillip says, downing a bite of the soufflé.

"Belle possess some sort of kitchen magic. I have yet to taste something she's made that didn't make my tummy happy." I slice my fork through the breakfast portion set upon my plate.

"Well, if you cook this great every time," Phillip says to Belle. "I would be more than happy to be your official food taster."

"Stop it." She waves her hand at him, feigning embarrassment. Secretly, I suspect she is eating up the compliments. Savoring every word.

When our bellies are full, I put the remaining soufflé into the fridge while Phillip helps Belle clear the table and wash the dishes.

"If you are willing to always clean up after my messes, you can come over anytime you wish," Belle says to Phillip.

He barks a laugh, tugging her lips into a smile.

Behind us, Mike edges from his bedroom, saying not a word

to any of us. He carries his basketball within a mesh sports bag, thrown over his shoulder. He quietly closes his door and sneaks down the stairs, acting as if his stealth-intended actions have rendered him invisible to us.

"I'm worried about him," Belle says. "I don't think he is well."

"I agree." I link my arm with Phillip's, tug him from the kitchen. "Phillip and I are going to go enjoy our morning in the Quarter."

"Um... okay. Well... thanks for the fun breakfast." Belle crosses her arms and shrugs her shoulders. "See you guys later."

"Later." I wave over my head and lead Phillip down the stairs. "Let's do it right this time," I say with my voice low.

He tilts his head and pinches his brows together. His eyes fill with questions regarding my statement.

"Let's figure out where my brother goes and what he's doing," I clarify.

"Right." Phillip nods. "Operation Follow Mike/Save Mike."

I can't tell if Phillip truly buys into my mission, but he goes along with the idea, nevertheless. Being nothing but encouraging. We cross the garage space and step outside.

"This time," he adds. "Failure is nonexistent."

CHAPTER NINETEEN

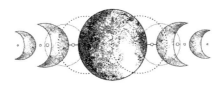

I am determined to help Mike, whether or not he wants my aid. From the front of the garage door, we move to the corner where we have a clear view of the cross streets in both directions. I catch sight of Mike turning onto the busy street north of us. He's moving in the direction of the community center basketball courts. Phillip holds my hand, and we move at a casual pace, keeping Mike in sight as much as possible.

"Where would you like to go when I get the bike operational?" He swings our clasped hands between us.

I hesitate to answer, try to think of someplace fun or exciting, but my brain fails to multitask between making plans with Phillip and keeping track of Mike's movements. "I don't know. Where would you like to go? You are, after all, the one putting in the time to make the bike work."

"It really depends on how much time you are willing to give me," he says.

We turn the corner and walk toward the community center, but Mike has already moved past the building. He crosses the street and heads down a smaller avenue to the east. Was the basketball thrown over his shoulder merely a ploy meant to confuse us of his true intentions? Or is Mike planning to play basketball somewhere else?

"Time?" I mumble. "How much of my time do you want?"

"I was thinking it could be fun to head down route 90 toward Avery Island. Maybe check out the jungle gardens and take a swamp tour. Of course, that's a bit of a drive and would make for a rather full day. Unless..."

"Unless what?" I say.

We cross the street and follow Mike into a residential area.

"Unless you'd be able to get away from more than a day," he replies.

My steps falter. Spend a night with Phillip? Mom would flip. "If we had more than a day of adventure, what more would you add to the itinerary?"

"Depends upon you and how much time we have. We could go further south and see the Chauvin Sculpture Garden." He smiles at me. "Or we could head to the state line and enjoy a day at the Sabine National Forest. Or... go the opposite direct and ride down into Venice, see the coast."

"Seems like you have given this a lot of thought."

We turn another corner, walk another block.

"I have, but I promise my intentions are pure. I merely want us to have a good time on a small adventure together." He squeezes my hand. "And if it interested you, you're more than welcome to come to my place and help with the bike restoration. Then its working condition would be the result of both or our efforts."

"Maybe." I've never worked on anything mechanical before.

"Cool." His head bobs in a happy nod.

Another block and another corner, and I no longer spy Mike walking anywhere up ahead.

"Did we lose my brother again?" I pull Phillip to a stop.

He swings around, taking in the full scope of the neighborhood. "It appears we may have done exactly that." He heaves a breath. "I was so sure we wouldn't lose him this time."

I glance up and down the street. "I've been so busy keeping watch over his movements, I can't believe I managed to lose sight of him this time."

"He has been turning a bunch of corners recently." Phillip's face tightens. "It's almost like he was trying to lose a tail... like he knew we were here."

"How could he," I say. "Not once did he look back."

"True." Phillip crosses an arm over his chest and taps his cheek with his other hand. "It is rather curious. Maybe he has eyes in the back of his head."

"I wasn't paying attention to the path." I study the direction from which we came. "Do you have any idea where we are?"

Phillip spins back toward the path we previously traveled. "Not a clue. But we can't be too far off a main street."

"I hope you're right." I shiver.

Something rubs against my ankle and I yelp, jump.

"What's wrong?" Phillip grabs my upper arm.

"Meow." A longhaired black cat circles the space beside me. "Meow."

"The cat surprised me, is all." I bend down and stroke the cat's back. He purrs and stretches, raises his tail high into the sky. "Silly kitty," I say. "Are you lost?"

"Meow."

"Wait a minute." I grab the cat's chin and turn his face toward mine, stare at him. "You aren't the same kitty that tried to sneak into the house with me the other night, are you?"

"Meow."

"Your brother definitely went this way," Phillip says, paying the cat no mind. "He must have immediately turned onto the next street. That's the only thing that makes sense." He grabs my hand again and tugs. "Come on."

We walk-jog to the next junction. It's another residential street packed with houses. There's no sign of Mike in either direction.

"Where could he have gone?" I bite my lip and my heart squeezes. I want to help Mike and yet the universe seems to be working against me.

"Meow." The black cat has followed us to the corner.

"Silly kitty," I say. "Don't you have someplace you should be?"

"What is it with you and cats?" Phillip asks. "The other night one tried to follow you inside. Then you tell me you were scratched up by a cat. And now this."

The second one is a lie, but I'm not going to confess to the truth, that I was scratched by people believing themselves to be vampires attracted to my blood. Not a cat.

"Boo!"

Phillip jerks and I jump. We both spin around and come face to face with my brother, Michael.

"Got you good," he says.

"Dammit, Mike. You scared the hair from my scalp." I press my hand to my heart, try to calm the erratic rhythm.

"Is that so?" Mike smirks. "I still see a ton of frizzy, black fibers stuck to the top of your head." He rubs my crown.

"Stop it." I push him away.

"Why are you guys following me?" His joking manner washes away into a solid mask of seriousness.

"We were not following you." I glance at Phillip. His lips are pulled tight. His eyes hide a dash of panic. I roll my head and sigh. "Alright. Maybe we were following you. But you have given us an endless supply of reasons to follow you and not one to leave you alone... or trust you."

"Really?" he blurts. "You find me untrustworthy?"

"That's not exactly what I said." I fluster. My hands flutter, raise, and wave at the basketball he has slung over his shoulder in a bag. "Why bring the ball if you didn't want to go to the courts at the community center?"

"You followed me because you thought I was going to play basketball?" Mike glances between Phillip and me. "Continued following me because I didn't stop at the courts? Is that what you are trying to say?"

"No." My head jerks back. "I just want to understand why you felt the need to lie."

Phillip pulls me to his side and wraps his arm around me and rubs. It's meant to comfort, and maybe it would, if I wasn't so wound up over this mystery of Mike.

"I don't feel a need to share everything I do with the family. I happen to savor my privacy, but if you must know, I am on my way to meet my girlfriend. I would prefer you keep that to yourself, though. I don't need Mom nagging me about it." He drops the mesh bag with the basketball to his side.

"A girlfriend?" I say. "You have a girlfriend? When did this happen?"

"Not all that long ago, and I have yet to determine if this is a relationship that will last or not. That's one of the reasons I'd like to keep this on the down-low." He leans forward. "Okay?"

"What's her name?" I blurt.

"Who?" he straightens.

"Your girlfriend," Phillip and I say in unison.

"Right." Mike laughs. "Fontella." The edge of his lips lift.

"That's an unusual name. Fontella who?" I ask.

"Fontella Bass. Satisfied?" His lips quark to the side.

"I guess." I bite my lip. I'm not a hundred percent sure

whether or not I am satisfied. But I feel better about Mike than I have in a while.

"Great. Then why don't the two of you beat it. I don't need my kid sister clinging to me when I go visit my girlfriend."

I frown.

"He's right," Phillip says. "We should head back."

I turn, narrow my gaze upon him. "You're probably right."

"Head that direction, and you'll exit this neighborhood, find yourself in familiar territory." Mike shifts and points in the direction at his back. He swings back and stares at us. "And Phillip," he says. "It is Phillip, isn't it?" He doesn't wait for an answer but continues. "Please help me discourage my sister from wandering all over the place. You guys have been doing a fine job at tempting the darker elements of fate to find you."

Phillip drops his head. "You're right."

"I certainly am." Mike moves past us and heads for the next street down the block. "Go home, Miri and please, stop wandering recklessly around the Quarter."

"Come on." Phillip tugs at my arm.

"Wait a minute." I resist his tug. "The way Mike spoke to you is totally uncool. He needs to apologize." I spin toward my brother, but he's no longer there. He has disappeared into the landscape of houses. "How does he do that?" I whisper.

"It's fine," Phillip says and tugs lightly. "Let's get out of here."

I allow him to lead us out of the unfamiliar neighborhood. Under his guidance, we move past the community center and toward Caleb's house.

"Your brother is right, you know." Phillip stops at the corner. The house is a mere block away. Visible at the corner.

"What do you mean?" I turn and stare at him. "In what way is Mike right?"

He releases my hand and shoves his fists into his pockets,

continues walking toward the house. "We shouldn't be wandering all over the Quarter and beyond, trying to follow him or figure out what he is doing. It's been one wildly massive goose chase. And it doesn't feel like the kind of things we should be doing with our time together."

"I admit that the missions may have been fruitless, but they haven't been all bad, have they?" I blink, once, two times rapidly. "We've been together which has made it more interesting... more meaningful."

Phillip scratches the back of his head and comes to a pause at the corner, beside Caleb's house. "Yeah... I guess... I don't know." He shifts to his left, looks away. "Something about it just doesn't feel right."

"But... but..." I stammer. "Mike is clearly into something he shouldn't be. It's written all over his face with the bloodshot eyes and dark circles. His all-too-often zombie like movements."

"Or, he could be lacking in sleep because he's trying to do it all. School, study time, maybe a job, and time for the girlfriend." Phillip jabs his arms wide, left and right, to accentuate his point. "He could be suffering from sleep deprivation. That would explain everything you've mentioned."

I shake my head. "I don't buy it."

"Maybe you refuse to see things that way because you want there to be something going on with your brother." Phillip sighs, and his shoulders drop. "Do you need something to fix? Is finding an issue with your brother more important than spending time on yourself and your happiness?"

I don't know how to respond to that. Any potential words get caught in my throat. My mouth pops open and only silence slips free.

Phillip studies the ground at his feet. Wavers. "I gotta get to work, anyway. Guess I'll catch you later."

"Wait. What?" I lunge forward and grab his arm. "I

thought you didn't have to work today?" My heart takes off like a runner at the start of a race.

He spins back toward me. "I thought you wanted to spend time with me, hang out, have fun, and get to know each other in a more meaningful way. Not use me as a buffer while chasing down your family members."

"I do. I want all those things." I tighten my hold on his arm.

His chest rises and falls. "You have a funny way of showing it. Maybe you need some time to think on this and decide if that really is how you feel." He yanks his arm free, turns, and walks away.

CHAPTER TWENTY

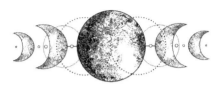

Phillip walks away, doesn't look back, his body language singing with frustration. I bite the inside of my lip and narrow my stare upon his backside. I've been spending my free time with him. I don't understand why he's so disturbed.

I cross my arms and huff. Decide not to dwell on him or his emotions... for now. Instead, I spin toward the house. Head inside and up the stairs.

Belle is sprawled across the sofa. The television is playing with the sound level on the low side. She's painting her nails while talking on the phone. At the sight of me, she pulls the phone away from her ear and presses her palm to the mouthpiece.

"I didn't expect you home so quickly. What happened? Phillip skip out on you?" she asks.

I wiggle my shoulders and press my hands deep into my pockets.

Her mouth jumps to the shape of an O, and her chin jerks back. "Just a sec," she says and returns to her call. She tells the person on the other end that she's got to go and hangs up the phone. Turns her full attention on me. "Seriously, what happened?"

I shift my weight and gaze over the room, pausing on the Christmas tree situated in the corner. The tree sits a tad crooked, and the decorations look as if they were thrown into place without thought.

"I'm feeling kind of edgy. You want to get out of here?" I say.

"Really?" She glances to the other side of the room as if she is expecting Mom or Caleb to be standing there, ready to protest an outing. "Okay."

She puts on her shoes, grabs her bag, and we head out for an unmapped walk of the nearby area. We head towards a spice shop Belle has been wanting to investigate.

"I can tell by the way you are acting that something happened between you and Phillip. When are you going to spill and shed some light on my confusion?" she says.

"I don't really know what happened between us." I scratch the back of my neck. "I've been spending a bunch of time with him and yet... he said I was using him. Insinuated that I am less interested in hanging out with him than I am in following Michael."

"Is he right?" Belle pauses to peruse items stocked in a store window.

"No," I balk. "Phillip definitely ranks higher than something so lame."

"I agree," she says, moving away from the window and resuming the trek to the spice shop. "Following your siblings is lame. But if you truly believe that, then how did Phillip get such a wrong impression?"

We round a corner and turn into the spice shop. The space is thick with the aroma of cinnamon, brown spice, black pepper, cayenne pepper, and so much more. I am unable to distinguish them all and, for a moment, the over stimulation of scents makes me dizzy.

Belle breezes through the shop, grabbing a spice, shaking a spice, sniffing a spice. I stay near the front door, allowing the occasional waft of fresh air to clear my senses. When Belle has decided upon her purchases and has paid, we leave the store and meander along the street without any true purpose.

"Wish there was a garden center nearby, but noooo. It has to be waaaay over there." Belle thrusts her arm out to accentuate the extreme distance to the nearest garden center.

"It's not really *that* bad," I say and frown. "We could probably walk there in less than an hour."

"Maybe. But I don't want to." She sighs. "Tell me more about Phillip and Michael. Why did you follow our brother?"

"Because I'm worried about him, of course," I say with snark.

"He *has* been strange ever since we relocated from Grandma's to Caleb's." She turns up the street and heads back toward the house. I follow.

"Exactly. So off from his norm, right?" I lean into the question and glance at Belle. She shrugs. "Apparently, he's been sneaking out to meet up with some new girlfriend," I blurt, then clamp my mouth shut.

Belle's forward motion abruptly stops. "Get out! Really?" She spins toward me. "I can't even believe it. That's crazy talk! Give me the 411. What's her name?"

I wasn't supposed to tell anyone anything. I'd sort of promised Mike. *Dang.* Now I'm trapped in the situation.

"Fontella Bass," I whisper and hope Mike won't get too upset. After all, it's Mom he doesn't want knowing.

Belle scoffs and continues her walk up the street. "Knew it was too good to be true."

"What do you mean?" I rush to catch up to her.

"Fontella Bass is a singer from the 1960's. You remember that song Mom used to sing when we were little?"

I stare at her, my expression blank.

"You remember." Belle snaps her fingers and swings her arms to a beat only she can hear. "Come on baby and rescue me," she sings.

"Right." I slice my finger through the air. My lips pull tight, and I shove my fists into my hips. "Why would Mike lie about having a girlfriend?"

"I don't know, but it looks more and more like he's hiding something." She initiates our forward motion, once more.

Dang it.

The rest of the way back to the house, I mull over all things Mike. His tired complexion. The bags under his eyes. The odd hours, sneaking out, and lies. He's been giving me nothing but lies. I chew and chew on the inside of my lip, extracting blood.

By the time we return to the house, Caleb has left for work. Belle and I take advantage of the quiet time by making the Christmas tree more presentable. More magical. We add more ornaments, a couple more strands of lights, and toss tinsel at the finished product.

The tree becomes less of an eye sore and something easier to digest.

Mom gets home at a semi-decent hour, and together, the three of us make dinner. Tonight's meal: skillet-grilled catfish with small potatoes and corn on the cob. We gather around the balcony table to enjoy our effort's delicious results.

"Isn't this nice," Mom says. "Things are really starting to fall into place. We are slowly becoming that strong family unit I want you girls to have."

"I guess," Belle responds.

"It's an adjustment, I know," Mom continues. "You girls

have had too many years without a father figure. But that's all changed now, and given time, you'll come to see how important a father figure is to have in your life."

Belle and I exchange a glance. Mom has been swallowing the happy-family Kool-Aid by the gallon. Having a complete family unit clearly means more to her than I ever realized.

After a short stint of television watching and ice cream devouring, everyone heads off to bed. Everyone, but me, that is. I race up to my room and pretend to get ready for bed, only I don't. I toss on my sweats, drag the phone from the hallway into my room, lay on the bed, and stare at the ceiling, the phone, the ceiling.

Phillip never calls to set things right.

My mind races. Spins around topics of Mike and Caleb and Phillip. Mostly Phillip. The house fades into silence, suggesting that Mom and Belle have ceased any busy work and are now tucked in for a long night's sleep.

I maneuver down the stairs with as much stealth as I can muster. I make my way to the stairs down into the garage. Take a seat on a step in the middle of the path. Roughly between the bottom landing and the main level, I wait for Mike. There isn't a chance of my brother slipping past me. Not here, where I have chosen to wait.

And I wait. And wait. And wait some more.

I prop my head on my hands. My eyelids droop. My head slips. I'm wide awake, sitting tall. And then I'm relaxing again. Slipping into a half-here, half-gone state.

My eyes droop to a close.

Something rubs against my leg.

My eyes snap open, and my hand shoots up, grabs Mike's pant leg. He stops, glances down at me, doesn't say a thing.

"You're late," I say.

"It's the weekend. I don't have a curfew," he rebuts.

He is right, on both occasions. But still, there is the matter of today and his big, fat lie. I want to know why he lied. Why he felt the need to lie.

"Why did you lie about having a girlfriend?" I blurt and push to a stand.

"I didn't. What makes you think I did?" He straightens his body against the side wall.

I imitate Belle, swinging my arms and singing, "Come on baby and rescue me...."

Mike's face falls. "Fine. You caught me, but I am only trying to keep you safe and out of business you have no part of. Do you get me?"

I fold my hands behind my back and lean against the opposing wall. Raise a brow.

"You are poking at dangerous things, and when one pokes at dangerous things, people could end up hurt... or worse." He folds his arms across his chest and tilts his head. "Do you hear me, Miri? I don't want to see you get hurt."

"But it's okay for your *girlfriend*, Fontella, to get involved in dangerous business?" I lean forward and jut my chin forward. We both know I am referring to him with regards to the dangerous business. After all, he pretty much just admitted there is no girlfriend.

"Stop it. Now you're just being difficult." He relaxes into the wall at his back and sighs.

"What is this I heard about a girlfriend?"

Mike and I jerk, snap our attention to the base of the stairs. Caleb stands on the bottom landing, gazing up at us. "Well," he says. "Tell me about this new girl of yours."

Mike's mouth drops open, and a tiny strangled noise escapes.

"Familiar got your tongue?" Caleb teases. "It's fine if you don't want to tell me all about her at this late hour. Instead, invite her to dinner tomorrow. I'd like to meet her, and I am sure your mother will feel the same way, once she has been informed."

"I don't think..." Mike stammers.

"Invite her to dinner. I'll expect you both here promptly at seven tomorrow evening." He turns and walks away. A moment later, a door bangs shut. Caleb has retired to his bedroom.

"This is your fault," Mike says to me.

I jerk back, my mouth dropping open and my splayed hands flying to my chest. I shake my head. "If you had never created the phony girlfriend, then this would not have become an issue."

Mike sneers and bolts up the stairs to his room. Slams the door shut.

I follow. Knock on his door. He doesn't answer. After waiting a minute or two, I head to bed.

The next morning, I catch no sign of my angry older brother, but I have other things to focus on... like Phillip and whatever it is I did to upset him. My mind is a flurry of thoughts, making concentration on anything else somewhat difficult.

I make no effort to start or sustain a conversation with anyone, so Belle and I walk to school in silence. She seems okay with that. Once we are on campus, we go our separate ways... I head straight into Phillip territory, hoping I'll find him at or near his locker.

I locate him at the edge of the locker block. He's talking with a few friends I have yet to meet. I stand back, cling to my backpack strap, and wait. He has his back to me, and therefore doesn't notice me. Not yet. But his friends do and one of them lifts his chin in my direction.

Phillip half-turns, glances my way.

He turns back to his friends. "Catch up with you guys

later," he says and swings around, walks toward me. "Hey." He rakes his hand through his hair and drops his gaze to his shoes. "How's your brother?"

"Honestly, I don't know," I blurt. "And right now, I don't care. You are the only one on my mind." His gaze slowly raises to my face. "I'm really sorry about yesterday." I dip my head and wring my fingers. "I'm sorry that I made you feel anything short of most important to me. I don't want to ruin what we have. Especially before it has truly begun."

Phillip's hand drops over my restless motion, instilling calm upon me.

I raise my gaze to his pale blue eyes. "Can we start over?"

A gentle smile warms his features. "Of course. Where do you suggest we start?"

"After school?" I pull my head back and bite the inside of my lip. "I no longer have detention, and I'd love to take you to meet my grandma. She's a rather insightful lady. Some say she's a tad crazy, but it only adds to her charm." A nervous smile cuts across my lips.

Phillip grins. "Sounds fun." His voice hints to skepticism.

"Great. Meet me after school?" I say.

"You got it," he replies. "I just need to be back by five thirty. That won't be a problem, will it?"

"Nah." I scrunch my nose and shake my head. Turn and head toward my first class for the day, by way of my locker. Phillip snags my arm and spins me back around. Cups my face and kisses me. Sweet, slow, and all too quick.

"See you after school," he says and walks in the opposite direction.

CHAPTER TWENTY-ONE

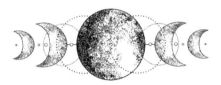

A fter the dismissal bell, I meet Phillip at the front of the school. We make our way to Canal Street and take the red streetcar toward the river, transferring to the green streetcar at St. Charles Avenue. Grandma's big, beautiful house is located on St. Charles, along the edge of the garden district. I take a seat on the right side of the streetcar. The side that will provide a decent view of the house as we approach.

The wood of the seat is still warm from the person who previously occupied the space. We settle in, and Phillip takes my hand in his.

"I'm going to let you lead this adventure," he says.

"It's pretty simple, really. We'll get off in the garden district. My grandma's house is on the corner between two of the stops. I recommend we exit at the second, since it's actually closer to the house." I press my hand to the window and gaze out.

"You're the boss," he says.

The streetcar lumbers along the line, around Lee Circle,

and beyond, onto the divided stretch of St. Charles. Phillip's warmth presses to my side, and I lay my head upon his shoulder.

"You used to live over here?" He leans past me and gazes out the window. "With your grandmother?"

"I did. Life sure was different a few weeks ago." I release a long breath. "Some days, living under Caleb's roof, my life feels like a disjointed dream."

"I'm sorry." He rubs the top of my hand.

"Don't be sorry. If we hadn't made the move, I wouldn't have met you, and you are one of the only things bringing any sense to my life right now." I press deeper into his side, and he stretches his arm around me, hugging me around my shoulders.

"About yesterday..." he says.

"I'm sorry for the way I acted... dragging you around while I followed Mike."

"You need to understand, the only reason I got bothered is because I am concerned about you. Concerned *for* you. There are a ton of things in this city you should be leery about. You need to be careful. More careful than I've seen you be." He drops his head against mine. "I'd like to see you be more cautious."

"I understand." I tilt my head upward. His expression is soft, relaxed. "It's just... my brother means the world to me, and if he's involved in something unhealthy or harmful, I want to help him get straight."

"I totally get that," Phillip says.

"And lately, there's something about Caleb that has been rubbing me the wrong way," I add. "There are actually several things about the Quarter that give me the heebie jeebies."

Grandma's house comes into view. A car is parked at the curb, and my brother is helping Grandma into the passenger seat. I jolt to the window, press my palms to the glass. Stare intently. Neither Mike nor Grandma glance at the streetcar. They don't notice me. Mike slips behind the wheel, starts the car, and pulls away from the curb. Waits for our streetcar to ramble by, then turns onto the street in the opposite direction. Disappears down the drive.

Where is Mike going with Grandma? What is he up to? What are they up to?

My breathing is tense. My palms warm and head pounds.

The streetcar pulls to a stop, and I don't move. Don't signal Phillip that this was the intended exit. That's no longer the case. Grandma's not home, and my mind is racing with a thousand and ten possible reasons why Mike would be taxiing Grandma about town.

"What's going on?" Phillip asks. "Are you alright."

The streetcar lurches forward, continues toward the next stop. He asked if I am alright. *Am I?* My skin tingles and warms. And my chest crowds with a heavy haze. The window glass beneath the press of my palms cracks.

Phillip yanks my hands away for the glass. "What the voodoo?" He examines my hands. Finds no abrasions over which to worry. "That was crazy," he says about the cracked window.

"Yeah." My voice is distant, lost in a fog of concerns and conspiracy theories. "Definitely strange."

"Are you alright?" He leans forward and tilts his head to gaze into my eyes. I nod to say that I am and fist my hand.

The streetcar slows to a stop. I blink, suck back a breath, and release it slowly. Motion to Phillip to get up. I follow him into the aisle and lead him off the railcar. We exit and watch the car roll away.

"We go this way?" Phillip asks, point in the direction from where we just came.

"Change of plans." I grab his hand, jog-run across St. Charles' divided avenue.

"What happened to meeting your Grandma?" He jogs a step behind me, allowing me to lead our adventure, as he had earlier promised.

"Grandma isn't home," I blurt and check for cars before crossing the second traffic lane.

"How do you know? We haven't knocked on the door. Haven't even walked by the house." We leap onto the sidewalk and stop. Phillip stares at me, confusion a heavy expression playing in his features.

"When the trolley was moving past the house, I saw her get into a car with my brother and drive away." I throw my hands up and shrug. "So... not home." I glance at the street signs. "The trip is salvageable, though. Do you trust me?"

Phillip grins. I take his hand in mine and lead him down the block to the local shopping center. It's not much more than a five-minute walk to the next intersection and the business building.

"Are you hungry? Because, if you are, the local coffee shop is pretty good." I point to the shop in front of us. It's situated at the corner of the mini mall. "We could grab a bite and then wander through the bookstore in search of a few good reads. Or..." I turn, glance down the street, then across the intersection to the Lafayette Cemetery. Turn my attention back at Phillip. "If you'd like more options to choose from, we can keep walking until we hit Magazine Street. There are more places to grab a meal down there."

I glance over Phillip's shoulder, once more, to the cemetery. Shiver. If I didn't know better, I'd think an army of spiders was scurrying over my skin. I'm overcome with the oddest feeling that, even though I don't hear any voices, the faceless ancestor from my nightmares is beckoning me to the adjacent burial ground.

My body jolts with a shutter, and I hug myself, spin around, and put my back to the city of the dead. Worms are slithering around my ankles, linking together to create a tether, pulling me toward the cemetery. Or... they might as well be.

I yank a step forward and rub my arms. I won't give power to the thoughts. Not now, anyway. I am here with Phillip, and I am going to enjoy the moments we have.

"Are you alright?" Phillip asks, stepping to my side and folding his arms around me.

"I got a crazy chill," I say.

"In this heat? You aren't catching a cold, are you?" He rubs my arms.

I bite the inside of my lip. Today is oddly warm for December. Definitely not shiver weather. And despite my shiver and shutter, I brush away a sweat bead from my temple with the side of my hand. The same hand that now prickles with a heat induced firecracker sting.

Chilly, cold, hot, sizzling. *Could I be coming down with something?* "I don't know. Maybe." I press the back of my hand to my forehead.

"You don't want to fall ill in time for the holidays. As fun as this outing is, I think we should get you home." He tugs my hand and pulls me along the sidewalk, back toward the St. Charles streetcar.

"I'm sure I'll be fine in a minute," I insist.

"We're not taking any chances." He squeezes my hand. Tugs me toward the streetcar on St. Charles. My gut constricts.

"Before we go..." I tug back and glance across the street. "Can we take a quick peek?" I tilt my head toward the cemetery.

"Really?" His face falls wide with surprise. "I guess. Since we are here." He weaves his fingers through mine, and we cross the street.

My blood turns to ice and muscles protest, scream at me to turn and run the other way. And yet, I am oddly pulled forward by some morbid sense of desire and curiosity. This cemetery makes my skin crawl, and I want to know why.

We pass through the iron gate and make our way down a path flanked by tight-set graves. Cracked cement and asphalt at our feet, aging brick and stone at our sides, and thick, suffocating history in every direction.

We walk to the center, turn and make our way to the far corner of the grounds. Phillip continues to allow me to lead, and I navigate as if I have a destination, which I'm not so sure I don't. My body moves as if drawn by a magnetic pull, one that is thirty times more powerful than my subconscious navigation.

Heat abandons me, and my skin explodes with goosebumps. My scalp itches and my mouth goes dry.

I don't want to be here.

And yet, I continue to advance.

I stop in front of a grave beaten and weathered by time. The engraving has softened, making the readability difficult... practically impossible. My fingers bump a line of what was once a name set into the stone. *Cath*-something.

Catherine, my mind answers. My head jerks back. How would I know that?

"You okay?" Phillip asks.

Because, she is me, just as you shall be me, a slight voice whispers on the wind... or... in my head. Memories from one of my nightmares drop over me. Me crawling, then falling out of a grave and onto the ground inside a cemetery. That was here, at this site... this grave.

My fingers snap to the safety of my chest.

"Miri?" Phillip prods.

"Yes, sorry." I spin toward him. "I'm... I'm okay, but I think I'd like to go home now." I shiver.

"Yeah. Okay," he says.

What I really want to say is that I want my grandma. I want the safety of her presence and the comfort of her company. But I already know she's not home, making my only option the top corner room of Caleb's place.

"Meow." A longhaired black cat appears at my feet. It looks a lot like... or exactly like... the cat I saw the other day in the Quarter... and at Caleb's door the day before. He purrs and rubs against my ankles. I reach down and stroke his fur.

"Are you following me?" I ask the cat. He meows in response.

"I think the cat likes you," Phillip says and motions for me to take the lead toward the exit.

"I gotta go now," I tell the cat and make haste moving us from the cemetery and up the street, back toward the streetcar.

The return trip is quiet, and Phillip escorts me all the way back to Caleb's garage door. We say our goodbyes, and I march inside. Up the stairs toward my room.

"Michael is bringing his girlfriend over for dinner tonight." Mom says as I swing past the kitchen. I already have one foot on the stairs to the next level. I pause and look back.

"Oh." *I doubt that.* I drop back to the floor and peer into the kitchen. "We finally get to meet this fantasy of his?" I act surprised.

"It would appear so." She smiles into her work. "I am making Michael's favorite."

"Red beans and rice," we say in unison. I've only just spoken the words, and I can smell the aroma filling the room. It's all in my mind, of course, but it sets my mouth to water. "Uh, Mom." I weave my fingers together and press them down the front of me. "Would you be alright with me inviting Phillip to join us?"

She pauses in her work and considers my request, her gaze dropping over me. "You are pretty fond of this guy, aren't you?"

My cheeks warm. "A little bit, yeah." I tilt my head into my shoulder.

She shrugs. "Very well. The more the merrier. Tell him dinner is at seven."

"Thanks, Mom!" I spin on the pads of my feet and race down the stairs and out onto the street, hoping to catch Phillip before he gets too far away.

Phillip lives outside of the Quarter, closer to the school, so I head north-*ish* and turn on the first street. Race along my usual path to school. Fewer tourists travel along the sidewalks here, making it easier to spot Phillip.

I call out to him. On the second time, he turns around, and I wave my hands in the air.

He makes his way back to me. "Is everything alright?" he asks.

My breath is heavy from the run, and I jog the remaining distance between us. "Everything is fine." I grab his arms for support. "I wanted to invite you to dinner tonight. Mom's making red beans and rice, and my brother is supposed to bring his girlfriend to meet the family."

"Dinner, huh?" A crease presses into the space between his eyes. "What time?"

"Seven. It should prove to be interesting and uncomfortable." I flash a nervous smile.

Phillip grimaces. "I promised my boss I would cover for the other busboy for a couple of hours this evening." He presses his fists into his hips. "I suppose I could come by for dessert, if that is alright?"

"I forgot you said you had to be back." My shoulders droop. "You have to work tonight?"

"Just for a bit, but I can come by afterward," he says.

"Yeah, sure. I'd like that. You'll probably miss the best part of the night, though." I rub my finger.

"You are the best part of my night," he replies, causing my face to flush. He reaches forward and touches my wrist. "And you're feeling better than earlier?" He makes reference to my reaction at the cemetery and the odd incident on the streetcar, when my body temperature rose unexpectedly. Strange as it may seem, I can't help but wonder if I caused the window to crack.

"I'm fine now. I don't know what was going on with me earlier." I glance to my feet.

"Okay. Good." He squeezes my wrist. "I'll see you later tonight, then. I'm going to try and fit in an hour of work on Dad's bike before I head to work."

"Okay, good luck with that."

I head home with a smile warming my core.

It's only a matter of minutes before thoughts of Phillip are replaced with notions and worries regarding Mike. I doubt he's currently getting into trouble since he is out with Grandma, but something strange is going on with him, and I don't like being on the outside.

I wonder how he's going to handle the girlfriend's expected appearance for dinner tonight. Bring a fake one or make an excuse?

When I get back to Caleb's, I have time to kill before the dinner drama is scheduled to begin. I hole up in my room and complete my homework, then start scratching together a list of all the strange things that have happened since my family moved into the Quarter.

I jot them down in the order remembered. First, there was

Belle manipulating the spices. I am fairly certain that happened, even if she denies it. Because she was definitely manipulating them the other night. No doubt about that. Then, whatever that was that happened on the school field trip, with the ghosts or hallucinations, and my fainting spell, that was definitely not normal.

There's also the vampic girl, who not only stared at my window on the day of our arrival but, later, dragged me into the vamp-themed store and tried to force me to touch a candle she said would hurt me. That wasn't only strange, but totally creepy. Especially considering where that encounter led me... to the freak show bar in the back... and all the weirdos there who worked incredibly hard to scare me. They were successful.

Something strange happened when I returned to the bar to retrieve my school ID. Something I still can't explain, and the experience doesn't sit well with me. A heat and light emanating from me. Sort of like today, when I may have cracked a window on the trolley with my emotions. Is such a thing even possible? And... of course... I can't forget to include the frequent nightmares of cemeteries and a disembodied voice. Something I experienced today in my waking hours at the cemetery. So, less nightmare and more... I don't know what.

I sigh and roll onto my back. Tap the end of my pencil against my temple. I really wish I had been able to talk to Grandma earlier today. My hands flop to the surface of the bed. Of course, the things I want to ask would best be asked without Phillip being present.

"Catch ya later, man." Mike's voice travels through my open window from the street below. It is followed by the slam of a car door.

I jump off the bed and climb on top of the cabinet, lean into the high window to get a view of the street. A car pulls away from the curb. It's the same car I saw stopped in front of Grand-ma's earlier.

Who else is involved with Mike and Grandma?

Mike heads into the house.

Time for the drama to begin.

I make my way toward the stairs. Belle falls into step behind me.

"Is it time?" she asks.

"Mike's here, if that's what you mean." I start descending the stairs, the thumps of Mike reaching the main landing carrying up the narrow stairwell.

"Right on time," Mom says. Pauses a moment. "Where is your young lady friend?"

"She can't make it," Mike says.

I stop at the bottom of the stairs and lean against the wall; uncertain I want to actually step into the questioning zone. I think I don't. I sit on the bottom step, and Belle settles at my side.

"But Caleb said..." Mom says.

"I know what Caleb said..." Mike opens the door to his bedroom and tosses a backpack inside. "He pretty much demanded she come tonight without giving me room to respond. And, as it turns out, tonight is a bad night for a meet-the-girlfriend dinner."

"Okay." Mom's voice is slow and deliberate, signaling she expects a further explanation. She leans back against the counter.

Mike drops his head back and sighs. "Okay. Here's the deal." He folds his hands over the top of his head. "Fontella is part of the school theatrical group, and they have a performance at the university tonight. It's something she can't miss."

"An actress? How thrilling." Mom folds her hands together, squeezing a towel in the clutch.

176

Fontella. An actress. I want to snicker, but I hold my tongue. The real act, the brilliant, deserves-an-award act is happening right here in front of us. Mike is laying the lie on thick.

"Is that red beans and rice I smell?" Caleb climbs the stairs from the ground level. "Can't wait to dig in." He steps onto the main level and slaps my brother upon the back. "Hey, there Mike, my boy. When can we expect your girlfriend to join us?"

"She can't make it tonight," Mom interjects.

"Is that so?" Caleb's eyes narrow, and he shoots Mike a suspicious glare.

"She is in a play tonight at the university," she adds.

"Really?" Caleb turns to face him. "If your girlfriend has a performance tonight, why aren't you there?"

"I went last night," Mike says, quick to cover. "And I am going to swing by tonight and see her afterwards."

"It makes me proud to see you being a supportive boyfriend." Mom smiles wide at Mike, and I believe I detect a hint of discomfort and tension in my brother's expression.

"Maybe we should all show our support and go see the performance this weekend," Caleb says, a wicked grin pressing to his lips.

"Can't," Mike deadpans. Shoves his hands into his pockets. "Tonight is the last one."

"What?" Mom startles. "Ending on a Monday? Why would they do that?"

"They performed all weekend, Mom. I'm not sure why the instructor added this Monday gig, but he did." He shrugs. "It is what it is."

"Such a shame," Mom says regarding the family's inability to attend Mike's fake girlfriend's theatrical performance.

Belle and I exchange a glance.

"I'll tell you what I think," Caleb interjects. "I don't think there is a girlfriend."

Uh oh.

"I think girlfriend..." Caleb uses air quotes. "...is an excuse for something else. Something he is trying to keep a secret."

"And why would I do that?" Mike counters.

Belle bolts to a stand. "Just because Michael's girlfriend couldn't make it tonight, doesn't mean she doesn't exist."

Caleb spins and jabs a finger at her. "Stay out of this."

"Caleb. Honey." Mom steps forward, hand outstretched as if to soothe.

"Back off, woman," He blurts and thrusts an open palm toward her.

"Seriously?" I bolt forward, hands clenched in tight fists. "What is your damage? You're not our father, and yet you have been acting like a jerk dictator since we moved in."

"Don't start with me, Miri." He slams a fist into his open palm. "You have plenty of things you should be answering for."

"Is that right?" My eyes narrow.

He raises a flat hand, appearing every bit ready to slap me.

The kitchen explodes. Spice jars shatter, filling the air with sugar and salt and every spice imaginable. Bits of glass ping off surfaces and settle upon the floor.

Everyone jolts. Mom throws her arms up and yelps.

"What the..." Caleb's eyes are as wide as quarters. His muscles have slackened, and his face morphed a pale grey.

I swivel toward Belle. Her face is beet red and tight with tension. "Belle?"

Her gaze snaps to me. Then she whirls around and darts up the stairs. A second later, her bedroom door slams shut. The sound is followed by a second bang. Mike has gone to his room. Likely locked the door.

I turn back to my mom. "Way to stand up for your kids," I

say. "You made me real proud tonight." She blinks wide. I turn and race up the stairs.

"Isn't anyone going to help me clean this mess up," she says at my back.

I don't bother to respond. I close myself off in my own room. Drop flat against my bed.

I chew on the inside of my lip. *This is a disaster.* I can't have Phillip show up and get subjected to the aftermath. If only I had a phone in my room, I could call the restaurant where he works and give him the heads-up. I sigh. Opt to take vigil at the window, in wait for his arrival.

Time moves with the speed of a snail. Forty minutes could have passed, or only ten, when Caleb's voice rises on the floor below. He is arguing with Mike, once more. I can't make out all the words passing between them, but bits and pieces stick in my ear, sharp and clear. Words like liar and trouble. My roof, my rules.

Jerk. I scratch at the window seal paint with my fingernail. Think I spot Phillip down the street heading my way.

"Get out of my house," Caleb yells. "I want you out. And I don't want you to come back."

My back jerks straight.

"Gladly," Mike retorts.

CHAPTER TWENTY-TWO

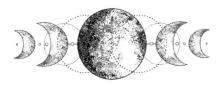

Thundering crashes and bangs ricochet through the house, marking Mike's progress toward the door.

My heart slams against its confines in bruise-worthy fashion. Pounds to break free. My chest presses in, deep and harsh... wanting to crash in upon itself. I push my palm to my breastbone and drag forth a struggling breath.

Mike bursts through the door and out onto the street.

"Oh, hey, man." Phillip's voice drifts to my ear.

I lean out the window. Mike steps back from Phillip, having plowed into him upon his quick exit.

"Don't take this the wrong way," Mike says. "But I've gotta go." He makes a sharp turn and moves away at a brisk pace.

"Um, yeah. Sure thing," Phillip says to his back.

"Phillip," I call out the window and wave. His blue eyes turn to me and blink with confusion. "Wait there. I'm coming down."

"Um. Okay." He scratches behind his ear.

I jump off the small cabinet, grab my sweater from the corner of the bed, and race down the stairs to meet Phillip.

Mom is still cleaning when I reach the main landing. Her gaze rises to meet mine, but I don't say a word. I turn toward the next flight of stairs.

"Where do you think you are going?" Caleb says.

I pause, glance back. "Phillip is here. I'm going to politely send him away." My expression is flat, camouflaging my fury at Caleb.

He takes a step toward me, his eyes narrowing to slits. Mom stands and grabs his arm, halting his motion. She nods at me, giving me the go ahead. I dart down the remaining stairs, through the garage, and out to the street where Phillip awaits.

"I take it, things didn't go well?" he says in way of a greeting.

"Total understatement, but yeah. Not well at all." I tug him into a hug and whisper at his ear. "Let's get out of here. I'll tell you while we walk."

"Where are we going?" He pushes back and gazes over me.

"I don't know. Anywhere not here." I wrench my arms through the sleeves of my sweater and pull the front straight.

"That I can deliver." He tips his head and extends his arm. I accept.

We head for the Quarter. I know Caleb will be upset. Possibly Mom, too. But I don't particularly care. Not right now. Things are seriously messed up in our home dynamics, and I need some space, time away.

At a corner convenience store, we grab a couple of sodas and a bag of chips. Not the red beans and rice I was anticipating, but it does the job of satisfying my tummy. Bourbon Street becomes our destination. The music, the tourists, and the location are a surefire distraction from my many issues.

When we reach Bourbon Street, I notice the vampic girl chatting with a couple of questionable-looking individuals.

They are planted just outside the corner bar, several feet from the curb.

I tug at Phillip's sleeve, prompting him to keep walking straight.

I don't want the girl, or her friends, to take notice of me, should we turn onto the street and walk past them.

"I thought we decided to walk down Bourbon?" he says.

"Change of plans." I glance past him, over his shoulder, to the vampic girl. She doesn't appear to notice our passing. I turn my gaze forward. "I saw someone I'd rather avoid. So... why don't we go another block down and turn there. We can swing back up to Bourbon in a block or two."

"Alright by me. I don't really care where we walk. I'm here for the company." He smiles wide, then pulls a chip from the bag and pops it in my mouth.

I chew and swallow, and my belly complains with want for something else. "In that case, why don't we go get some beignets, like our first night together," I say.

His face lights up. "The day I saved you from all the scary people in the Quarter?" A grin spreads across his face, stretching from ear to ear. I nod. Silently laugh. "Café Du Monde, it is." His gaze drops over me. "That outfit is going to look superb covered in powdered sugar.

A laugh bursts from my lips, and I swat him. Hug him to my side. Walk a joyful gait toward the river, my arm linked with his.

We follow the streets to St. Louis Cathedral, cross the front of the church, and turn down the side of Jackson Square. As usual, the perimeter of the square is populated with art peddlers, but it is a woman from a small table, unadorned by products for sale, that jogs to my side and grabs my hand.

"Excuse me." I yank my hand away. "What are you doing?"

"Sweet thing, let me read your palm." She motions for me to raise my palm to her.

Phillip tilts his head to me. "Do you want to?"

"I don't know." My face pinches, and I hold my hands tightly to my chest.

"I do it for free." She waves me forward.

"Nah." I shake my head. "Too many strange things have happened to me lately, and you are just one more in the string of oddness. I'm going to pass."

"Yes. You are surrounded by discord." She waves her hands around my silhouette.

"I just told you that," I snap.

"Then let me tell you something you don't know." She leans forward. "I no charge you. What will it hurt?" She waves me forward with one hand. I narrow my gaze upon her.

"It's totally up to you," Phillip says, tilting into me. "If you want me to get rid of her, just say the word."

His proposition makes me snort. Still, I don't shift my gaze from her. She motions me forward, once more. I drop my gaze to my open palm. Reluctantly reveal it to her. She grabs at my hand, yanks it close, and studies it with great intensity. Traces the tip of her finger along a line crossing my palm.

"You descend from a powerful line, no?" She glimpses at me. I shrug. "You do. Don't doubt. But..." She steps back and presses a finger to her lips. Glances to either side of us. "They fear you." Her face tints with a touch of depravity. "And you know not why." She tsks and wags a finger at me. "You know not the power at your disposal. You are bound, child. You must free yourself, or the Quarter will be the end of you." She releases a wicked laugh. It rises up her throat and rolls off her tongue in an ear-splintering cackle.

Phillip grabs my shoulders and guides me backwards, away from the crazed psychic. We turn and dodge down the walk and around the corner in a fit of laughter. At the edge of the corner, we stop and stare at each other

"That was... different," Phillip says with a roll of his eyes and a shake of his head. "A bit intense."

"I think the word you meant is bizarre, crazy, insane." I glance back to confirm she isn't coming to fetch us. So far, so clear.

"Yes. All of that." Phillip's back straightens. "Hey. Isn't that your brother?" He points toward the street at the front of Jackson Circle.

Mike has emerged from Artillery Park and is briskly making his way toward, and through, Jackson Circle. The hunch of his shoulders and the tightness of his muscles suggest he is still holding strong to the anger buildup from earlier. He sulks past with his head down, taking notice of little, if anything.

"He looks pretty preoccupied," Phillip says. "Now is probably an excellent chance to follow him unnoticed, if that still interests you?"

I stare at Phillip, blinking twice. Last time the two of us tried to follow my brother, things got awkward and Phillip got mad at me. I glance at my brother and then back to Phillip. And now he is suggesting we make another attempt.

"Okay," I say. "If you're game, let's do it."

He grins, grabs my hand, and drags me in chase to catch up to Mike... beignets from Café Du Monde forgotten. Keeping a decent buffer between us, we follow my brother through the Quarter. Not once does he look back or take notice of our presence. At the far end of the district he climbs the steps to a house and, after one knock, is ushered inside.

Phillip pulls me against a tree. Presses his hand against the trunk and leans into me. "Do you know this place?"

"No." I shake my head. "Never been here. What do you think it is? A friend's house? A drug den? Something else?"

"Not my area of expertise. Could be anything as far as I'm concerned." His watchful gaze shifts back and forth between me and the front of the house.

"Well, Mike went in there so I'm simply going to follow him." I duck down and shift beneath Phillip's outstretched arm. Pop free and start for the house. He grabs my arm, yanking me to a stop.

"Just like that? You're just going to walk up there?" he says. "You don't know who's inside."

"My brother is." I smile at him and pull free of his hold, cross the sidewalk and head up the front steps. Phillip jolts to a quick follow.

Before I can get to the top of the stoop, the front door opens and a woman steps outside. She grabs my upper arm. I startle and meet her gaze. Dark circles weight from her cold, hard eyes and a large, jagged claw-like scar cuts across her left cheek. Her hair is jet black with a thick streak of grey.

"Where do you think you're going?" Her gaze shifts from me to Phillip.

"Inside." I attempt to sound confident and unwavering, but detect a tiny wobble in my delivery.

"Oh no you're not." She moves down the steps, intimidating us into backstepping. "You should go home. You do not belong here."

"I'm sorry, but..." Phillip presses forward.

"Isn't it past your bedtime?" she interrupts. "I do believe the sun has set. And curfew is quickly approaching."

"I don't care if it is nighttime or not. I am going in there." I shift to move around her, and her arm juts out in my path. I halt and close my eyes. Take a deep breath and pull my lips into a tight line. Allow my frustration to settle, dissipate a fraction.

"Why do you think I don't belong in there?" I point to the house.

"Because I know all the pupils, and you are not one of them." She hooks her hands on her hips.

Pupils? My mouth falls slack. Is Mike attending some sort of private schooling thing he hasn't told me about? *Highly possible.* He hasn't told me much of anything.

"What kind of pupils?" I ask.

"If you belonged here you wouldn't have to ask." She smirks.

"Okay, you got me." I fold my arms. "But the question still remains. I want to know what it is that you teach here. This place doesn't look like any kind of school I'm familiar with."

"I suspect what we teach is nothing you need to worry about, for if it was something you needed, it is fairly likely you would know about us and what we offer," she says.

My shoulders drop. The woman is an expert at stonewalling, and I am getting nowhere fast. "We're not leaving until you let us in." I square my jaw.

She laughs and in that instant, her eyes sparkle. "Well, then. I guess we have ourselves a new set of lawn ornaments."

"Come on, Miri." Phillip tugs at my elbow. "We can wait for him over there." He motions to the spot by the tree.

"No," I rebut. "Not good enough."

"I will not have you waiting to jump one of ours." The gal with her cold eyes and scary scar pins a harsh glare upon me.

"You don't understand." I clench my fists.

"Then explain it to me." She flashes a glance at Phillip

I lurch forward. Push up in her face. "We need to get in there. So you are going to let us pass."

"I fail to see that as an explanation." She shifts her attention to Phillip. "Are you going to let your woman dictate the situation?"

Phillip grins and then smiles at me. "She's her own person. She can do whatever she wants. I'm simply here to add my support."

The front door to the house opens, and a large man steps onto the stoop. Stations himself, door-side, with thick, muscular arms crossed. His face is a wild display of black ink.

I swallow hard. Try not to stare but return my attention to the woman. Phillip softly clears his throat and tilts his head to my ear. "Maybe this wasn't such a good idea."

My gaze flitters to him for a flash. Then to the giant standing beside the door. And finally, back to the woman positioned in front of me. I understand Phillip's thoughts on this matter, but too many times, I have attempted to follow Mike and have failed. Now that I have finally managed to make it this far, I need more answers than the outside of this little brick house has to offer.

"The thing is..." I throw my hands out at my side. "My brother has been having a rather difficult time of it lately. Acting strange. Sleeping super late. Sneaking off to places unknown."

She raises a brow but doesn't interrupt.

"Anyway. A few minutes ago, I saw him go inside, and I thought maybe this place could help me understand what is going on with him." I frown.

"Your brother is inside?" she asks. I nod. "And you don't know what this place is?" I shake. "Well, isn't that the cat's meow?" She taps her finger to the underside of her chin.

"His name is Mi..."

She slams a flat palm in front of me, cutting off my sentence.

"We don't use real names here." She narrows her gaze, as if judging my level of understanding. I gulp and nod.

"Oookaaay. Then he's the tall guy with short-short hair, dressed in orange," I say.

She laughs. "Honey, you just described an enormous amount of the local population." She shifts her weight. Folds her arms across her chest. Scrutinizes me. "Let's say I take you inside to find your brother. Then what?"

"I talk to him," I blurt. "That's all I want. Honestly."

"Talk and nothing more," she says. "No looking around or gathering secrets."

My face wrinkles. "What secrets?"

"Very well. I shall allow it, but we do it my way." She motions to the man standing beside the door.

I release a sigh of relief. "Thank you," I say. "Thank you so much."

She swings her finger in the air. "Blindfolds."

Cloth drops over my face, blocking my sight.

CHAPTER TWENTY-THREE

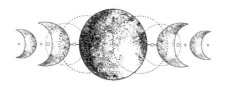

Someone has blindfolded me. *Where did they come from, and how did I not notice?* I touch my fingers to the fabric. Cotton.

"Not digging this plan," Phillip says.

"You are more than welcome to stay out here and wait," the woman says.

"No way. I'm not leaving her to go inside alone." Phillip brushes against the back of my hand, searching for the twine of our fingers. I take hold of his hand.

"Very well. Come along." She climbs the steps, her heels clicking upon the marble. A second later, the groan of door hinges. Someone at my back pushes me forward, guides me up the steps and into the house.

The clomp of shoes upon cement and marble is replaced with the creak of wood floors and the shuffle of footsteps... people shifting out of the way. I drag my fingers along a wall at my side. It feels thick with a multitude of paint layers. The air is thick with the scent of frankincense and sage.

"Would anyone like to claim these stragglers?" the woman asks. "The girl claims to have family among one of you."

Someone clears their throat. I imagine Mike standing in a corner or at the back of the room, sheepishly raising his hand. The woman makes a humph of acknowledgement.

"Follow me," she says.

Several whispers travel the far side of the room, followed by soft shoe shuffles.

I am shoved forward and maneuvered deeper into the house, past a humming light, around a corner, through a doorway, and pushed to sit in a chair. The fabric is soft to the touch. Velveteen, maybe? More feet shuffle in, and a door closes. The blindfold removed.

Phillip sits in a chair beside me, a small side table between us, and Mike stands before us, leaning against an ornate wooden desk. The space isn't overly large. Just enough room for a wall-to-wall bookcase at our back, the two chairs we occupy, and the desk supporting Mike's weight. The entire room is wallpapered in a giant grey scale mural. The charcoal curtains are pulled shut, and the overhead chandelier bathes the room in a warm glow.

"I shall leave you to it, then." The woman and her helping guides leave the room.

Mike frowns at me and remains silent, his gaze shifting to the door and back. He's waiting and listening. A line of footsteps moves up the stairs. My guess, the woman is relocating everyone out of sight in case Phillip or I step out of the room.

So secretive.

Once all the sounds of movement have settled on the upper level, Mike crosses his arms and turns his undivided attention upon me. "What are you doing here, Miri? Did Caleb hurt you?"

"No. No. I left before he even had a chance to do

190

anything." I shake my head. "I..." I start to stand, and he points to the chair, suggesting I remain seated. I glance around and drop back to the chair. "I'm worried about you?" I say. "*Been* worried about you." My hand swings toward the door in weak reference to the situation. "What is going on here?"

"I don't want you worrying about any of this. You shouldn't be here." He glances at Phillip. "Neither of you should be. If Caleb finds out..." He steadies his stare upon me.

"None of this is sanctioned by him or Mom, is it?" I lean into my knees.

"Does this look like something Mom would approve of?" He blurts. "No. It's because of what I am doing, and what this place is helping me do, that Mom moved us out of Grandma's."

"What... what?" I jerk back in my seat.

"What are you doing?" Phillip interjects. "What is this place?" He swings his hands out in reference to the room and the house beyond.

"These matters and this place are not for your kind." Mike jabs a finger a Phillip. Phillip clamps his jaw shut.

"Mike!" I bolt out of my seat, ignoring his stay-put request. Mike rolls his head back.

"Come on, Miri. You've got to know Mom has been lying to us, been working to keep us in the dark. You must feel it in your bones... what we are." He sighs and his shoulders slump. "I saw what you did in the kitchen this evening."

"You mean the spice explosion?" My hands flair at my side. "I kind of wish I could take credit, but I'm pretty sure that was Belle."

Mike's brows raise, and his lips quark to the side. "And you?"

And me, what? Harbor superpowers? I shrug.

"Okay. Listen." He places his hand upon my shoulder and gently pushes me back to the seat. "Grandma wasn't lying. Our lineage is powerful. Crazy powerful, and, for whatever reason, Mom doesn't want us to know. Caleb supports her in the quest to keep us contained in ignorance. But Grandma and I have been working in secret for a few years. She's been teaching me how to harness my power. Accentuate my strengths and overcome my weaknesses. When Mom found out..." He spreads his arms wide. "Caleb's."

"If what you say is true, wouldn't we all be feeling and experiencing strange magical things... supernatural mistakes?" I ask.

"Aren't we?" he counters.

I sigh and lean into the back of my chair. Recall the things I thought I saw magically happen in Belle's presence. Think about the list of oddities I made earlier today. "Let's say all that you are telling me is true. What does that mean for us?"

"It means we need to be careful." Mike's chin juts forward. "I don't trust Caleb, and neither should you. He knows what I am up to. I don't know how, but he knows, and he hasn't told Mom. I find that suspicious."

I suck back a breath. Caleb also knows things about me he hasn't yet shared with Mom.

"I think he has informants all over the Quarter. Maybe that's why he was so keen on moving us in... so that he could keep a closer eye on us. All of us." Mike leans against the back wall. "I have seen him places, doing things. Like lurking outside that seedy vampire bar, for one."

The vampic bar across from where Phillip works. The one where I had *two* scary encounters. And the same one where I thought I saw Caleb witnessing my attack, my fright, but do nothing.

"I've also seen him hanging about with a local voodoo priestess. I doubt Mom would approve, if she would listen."

"What does that mean?" I lean forward.

"I've known about some of Caleb's extra-curricular activities for a while now. The night Mom moved us under his roof, I tried to tell her when we were alone in the car. She refused to hear a word I said. It was almost like..." His face pinches with thought and he stretches one arm out as if trying to pull the answer from his mind. "It was almost like she was brainwashed." His eyes widen, body straightens.

He steps forward and motions for us to stand. Phillip and I both comply. Mike moves to the door, opens it a crack, and peeks out.

"You should get back," he says to me. "Before Caleb suspects anything. I don't want him targeting you next." He grabs my arm and pulls me toward the door.

"What about you?" I resist his pull, unwilling to leave his side so easily.

"This is a safe place for me." He smiles. "They're helping me gain better control my powers, and they have already agreed to let me crash here for the next several nights. Until I figure something else out."

"What about Grandma's? Why not go there?" I ask and reach for Phillip's reassuring handhold.

"I would love to," he says. "But I can't afford to bring any trouble down upon her, and I have a strong sense trouble is headed our way."

I suck back a sudden breath. It lodges in my throat. How does one prepare for trouble from an unknown source? The source could be Caleb, or it could be something else entirely. "What should we do? How do we prepare?"

"The first thing we do is not give Caleb any reason to raise his suspicions." Mike rolls his eyes. "Something that has gone sensationally well so far, wouldn't you agree?"

"Do you mean because of the fight you guys had tonight?" I

brace my hand against the doorframe, preventing Mike from ushering me out.

"That and so many other big and little things. Come on." He yanks the door open and nudges me into the hallway. The space is tight, with wainscoting on the lower half and the upper portion of the wall painted in a greyish green.

"Best you get home," Mike continues. "After what happened this evening, the more time you spend away, the more cause you give him to get angry. And I don't want him taking his wrath out on you while I'm trying to figure out how we should best deal with him." Mike prompts me and Phillip down the hallway and toward the front door. A glance over my shoulder into areas not wandered brings me a slight whiff of roasted chicken, as well as informs me the kitchen is in desperate need of updating.

"Watch it, man." Phillip yanks free of Mike's touch, but continues to move toward the exit. He grabs my arm and pulls me at a quicker pace, clearly anxious to get out of here.

We move into and through the front room. Probably once a nice little parlor, it now looks to be set up more in an informal classroom style with several table and chair arrangements. One table hosts a medium-sized cauldron. On one of the others, a clutter of stones and dried bones sit.

"I'll walk you home," Mike says. "To make sure you get there without any issues. Once you are there, keep your head down and try not to draw his attention."

"Because you fear for my life?" I glance over my shoulder at him. "I'm a big girl, you know. I can take care of myself. Plus..." I glance to Phillip, tap a comforting pat upon his guiding hand. "I've got this guy."

"I know. I know you're quite capable. I just worry about you and Belle." Mike shrugs.

A smile warms my heart, and I turn my attention forward,

to where I am going. The woman from earlier, stands beside the front door. She pushes it open and steps aside, allowing us to pass. Phillip tugs me into the open air.

"El," she says to my brother. He motions for us to wait a moment, and he nods at the woman. Nods. "Saddler would like to see you upstairs."

"Now?" Mike's eyes widen. He glances back into the house, then shifts his gaze to me. "But I told my sister I'd walk her home."

"He says it's important," she deadpans.

Mike's lips press together in a tight pucker. His brow pinches with thought.

"It's alright," I say. "Do what you need to do. I'll be fine." I clasp Phillip's arm. "Like I said, I have this guy to keep me safe."

Mike's face pulls into a downward frown. He is far from glowing with confidence in Phillip. What was it he said about Phillip a few minutes ago? *"These matters... are not for your kind."* What exactly did he mean by that? Was he referring to skin tone or something else?

"Okay. Fine," Mike blurts. "But don't do anything stupid, and head straight back to the house. I'll check in with you later. Understand?" I nod that I do, and he disappears back into the house. I watch him jog down the hallway and up the stairs.

"Don't you have someplace you should be?" The woman asks.

"Did anyone ever tell you how warm and fuzzy you are? You make me tingle with welcoming comfort." I hug myself with sarcastic overacting.

She snorts a laugh. "Clearly, you have fallen from the same tree as El," she says of my brother.

"What is with the name El, anyway?" I lean closer.

"I told you we don't use our real names. El is the one your brother goes by."

"But what does it mean?" I ask.

"You'll have to ask him." She motions toward the street. "Now get off my stoop before the neighbors start to get curious."

"Nice talking to you." I make no effort to hide my sarcasm, and I descend the steps. Phillip wraps his arm around me and rubs my arm. Glances over his shoulder.

"Thanks for the top-notch hospitality," he says.

"Anytime," she responds. "But we best not see you back here."

I huff and cross my arms. Something at the edge of my vision jumps, catching my attention. *It's the vampic girl. She followed us...* or managed to find us. My insides liquefy. I spin on Phillip. Press my hand to his chest.

"Give me a second." I dash back to the woman still standing at the door.

"Can't get enough of our unique torture?" she says.

"Something like that." I glance across the street. The vampic girl is backing into the shadows beside one of the homes, but she's definitely there, and she's definitely watching me. "Can you give my brother a message? It's important."

"And you didn't think to deliver this message when you were talking to him two minutes ago?" She scowls.

"It wasn't an issue two minutes ago." I slam my fists into my hips.

Her eyebrows raise. "Okay, kid. You've got me curious now. What is it you want me to tell him?"

"Tell him that some vampire-wannabe girl is following me." I cross my arms and carefully glance toward the girl again.

"Are you saying she's here now?" the woman asks. I nod.

Her gaze shifts over the surroundings. "Anything else I should tell him?"

"That should be enough," I say. "I'm certain he'll know what to do with the information."

"Very well. Consider him told." The woman opens the door, steps into the house, and allows the screen door to close between us. "Now don't let me keep you from getting home."

Right. I glare at her and then turn and dash back to Phillip, stay close to his side for the walk home. Our walk is quiet, and thoughts of Mike's disclosure, and of our stalker vampic girl, fill my head. Mike said he thought Caleb had informants throughout the Quarter. *What if the creepy vampic girl is one of his informants? What if she tells Caleb where I have been and what I have been doing?* Will he kick me out of the house like he did Mike?

We turn the corner, putting Caleb's house in sight. Nothing appears amiss. All is relatively quiet, and I am hoping, hoping, hoping Caleb went out without bothering to first verify my presence.

I shiver. A combination of trepidation and apprehension. Phillip pulls me to a slow stop in front of the home, and my gaze wanders to my bedroom window.

"Meow." Something rubs against my ankle.

A black cat drops to the ground at my feet, rolls onto his back, exposing his belly. I blink wide. It seems inconceivable to me, but the cat requesting my attention appears to be the same cat from both the cemetery and from deeper in the Quarter the other day. In fact, he has shown up several times now. What is with him?

"Meow." He begs for my attention.

CHAPTER TWENTY-FOUR

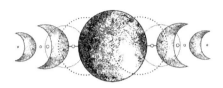

"You again?" I kneel and rub the cat's belly. "You are relentless. What are you doing here?" The cat rolls back and forth upon the sidewalk. Meows some more.

"What is it with you and cats?" Phillip asks.

"You know what's strange?" I say, ignoring his question. "I think this might be the same cat we saw at the cemetery earlier today."

"That is strange. And rather improbable." He kneels and pets the cat. "That's too far away for a cat to travel."

"How would you know? Are you a cat expert?" I shoot him a sideways glance.

"No." His face crumples. "I had a dog when I was younger, but no cats. And currently, no pets whatsoever."

I frown. Feel slightly sad for him. But why? It's not like I have a pet, or even had many growing up. I return my attention to the cat demanding my love.

"Then it's plausible this cat traveled the distance from there to here." I drag my fingers through the cat's hair one last time. Pushing to a stand, I stare up at the windows. The top level is dark, but a dim light carries through the glass balcony doors on the second landing. Either someone is hanging out in the family room or Mom left a light on. Either option is viable.

"It's been an interesting evening," Phillip says. "I got the impression that neither Caleb, nor your brother Mike, are very fond of me."

"I didn't necessarily get that impression from Mike. And as for Caleb... who cares what he thinks." I grab Phillip and pull him closer. Wrap my arms around him. "It's not up to anyone other than me as to who I choose to see." I smile and press my forehead to his. "You bring sense to my life. Plus an all-consuming warmth, and don't you dare think anything otherwise."

"Yes, ma'am." His lips tease me, brushing against the edge of mine ever slightly. The tip of his nose traces along the edge of mine, and his lips press against my mouth in a soft and all-too-quick kiss. "There's no school next week," he says, veering the topic away from our previous discussion. "Maybe we can take a day trip on my dad's bike. Whadaya say?"

I jolt straight. "Did you get it running? Because, if you did, I believe the terms dictate the bike is now yours and no longer your dad's."

"You may be right about that." His voice is soft. His attention less on the conversation than on my face, my mouth. He pulls me closer, and our bodies lock in a connection rooted strong upon our lips and deep within our hearts. A whirlwind of mouthwatering emotions.

A catcall and a whistle comes from across the street, and I reluctantly pull away, allowing space between us. "Guess I had better get inside."

"Yeah, guess so." He makes no effort to release his hold upon me.

"See you tomorrow at school," I prompt and gently take a step back. His hands slip from my back, pull into the refuge of his pockets.

"Definitely." His smile is gentle. Sexy. I take a step toward the door and wave goodbye. "I'll just hang out here for a few minutes to make sure everything goes alright in there and you don't get in trouble."

"And if I do... get in trouble. What could you do?" My hands splay at my sides.

"Well I could..."

"You couldn't do anything," I interject. "If Caleb yells at me, he yells at me. It's not like you'd bust down the door and come racing up the stairs to my rescue."

"I might." His nose wrinkles.

I fight the smile threatening to spread across my lips. It warms my heart hearing Phillip professing to become a hero should I require one. But if what Mike said is true, and magic truly does run in my family's blood, then I should be all the hero I need.

"Stop it," I say and swat a hand at him. "I'm already tightly tangled in your devilish device. I don't need to be dragged deeper." My hand presses to my chest.

"You can fall far and deep. I promise to catch you." He smiles.

I strangle a giggle. "Go home, Phillip. I'll see you at school tomorrow."

"Right." He lifts his chin in acknowledgement. "See you in the morning." He waits for me to step inside and close the door.

Making my way through the house with silent motion, I climb to my room on the third floor and peek out the window. Phillip waits on the street below. One quick wave from me lets him know all is well. He swings his arm through the air in parting and heads down the street.

I spin around and drop to my butt upon the cabinet. Stare at the clock upon my nightstand. Time has flown since the debacle at dinner. Or, the dinner that didn't happen. Because it is approaching the eleven o'clock hour, I was able to slip up to my room unnoticed. Belle is in bed because it is a school night, and Mom, because she has to work in the morning.

My skin burns at the thought of my mom. Damn her for not sticking up for Mike. For any of us, really. So glad I didn't run into her. I'm not sure what I would say to her. I want to talk to Grandma, but it's too late to call her. She's likely sound asleep at this hour.

I creep through the adjoining bathroom and peek in on Belle. She is in deep, as identified by her heavy breaths. Any need to talk will have to wait until tomorrow. But can I sleep with so many thoughts plaguing my mind? Caleb's behavior, Mom's lack of a backbone in the face of Caleb's fury, the stalking vampic following me, Mike and his *school*, Belle and the spices, me and... and... whatever I did to the glass window earlier today.

I close the door to her room and prep for bed. Decide to take a shower, in an attempt to loosen my tension and wash away my frustrations. The beat of the water and the caress of the steam soften the thrush of my blood... a smidgen.

If Mike has witchy powers as he professes, and I've witnessed Belle's magic at work, what about me? What do I have? There must be something running through my blood. Something I can summon to keep me safe from Caleb and his anger. Possibly something I've already caught hints of these last few weeks.

I turn off the water. Towel dry and dress for bed.

I guess the larger question is... *how do I summon the power, and how do I control it?*

I need to talk to Grandma.

I'll call her in the morning, before I leave for school.

I slip beneath the covers and close my eyes. Breathe deep and direct my focus to nothing. Utter darkness, yet sleep does not come to me willingly. I toss to my right, think of the glass breaking beneath my touch. Toss to my left, recall the orange glow that appeared to emanate from my palm in the club that crazy night. I twist flat on my back, remember an earlier conversation with Mike.

"Dad didn't just leave," he said. If Dad didn't *just* leave... leave us to end up in this crappy situation with Caleb... then what happened to him? Why was our dad *forced* to leave? Where did he go? And why hasn't he at least visited us?

The thoughts consume my mind until sleep finally wins, and I succumb to the darkness of my bodily slumber.

Though, rest is not had.

My mind is ever active, and a voice at the back of my head taunts me, calls me to it. The disembodied voice that has haunted so many of my nights.

"Go away," I tell it. "Leave me alone. I want nothing to do with you."

"Do you honestly believe your participation is a choice?" the voice answers.

A thick fog swoops forward and engulfs me, pulls me backward into the confines of the dream. The growing nightmare. The cemetery.

The fog drops to a low-lying mist, from which the city of the dead rises into the starless, night sky. The aroma of earth and brick and dying flowers is heavy upon the damp air. The ground, muddy and spotted with rain puddles.

The fog wisps away from me, leading through the maze of concrete resting places. With a quiver and a tight hug, I follow. Terrified to discover where the misty element will lead me. Terrified not to know.

The cemetery I now wander in my nightmare is not the same one I explored earlier in the day with Phillip. That one had been in the Garden District, and this one I recognize as being located on the outer edge of the Quarter.

The spiraling haze leads me to a decrepit brick tomb. Any identification markings lost to time. At the front of the grave, the haze shifts and takes on the shape of a tall cylinder.

"Come to me, my dear," the mist says. "Come to me as your family before you has done. Combine our life forces, our power, and grow stronger than you can possibly imagine."

My muscles tense, and I stare at the circling murk, my eyes widening and my feet moving, moving me backwards. "My family didn't come to you," I say. "I know my grandma didn't. She's not possessed. And my mom doesn't believe in witches or their power. She doesn't believe in whatever it is you stand for."

"When you look at your world, do you only see the things that are in your immediate sight?" the disembodied voice says. "Such a limited view of life, should that be so. There is infinite worthiness beyond that which you can see. A vast network of power and energy connecting our family through the threads of time." The shifting mist thins, displaying a hint of a female within. A woman dressed for a time long since gone. "Your grandmother was never a good match for me. Her magical strength, lacking. And your mother interests me not. But you. You are strong in all the ways that they are not. You and I are a good match."

Rain drops from the sky. A slow sprinkle building in intensity. The mist among the graves thickens, drops lower, and the outline of buildings upon the horizon vanishes, the density of graves thin.

The tomb standing before me transforms into a monument with fewer years in age. I glance around me and everywhere I look, the cemetery and the city beyond its walls has changed. Have I slipped through time in this vivid nightmare of mine?

The smell of sewage and rotten water rises around me and wafts through the air.

"It began long ago," the voice says. "Long before our family reached this land. Long before the new world and your generational innovations. What has been for thousands of years cannot be denied by one as young and naïve as you." The swirling mist drifts closer. "Fighting me will do you no good. In the end, I will win, and you will be mine."

The mist separates, and a hand presses forward from the cloud, points toward the ground.

"Take it," she says. "It is for you."

Lying in the mud, upon the newly exposed ground, is a necklace—silver with a large black stone and a slithering serpent.

"It has been passed down through the family, and now it is yours."

"If it has been passed down through the family, then why is it here, in this nightmare of a cemetery and not in my mother's possession?"

"It is not for your mother to have." For the first time since my nightmare began, the voice is harsh, bordering on angry. "The necklace is to follow the bloodline and belong to no other."

I suck back a breath and bolt awake. I lay upon my bed, eyes wide and body weighted, frozen.

Follow the bloodline. *Why had I not seen it before?*

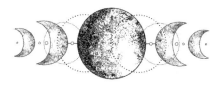

om and Grandma were always so careful with their word choices, but it's now all incredibly clear to me. We lived with Grandma because we, Michael, Belle, and me, are her grandchildren. Not because of any blood relation with Mom. We are related to our Grandma through our dad, not our mom. How did I miss that before now?

I think about Mike's attachment to his memory of Dad. Something I do not share with him. Did he know? He probably did. It explains a lot. The tension between Mom and Grandma. The lack of childhood stories from either of them. Mike's friction with Mom.

I sit up and turn my gaze to the clock. The alarm is due to go off in a few minutes. The school hour is approaching. I wonder... *is it too early to call Grandma?*

I rub my eyes, turn off the alarm, slip out of bed, and step out onto the landing between Belle's and my bedroom. Neither one of us has a phone in our room, but there is one on each level of the home. One in Caleb and Mom's room, another with a forever long cord hanging on the wall in the kitchen, and one set upon a small table between the top-most bedrooms. I pick up the receiver and dial Grandma's number.

Grandma picks up on the fourth ring, and I am quick to ask if she is free in the afternoon. Turns out, she isn't. Not the answer I was expecting. She has a doctor's appointment and although she doesn't outright say it's an important one, I get the sense that it is. So, when she asks me if I would like her to reschedule so that we may meet, I tell her to leave everything as it is. We make plans to meet after school tomorrow, instead.

Disappointed, and slightly concerned for my grandma's health, I hang up the phone and go get ready for the day. Still steaming about Caleb and his horrid behavior the night before, plus mad at Mom for not standing up for her own kids, I quietly pack my school bag, hole up at the top of the stairs while she pours her coffee, and move out once she is in the bathroom with the shower running.

Thankfully, Caleb is oblivious, deep in *snoreville*, having stayed out late the night before. A behavior that appears to be rather routine for him. Belle joins me at the front of the home, and we walk to school together.

"That was you last night... with the exploding spices and all?" I ask after several moments of awkward silence.

"Why would you think that?" She tries to act surprised, but I see through her game.

"You don't need to hide the truth from me." I glance around to make sure no one is walking close. "I followed Mike last night. Did you know he's been going to some sort of *school* where they are helping him master his magical abilities?"

"What?" Belle stumbles to a stop and stares at me. "What are you talking about? What kind of school?"

"I don't know much beyond what I just told you. They were terribly hush-hush when I showed up. Even blindfolded me and shoved me in a room to meet Mike, making sure I didn't see the other people present."

"Where is it?" she asks.

"Come on." I tug her elbow and resume our walk to school. "It's at the far corner of the Quarter. If we take a different route to school, I'll point out the general area." She agrees and we continue straight when we would normally turn north. "So, you can tell me," I continue. "Did you cause all the spice jars in the kitchen to explode last night?"

She sighs. "The situation was getting rather heated, and it made me uncomfortable. I just. I don't know. Popped." She bursts her hands wide at the side of her head.

"So, you did do it?" I push.

"I think so. Yes." She drops her head. "Listen," she says. "I'm just trying to figure it all out. You can understand that, can't you?"

I guess so." I avert my gaze to the sidewalk at our feet.

"I can't always make the magic work, and when I do, I'm not always sure what factor made it work."

"That must be frustrating." My frown is filled with internal thoughts. At least she's getting some results, even if they aren't consistent. "Are you having any spooky cemetery dreams?"

She jerks sideways, allowing more space between us. "No. Thank god."

Right. My insides drop. We near the far edge of the French Quarter, and I stop at a corner and point down the street. "Mike's school is down there, about a block."

"But they're houses," she says.

"Yep. An undercover magical school disguised as an unassuming house." I smirk. Cross the street. Head north toward the school.

Belle follows me in silence, and any continued conversation drops into nonexistence. The school day falls into a rhythm of study and rush. With winter break fast approaching, most of my classes are prepping for tests. I catch up with Phillip at lunch and again after school. He has to work, so I take my books and, not wanting to go home, follow him to the restaurant, where I sit at a table in the back corner and refresh my knowledge of American history. During his break, he sits with me, and I explain to him my plans to meet with my grandma the following day. I want to gain a better understanding of my family. Our truth and our history.

That night, I take a sleeping pill to avoid any unwanted nightmares, and it works. On Wednesday morning, I awake more refreshed than usual. Yet, even in my renewed state, the school day drags with the pace of a slug. When the final class bell rings, I'm eager to race across town and meet up with Grandma.

Phillip catches me at the front of the school, asks me to be careful and to call him when I get home later. I agree and make my way to the Garden District. When I walk up to the house, my grandma is standing on the front porch waiting for me.

"Miri, sweetheart. Come here." She opens her arms wide, welcoming me into her loving embrace. I throw my arms around my grandma and hug her close.

"I've missed you so much," I say and fight tears wanting to flow.

"And I, you." She kisses my forehead. "Come inside and tell me what is on your mind." She opens the front door and motions for me to enter. The mouthwatering aroma of chicken gumbo invites me into the home, and I go eagerly. Grandma ushers me toward the kitchen, directs me to a seat at the table. She hands me a soda from the refrigerator and takes a seat at my side. I pop open the can, take a sip.

"You're having nightmares, aren't you? She has been calling to you in your sleep?" Grandma lays her hand upon mine.

"How did you know?" My jaw drops and head lurches forward.

She dips her head into her shoulder. "It makes sense. You're of age. And... I suspect, both unprepared and unprotected."

I pull back into my chair. "You do know how crazy this all sounds, right? My life has been unrealistically weird since we moved out. You always warned Belle and me to stay out of the Quarter, but I never expected to find the kind of strange I've experienced. There is so much I don't understand, and I want desperately to make sense of it all." I shake my head and rub my forehead. "I get the unprepared bit. With all your talk about witches, you really didn't tell me anything. But how am I unprotected?"

"By your lack of knowledge and lack of access to your power," she says.

"I have no power. Belle has more magic in her blood than I do. I've got nothing."

"I doubt that is true," she says. "I suspect you are far more powerful than you realize." She pulls something from her pocket and drops a small, ugly doll upon the table. The doll and its clothing are rudely sewn together and tied with yellow twine. "I found this in your mother's old room after you all left. In her rush, I guess she forgot to take it."

"What is it?" My fingers inch forward with desire to touch the doll, and equal disgust of its existence.

"This is magic," she says. "Magic used to bind your magic, to be precise."

"But Mom doesn't believe in magic, so why would she have any such thing among her belongings?" I tap the doll with my fingernail and then pull my hand back. Clench into a fist.

"Your mother doesn't want to believe, but deep down she knows of the power. Knows it to be real." Grandma nods. "She comes from a line of witches, as do you. She may be weaker, but she has witnessed greatness."

"That, right there." I point at Grandma. "Mom is not your daughter, is she? You basically just admitted as such. How come you never told me this growing up?" I ask. "Why keep the truth from us and lead us to believe that Mom was *your* daughter?"

"To protect you and your siblings, of course."

My nose wrinkles and head shakes. "I fail to see how a lie was meant to protect us."

"Because my son, your father, was swayed to something unnatural and completely unsafe to be around." She heaves a heavy breath. "I needed to keep you safe from that element, and your mother agreed. We decided on a story that was meant to satisfy you and your siblings just enough to evade too many questions and avoid the desire to find your missing father."

"But Michael knew," I say. "You told him."

"He didn't always know. Over time, he figured it out. He's a smart kid... as are you," she says.

"And powerful?" I prompt. "Magically powerful? Did you know he is going to some sort of school to help him learn and control his craft?"

"Yes. Powerful like your father." Her gaze shifts, and she stares with a dreamy eye at the far wall. "Strength runs deep in his veins. He reminds me of your father in so many ways." Her attention snaps to me. "I helped Michael find the school, since your mother forbid him to continue spending time with me. Before the school, I was helping him where I could." She sighs. "But the path for each witch is different. Personal. And he has to discover and learn things that are beyond me." She squeezes my shoulder. "His journey is his own. As is yours."

"And what of my journey?" I press my elbow into the table. "I'm having nightmares. Weirdos are following me around the

Quarter. And I appear to have no magical ability of my own. Only strange occurrences."

"What kind of strange occurrences?" Grandma narrows her gaze upon me.

"An odd glow and heat coming from my hands," I say.

"And the people following you?" she asks.

"They may be spies for Caleb. I'm not sure, but there is a creepy vampire-wannabe girl." I frown.

"And the frequency of your nightmares?" she presses.

"Every couple nights." I bite the inside of my lip and study my grandma. Her brow is crinkled with deep thought.

She nods, several times, her mouth pressing into a firm line. "That ancestor of ours is a persistent one. She lived in my grandmother all the years that I knew her, and..." She raises a pointed finger. "I paid attention. Kept my ears open and learned." She squeezes my hand. "She is powerful, indeed. But she can be thwarted. Held at bay. She need not control you as I am sure she seeks to do."

"I don't understand why she would want to control me. I don't have any abilities that I've noticed," I say.

"Aw... but you do." She raises a pointed finger in the air. "You have been magically bound by your mother, who has come to fear the power running in our bloodline. Her constant denial of her own ability has cut her off from the source." She pushes away from the table and walks into the kitchen, still talking. "I think her influence upon you has resulted in you stifling your own ability. Because I doubt her little binding magic would fully hold you down. Clearly it hasn't." She grabs a small box off the counter and returns to the table.

"What do you mean the binding didn't work?" I say. "I have no magic so that clearly isn't true."

"Your magic is attempting to break free and is succeeding to

211

some degree," she replies. "You experienced it yourself with the heat and glow emanating from your hands."

"I don't know." I shake my head.

"You will," Grandma says and sets the box upon the table. "You'll understand soon enough. And when you do, you will begin to grow into the strength and power necessary to keep that pesky ancestor in her grave."

"I wouldn't mind that." I rest my arms upon the table and fold my hands together.

"You will also begin to understand why the less powerful in the Quarter fear you," she says. "It is fear that has them following you. They fear your power. Your potential. The potential downfall you could bring upon them."

"You're saying the creepy vampire girl is correct in assuming I'm a witch and she's toying with me because she's afraid of me?" My brow crinkles, and my mind struggles with the waves of doubt thrashing over me.

"What better way to hide outward fear than to tease and taunt that which you are afraid of?" she says.

"Avoidance?" I blurt.

She smiles wide. Pushed the box between us. "Everything we need to break the binding spell is here in this box. Would you like to see what happens when we remove the chains upon you?"

CHAPTER TWENTY-SIX

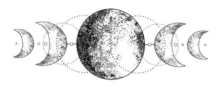

I stare at the box. Study its unassuming appearance and think about the many things Mike has told me... and then consider Belle's manipulation of kitchen gadgets and spices.

"What's inside?" I lean closer.

"Everything necessary to break any binding spell cast upon you." Grandma rests her hand on the top of the box. "Do you want to find out what it feels like to be free of any magical shackles?"

Very much so. "What do I need to do?" I bite my lip and glance between the box and my grandma.

She stands and pulls the box into her clutch. "Follow me." She sweeps her hand in a follow motion. "It's time for you to wash the attachments away."

With her in the lead, we climb the stairs and make our way to the bathroom Belle and I used to share. She places the box on top of the toilet and removes the lid. Pulls free several items from the box and sets them upon the counter. Among the items is a large, white pillar candle, a jar of salt, and a bundle of mixed herbs.

"For this cleansing ritual, you are going to take a bath. It is neither the ideal day nor the ideal time of day..." She glances out the bathroom window. "But I believe our combined magic will be more than sufficient to break the binds your mother has placed upon you."

"If everything you say is true, why did my mom bind my magic in the first place?" My shoulders drop.

She turns to face me and drags her hold down the length of my arms. "My dear, you have done nothing wrong."

"Okay. But why did she bind me?" I push. "Why didn't she bind Belle or Mike or all of us?"

"Because it was your magic that scared her the most." She squeezes my wrists. "Belle and Michael are fine witches, but neither one of them pull from a well of magic as deep and as rich as yours. Unbound, your magic is intense, powerful, and a threat to those who don't understand."

I bite my lip and blink, struggle to comprehend what she is telling me. Not only am I a witch by blood, but I am a powerful witch. And yet, I haven't experienced any hint of this supposed power until recently.

"In all the years that I lived under your roof, why didn't you tell me any of this?" I cross my arms.

"Your mother strictly forbade it," she says. "I threw information and hints at you kids, but that was all I could do. I couldn't risk her taking you three away from me." She tosses a hand at her side. "Of course, that is exactly what she eventually did." She turns on the water and starts filling the tub.

"But what about Mike? You told him things?" I blurt.

"Michael came to me. I did not initiate the conversation. Just as I did not initiate the one we now have." She tests and adjusts the temperature, sits on the tub's edge. "I could not turn him away, just as I will not turn you away. Of course, your mother found out and then moved you away."

My jaw drops, and I suck back a breath.

"Why don't you go get ready for your bath," she says. "I left your robe on the bed." She waves me out the door. "I'll continue to prep the bath."

"Right." I head to my old room. Sure enough, my robe is laid out across my old bed. I inhale deep and take in the space. When Belle and I shared this room, mere weeks ago, I wanted little more than a room to myself. Now, under my current living conditions, I think I would prefer to come back to this house and this arrangement. Sure, my own room and bathroom sink is nice, super nice even, but I'm not sure it's worth living under Caleb's watchful eye, or with the tension created by him and Mike.

I shed my clothing and slip into my robe, pull my hair up and secure it with a tie. Return to the bathroom. The tub is full, and Grandma leans over the water, mumbling a chant. She has sprinkled a few herbs into the tub, but the majority of the bundled herbs are now mixed with the salt, and remain in the jar.

"What is all this stuff?" I step into the bathroom beside her and motion to the herbs floating upon the surface of the bath.

"It's all rather natural." Her hands fluster at her side. "We will be calling upon the energies of the earth for this ritual. Each element is presented here, and builds upon the others, working together to reinforce the strength of each. Sage, rosemary, and hyssop have been mixed with the salt to add support."

My lips pull into a lopsided frown.

"You really should start studying your herbs." She pats my upper arm. "There is a fair amount of overlapping in these herbs magical uses, but they should do a fine job with the task at hand. One thing you should learn is that salt can be your best friend. It can serve to purify you and protect you." She dips her hand into the water and swishes back and forth. "The addition of the herbs serves to further banish unwanted attachments. They will work to heal you, purify and protect you."

She raises her hand from the water and allows it to drip dry for a moment before turning back to the bathroom counter. "We will burn the sandalwood to add an element of healing and protection to the air around you. In addition, the candle calls for the energies to grant you truth, purity, and a connection with your divine self." She strikes a match and, murmuring a chant, sets the incense and then the candle to burn. Flips off the overhead light.

The room fills with the aroma of sandalwood, sulfur, and the slight hint of water lily.

"This is a lot of stuff," I say. "How am I supposed to make the magic work?"

"Keep your intentions pure. Focus on severing any unwanted attachments and realizing your true potential." She takes my hand and turns me toward the water. "Clear your mind and focus now on those intentions."

I breathe deep, close my eyes and focus. Focus on clearing my mind, body, and soul of any unwanted baggage and tethers. Focus on discovering who I am and all the things of which I am capable.

The glass jar scrapes upon the surface of the counter, and my eyes pop open. Grandma holds the jar over the bath water. "In the name of the energies, our ancestors, our god, and ourselves, we call upon thee, oh elements of the earth and water. Come forth and cleanse our Miriam of all evil and unwanted magicks; restore her to balance and health. By our wills combined, so mote it be."

She tilts the jar and sprinkles some of the contents into the bath. Hands me the jar.

"Now you," she says. "Speak the request, and add the rest of the salt and herbs to the water."

I take the jar, and with her guidance with the wordage, I repeat the spell, asking the elements to unbind me and heal me. I empty the jar into the bathwater. When complete, Grandma takes the empty jar from my care and pats my back, smiles.

"I am going to leave you alone for this next part. I want you to soak in the tub for about twenty minutes or so, being mindful to keep yourself calm and in a meditative state. Submerge yourself completely at least once, and then relax... allow the process to work. In your relaxed, cleansed state, all the attachments should simply slip away."

She pulls a piece of paper free from the box and sets it upon the bathroom counter. "When you are done soaking, drain and rinse everything away, and make sure none of the saltwater remains, on you or in the tub. With the rinsing of the saltwater, so shall any remaining attachments be cleansed." She lifts the paper between us. "When that is complete, read the words upon this paper, while making sure to hold intention in your heart." I nod, pull my lips tight. "I shall leave you to it, then." She kisses my forehead and exits the room, closing the door behind her.

"Let the magick begin," I whisper and drop my robe, slip into the bath. The perfume of rosemary overpowers that of the sage and hyssop. Combined, the aroma tugs a smile to my heart. The water caresses my skin, and the warmth relaxes my muscles. Flickering off the surrounding walls, the dim glow of the candle sets the room in a calm, atmospheric light.

I dunk beneath the water and soak every inch of my body, then settle into a comfortable position, resting my head against the back of the tub. Close my eyes, rest my mind, and allow the minutes to tick away. A sense of heaviness slushes off my body, and I begin to feel lighter. A fog within my mind lifts, and a new tingle of energy dances through my veins. Across my skin.

I fold my arms over the side of the tub and drop my fingers into the water with a *pling*. The constant shift between light and dark, caused by the candle's flame, plays upon my closed eyelids. When the heat against my skin fades to a dull warmth and the sunlight beyond the window softens, I decide it has been long enough. Surely, longer than twenty minutes.

Following my grandma's directions, I rinse the saltwater from my skin and down the drain. Wrap the towel around me and read from the slip of paper the words meant to conclude my binding cleanse ritual.

"I thank thee, oh elements of earth and water, in the name of myself, my god, my ancestors, and the energies," I say. "Be released to your homes, doing no harm along your way, and return to me with glad hearts when next you are summoned. By our wills combined, so mote it be."

The air in the room lightens, as if a heavy weight has been lifted, and I would almost swear that somewhere, in the house or in my head, I hear a tiny bell.

I dry off, get dressed, and meet Grandma downstairs in the kitchen.

"Your aura is much cleaner now," she says. "You will start to experience the awakening of your senses. They have been stifled for too many years. Thrust into a dormant state. Now that they can breathe, they will begin to expand and show themselves."

My forehead tightens and stomach knots. *In what way should I expect my senses to show themselves?* The mere contemplation of magic happening randomly around me chokes the air from my lungs.

"You are going to do just fine," Grandma says. "Just don't pinch yourself off to the possibilities."

"Can you show me how to..." I wave my hands before me. "I don't know... do magick?"

"Why don't we give your body some time to acclimate to the change?" She narrows her gaze upon me. "How about you come back tomorrow after school. We'll see where your energy has settled by then."

I frown and she laughs. Hugs me tight.

"These things take time. You can't rush the process." She releases me and steps back. "The magic coursing through your veins works like any muscle in your body. It will grow stronger the more you use it. But given the fact you've been bound and not using any, you'll likely be weak at first. I recommend you get home, get your schoolwork done, and get a good night's sleep. I want you well-rested when we start tomorrow."

I nod, somewhat reluctantly, and say my goodbyes. Promise Grandma I'll return after school tomorrow. Her words make me think I should be presently tired or weak, but I feel neither.

I head back to Caleb's with a bit of a nervous bounce in my step. My blood races with concern for my living circumstances. Mike's situation... and Caleb's clear irritation. At what exactly he is irritated with, I'm not a hundred percent certain. I catch the St. Charles trolley, take it to the one running along Canal Street.

I settle into a seat near the back, and sit sideways on the bench. Pulling my legs into my chest and my hoodie over my damp hair, I rest my head against my knees. The trolley lurches forward, and two men, a few seats ahead of me, jump into conversation. They may be trying to be quiet, but their words and familiar tones carry softly to my ear.

Caleb. Caleb is one of the men.

My insides jolt, even as I attempt to hold my body still.

Possibly turn invisible. I sink deeper into the seat and tug my hoodie farther over my head, dropping my face into shadows. Only, curiosity is nagging, nagging at me. So I twist, in an attempt to get a better view of the person with whom Caleb is chatting. It's someone Mike pointed out to me as a serious avoidance. A terribly bad element. A voodoo witch for hire, a bokor.

My shoulders stiffen and stomach flops, and yet, I don't move. I avoid doing anything that may draw attention to me.

"It should be fire," the bokor says. "It is the best chance you have to cleanse the evil for good."

His words spark a memory, and I flash back to the day the creepy vampic dragged me into the French Quarter store, pushed me to touch the candle. The candle I wanted nothing to do with.

"I know." Caleb nods. "I wish it weren't so."

"There is no other way, brother. The whole lot of them are a threat to order within the Quarter. We cannot allow them to destroy the balance of power we have established."

The whole lot? They couldn't possibly be talking about me and my siblings, could they? Something within me harps at my intuition, suggesting that my family is *exactly* what they are discussing. Grandma told us to stay out of the Quarter, and still Mom moved us to the outer edges. Did Grandma want us to stay clear of the Quarter because other factions, be it witches or voodoo priestesses, don't like my father's family and would seek to destroy us?

Crap. I forgot to push for further information about our family history. I bite my lip. I was too narrow sighted. Too caught up in the whole magically bound situation.

Tomorrow. Tomorrow I will press Grandma for more information.

"Then fire it shall be," Caleb says. Shakes his head.

My breath lodges in my throat. *If there is a tomorrow.*

"Edith will be heartbroken." Caleb's head dips.

My heart jumps. Edith. My mom. They *are* talking about my family. About my family and fire.

The trolley rolls to a stop, and the doors at the front and back swing open. Keeping my head low, I push into the aisle, swirl toward the back, and make a quick exit, jogging down the steps and jumping into a speed walk. I need to get home, like, yesterday. I need to warn my family about Caleb.

I take three brisk strides, and someone steps into my path. No time to react, I bump into them. Apologize. Move to step around. But they grab my arm.

"What's the rush, little witch?"

My head snaps up, and I come face to face with the vampic. I gasp.

"Your broom on fire or something?" She tilts her head. "Possibly running from a pack of witch hunters?" She glances past me, and a wicked grin spreads across her lips. "Or witch cleanser." She lifts her chin to someone at my back.

My blood freezes over, and rigor mortis sets in. I force my head to turn, glance to the space at my back. Caleb stands a few feet yonder, his gaze narrowed and tight upon me. A festering, dark emotion swirling behind his eyes.

His fists clench, and he pivots, storms away.

Ohmygosh. A plethora of emotions explode throughout my system. He's going to cleanse me, kill me and my siblings in some sort of Salem witch trial manner. I shove the vampic chick out of the way and dash up the street. Run across the intersection and head in the direction of the house. I need to get home before Caleb. I need to warn my family and get them to safety... before it's too late.

The tip of my shoe catches on something, and I trip. Slam to the ground. My knee throbs, and I suspect I'll see damaged skin and possibly blood should I lift my pant leg and check... which I don't.

Behind me there is a wicked chuckle. One glance over my shoulder informs me the creepy vampic chick is following me.

What's her deal?

I pull myself to a stand and limp-run toward my family.

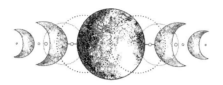

CHAPTER TWENTY-SEVEN

My shoes slam against the pavement, the pads of my feet crying for relief, a stay of motion. But I can't stop. I must get to my family before Caleb. I need to make sure they are safe. Then keep them that way.

My heart throbs, pounds a dent at the back of my ribs, and my newly washed skin dimples with beads of sweat.

Oh, and the smells...

The smells of the Quarter are particularly assaulting right now. A nauseating mix of body odor, perfume, sweet alcohol, stale beer, and vomit. But there's something more. The scent of earth, a hint of flowers. Aromas reminiscent of the cemetery. Does death follow me?

If the ritual to eliminate the binding was successful, does that mean my witchy ancestor has easier access to me, to control me, and my unknown ability? Or is she more restricted?

I turn a corner, bringing Caleb's home into view. It stands a block away, at the edge of the intersection. Swerving around bodies, left and right, I dash to the door at the front of the garage. Toss it open and start screaming for Mom, Belle, and

Mike. I take the stairs to the second level, two at a time. Slam into Mom in the space just outside the kitchen.

"What has gotten into you?" She grabs my arms, yanking me to a hard stop. "Why are you carrying on like this?"

"Mom." I drop my head and gasp for air. "Where is Belle? Mike?"

"I'm here.' Belle peeks her head out of the kitchen. "Wanna help me with dinner?" She straightens. "Oh yeah. Your boyfriend called about an hour ago."

Phillip called? My eyes widen, and I bite my lip. I had promised him I'd call when I got home. Guess I took longer than I had intended.

"He said he'd call back later," Belle says.

I shake my head, my gaze bouncing between my mom and sister. "Where's Mike?"

"He's not here. Remember?" Mom says, triggering my memory of Caleb and Mike's raised voices. That's right, he wouldn't be here. Caleb kicked Mike out. "What is going on here, Miri?" Mom prods.

"Not here. That's good. I think," I say of Mike, my gaze flitting toward his bedroom door.

"What has gotten into you?" Mom shakes me ever so slightly.

I jostle her hold free from my arms and shift to her side, gaining a clearer view of Belle in the kitchen. The thick scent of jambalaya permeates the space. "Listen." I flatten my hands in the empty air between me and my family. "I know this might sound a tad crazy, but Caleb is on his way here with the intention of hurting all of us. I heard him when he didn't know I was nearby or within earshot. He plans on getting rid of our *evil* with fire. So..." I motion toward the stairs. "We need to get out right away."

"Caleb wants to hurt us?" Belle lurches forward. "Why?"

"Because of what we are."

"Don't be ridiculous." Mom grabs my upper arm and yanks me. "Caleb is like a father to you. He would never hurt any of you. He loves you."

"Stop being so naive when it comes to Caleb, Mom. Honestly." I yank free of her hold once more. "I expect better from you."

Belle removes the pan from the burner, turns off the heat, and wipes her hands with a kitchen towel. Heads into the family room area.

"What are you doing?" Mom calls after her.

"Getting my bag so that we can go," she says.

"We aren't going anywhere until we straighten this massive misconception out." Mom drops her hands on her hips and glares.

"If Miri says we need to go, then that's good enough for me," Belle counters. "I believe in my sister."

"Above your own mother?" Mom shifts to face her.

"It's not like that," Belle blurts.

"It shouldn't need to be like that," I interject and shove past Mom, placing myself between Mom and Belle. "We can work this all out somewhere else. Somewhere away from here." I turn my attention tight on my mom. "Grandma told me everything. I know about the family line *and* the binding."

"Is that so?" Mom leans into the side wall. "When did you talk to your all-knowing grandmother?"

"Today. Just came from her place." I cross my arms.

"Miri!" Her voice pitches, bounces off the walls of the room. "How could you? I thought I made my wishes blatantly clear. You are not to visit her without my supervision. Her delusions are dangerous."

"You saw Grandma?" Belle's voice is tiny at my back.

"That's just it, Mom. I have decided she isn't so crazy after all. And I choose to walk without the blinders on anymore." I inhale, exhale deep. "I get that you are scared of the power my father's side professes to possess, but we are still your children. How could you keep us in the dark for so long?"

"Do not try to stand strong on things you do not understand," Mom says. "There are witches and then there are those... your grandmother, for example... who want to be more. Want it so badly that they create a mystic around themselves. Craft an illusion so grand that everyone begins to believe the falsehood, themselves included. Do not follow in her footsteps. I beg you."

"I know about the binding spell you cast on me." I shift my foot to the side and lean into my hip.

"I don't know what you are talking about." Mom lowers her chin.

"What binding spell?" Belle whispers at my back.

"Grandma was cleaning the house and found it. I saw it with my own eyes."

Mom flinches and her posture loosens. Her demeanor giving away the truth she's been hiding for years. Heat rushes through my chest and burns my eyes.

"Do you have any idea how confusing my life has been, growing up in the shadow of you, Grandma, my missing dad?" My shoulders drop. Mom doesn't say anything. She merely stares at me with her mouth slightly agape. "I don't suppose you do. You weren't the one being made to feel the awkward outcast. The unworthy witch. The unwanted daughter."

"I have never done anything to make you feel unwanted..." Mom interjects.

"No, but Dad has been missing forever, and no one has ever bothered to explain his absence. Until today." My shoulders tighten.

"Your grandmother told you about Isaac?" Her hands drop to her side.

"I don't understand. What's happening here? Can someone please clue me in?" Belle says.

"Grandma held back no secrets," I say. "And she helped me undo the stupid spell you cast upon me. My magic is finally free to grow. To flourish."

"You have no idea what you have done." Mom's voice pitches. "It's dangerous for you to be unbound."

"Why so?" My lips pucker into a tight frown.

"Um..." Belle tugs at my shoulder. "Does anyone else smell smoke?"

"Turn off the kitchen burner," Mom orders Belle.

"I did," she says. "A while ago."

I spin toward the stairwell. Mom and Belle follow suit. A thin layer of smoke snakes up the stairs and into the room. Mom throws her arms out and backs away, pushing Belle and me backward in the process.

"Oh my gosh!" Belle grabs my wrist. "Is that fire? Is the house on fire?"

The house phone rings.

CHAPTER TWENTY-EIGHT

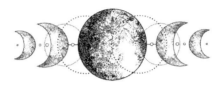

Belle leaps across the room and grabs the phone from the cradle, shoves it to her ear. "Call the fire department," she says and drops the receiver.

"What did I tell you?" I blurt and glance from the stairwell to the balcony. Which direction is our best option?

"This is not what you think it is," Mom yells. "It has to be an electrical fire or something." She spins in a circle, taking in the room and situation.

"Maybe. Maybe not." I glare at her and then dash into the kitchen, grab several clean towels from the bottom drawer. I hand one to Belle and one to Mom. "Breathe through these if the smoke gets any worse.

"I think it's past time to get out of here," Belle says, a serious sense of urgency to her tone. She spins toward the balcony doors.

"Right there with you." I dash past her and push open the French doors, take a step forward, and... *Blam...* smack into an invisible barrier. I shake my head. *That can't be right.* I step forward again.

Energy snaps across my skin, stretching tight, and thrusting me backward.

"What's wrong?" Belle steps forward, intending to move out onto the balcony, but she, too, is shoved backward, forced to remain inside the house. She shoves her hand against the unseen wall of energy. "Magic," she whispers.

"Magic fueled by ignorance and stupidity," I add. "Can you break through it?"

Belle blinks at me. "No. I struggle with simple kitchen spells. Something like this is far beyond me."

We both glance over our shoulder to our mom. She has plopped onto the sofa and dropped her face into her hands. Tears rain down her cheeks and across her palms. "I wanted to believe in him so badly." Her words choke through sobs. "When Isaac left me alone with three children, I wanted to believe another could love and accept my children as I do."

"That's the thing, Mom. If you truly accepted us, you wouldn't have bound me, forbid Mike, or restricted our knowledge of the family lineage." I attempt to push through the invisible barrier once more. "Instead, you would have worked with us to become the best versions of ourselves that we could be."

"Is that Caleb across the street?" Belle points beyond the balcony to the opposing building. My gaze follows. Caleb is indeed outside of the home, making no effort to come to our aid. He is leaning against the building on the other side of the road, whispering into his hands. "It looks like he is talking to himself," Belle says.

Reciting some sort of spell to keep us trapped in this hell, is more like it.

Mom shakes her head into her open palms. "Why Caleb? Why?"

I cross the room. "So... you believe me now?" Grabbing her

upper arm, I yank her to a stand. "It's not going to do any of us any good to sit down and give up. Cry over mistakes made."

"What are we going to do?" Belle grabs Mom's other arm and we pull her away from the sofa.

"The only thing we can do," I say. "We are going out through the garage."

"No." Mom thrust backward, out of our hold. "We can't."

"The fire is coming from the garage." Belle says, voice raised. "Won't that way be blocked too?"

"Most likely." I snap Mom's arm into my hold once more and yank her forward. "But what choice do we have. We need to break through the magic or burn to death. And I'm hoping the majority of his magical prison cell is focused on the exits not complicated by fire."

"I don't want to die," Belle says.

"Neither do I."

Belle and I pull our struggling Mom toward the garage. Halfway down the stairs, the smoke engulfs us. Heavy coughs rip through Belle's chest. I press my kitchen towel to my face and motion for her to do the same. We near the opening to the garage. The space is crowded with smoke, but the flames appear to be confined to the parked car in the center of the garage. At least, they remain so for now.

Mom halts, pulling Belle and me to a stop. "Come on." I tug.

"We shouldn't get so close to the fire." She takes a backstep up the stairs.

"What other choice do we have?" I ask. "Can you break through the magic keeping us from the balcony?"

She shakes. Sniffles. "No, but you can." She spins and runs up the stairs.

Belle coughs. Stares at me. I stare, wide-eyed, back at her. We don't have time for this foolish bickering and indecision.

My teeth clench and my gaze bounces from the garage door to the space were my mom disappeared up the stairs and back to our potential exit.

I grab my sister's hand and tug her toward our path free of the house, toward the exit to the street. A massive flickering finger of fire lashes across our path. I yelp and stumble backward. Belle pushes forward in a second attempt. Again, she is thwarted by the blaze, its sizzling resistance blocking our path.

"It's no good," she says through the filtering cloth held over her mouth. She turns and dashes up the stairs after Mom. My heart hammers. Every bone and muscle in my body is tightening, crying. My jaw aches and I want for release. Want to be free of this hell that is Caleb's burning curse of a home. I want to race past the fire and crash through the magic binding the exits. But it's no use. I won't leave my family. Reluctantly, I follow Belle and Mom back to the second level.

"Okay. You win," I say to my mom and bound from the stairs toward the balcony doors. "How do we break the magic holding us inside this inferno? How do we get out of here?"

Mom stands in front of the invisible boundary, her fingertips lightly tracing the energy holding us hostage. "Neither Belle, nor I have the strength of power to breakdown what has been created here. And you have been bound against performing any type of magic." She lowers her head. "There is no way around it. This is our fate."

"Mom!" Belle's voice pitches with fear.

"Morbid much." I grab her shoulder and spin her to face me. "Your binding spell has been broken. Tell me what to do."

"How did you..." She stammers, stares at me.

"Grandma told me what to do, and I did it. I gotta say, I felt oddly refreshed." I toss my hands out at my side and then allow them to drop straight.

"When?" She blinks.

"Earlier today." I frown. "Now tell me what to do."

"Channel us." She extends her left hand, and with her right, she drags Belle's hand forward in a silent suggestion that I take hold of both.

I grab their hands. "Now what?"

"Concentrate and focus your desire. Speak your wishes to the elemental energies guiding and watching over us." She squeezes my hand.

"Okay. I got it. Okay." I nod. But the truth is, I feel beyond foolish, talking to the elements and trying to create magic. "I don't know what to say."

"Follow my lead," she says, and both Belle and I stare at her, blink to each other. The magic in our lives is getting real. I shift my weight and hold firm to my family.

"Elemental energies that command this earth, hear our plea and break this curse," Mom says. She turns to me. "Now you."

I bite my lip and suck back a deep breath. The floor beneath my feet warms to an uncomfortable level. Soon, I'll be chicken dancing or looking to retreat to the third level. We need to get out of here before the fire either comes through to our level or destroys the structure and brings us crashing down into its hungry flames.

Here goes nothing.

I tighten my hold upon Belle and Mom. "Elemental energies that command this earth, hear our plea and break this curse," I say. My hands tingle and my body hums. I repeat the request. "Elemental energies that command this earth, hear our plea and break this curse." The verve thrumming through my system increases. I repeat the chant again and again and again, each time experiencing a stronger zing of potency racing through my blood and along my skin, a deeper connection to the world around me. Mom and Belle join me in the chant.

The invisible wall holding us hostage fizzles and hisses.

Waves of blue electric light flash across the surface. The fizz and hiss morphs to crackles and pops. A wave of energy explodes through the room, knocking us off our feet, and thrusting us backward. The three of us collapse onto the floor.

"What just happened," Belle says.

I twist onto my back and wipe the sweat from my brow. The room is smoldering, and I want for an endless supply of water to crash over me.

"I believe Miri was successful. I think she broke the spell." Mom stands, extends her hand to Belle, and helps lift her to her feet.

"Really? Did I really do it?" I rush toward the balcony door, slowing at the entrance, hesitant to slam into a stinging forceful stop, once more. I reach forward, into the open space of the doorway and meet no resistance. I jump onto the balcony. "I did it!" I spin to face my mom and Belle. "Let's go."

They rush onto the balcony and we move toward the corner, away from the burning car in the garage. I catch sight of Caleb turning and running away. Guess he's not interested in facing the consequences of his attempted destruction.

Belle, Mom, and I climb over the balcony railing and lower ourselves as close to the sidewalk as possible. We release and drop hard to the ground.

The heavy scent of sulfur and rubber and rotten eggs permeates the air around us. Plumes of smoke rise from the home, but any hint of fire has yet to show itself. So far, it has remained trapped in the garage.

"What the devil's hell is going on?" Mike slams into me. Grabs me. Rakes his investigative gaze over me. "Are you alright?" He turns toward my mom and Belle. "Are all of you alright?"

"We're alright," Mom says.

"But we almost weren't," Belle adds.

"Okay." He smacks my shoulder blade and moves past me, toward the garage door.

I grab his arm, yanking him to a stop. "What are you doing?"

"There is something I need to get." He jerks, attempts to pull free of my hold.

"In there?" I point to the curls of smoke escaping the house. "You can't. It's crazy."

"I can and I will." He extracts his arm from my detention and throws open the door, darts inside.

My mom screams after him, but he disappears into the cloud of fumes without a glance back. Through the now open gateway into the historical home, a vision of flames dances and consumes.

"What is he doing?" Belle grabs me and clings to my side.

"I don't know," I say. "It's a crazy and deadly move." My heart is hammering to a rib-cracking rate. My blood is congealing, my muscles and bones, fossilizing. With Belle and Mom at my sides, I stare up at the house and wish Mike safe... wish Mike back out on the sidewalk.

Far off in the distance, the sound of sirens wail. Can we wait for their arrival? Will Mike survive in the house that long?

Tears burst from Mom's broken composure. Her head drops into her hands and she wails. Wails for my brother, for us, for Caleb, and the wretched situation we are all in because of him. Because of my mom's relationship with him.

"I'm going after him," I say, regarding my brother. "I'll bring him back." I slip from my families hold, much to Belle's complaint, and head for the garage opening. Push forward through the door, into the smoke and toward the fire.

Someone grabs my wrist, tugging me to a stop. I spin, expecting to come face to face with Belle or Mom. Standing before me is Phillip, his eyes wide and wild. "What are you doing?" he blurts.

"Mike is in there." I jab a pointed finger toward the house. "I need to make sure he is alright and get him out."

"Commendable." Phillip wraps his other hand around mind. "But it isn't safe for either of you. It could get you killed."

"I can take care of myself," I say.

"Something you have proven time and time again." He frowns. "But this time is different. Fire can't be reasoned with." I strain at his hold. "I know our relationship is extremely new, but I'm not ready to lose you." With a gentle pull, he tugs me toward the door. "Please, Miri. Don't endanger yourself like this."

I glance toward the burning car in the garage, the fire skimming across the ceiling, the smoke-laden stairwell. Fire. So much fire. The element Caleb meant to cleanse the evil... the evil he sees in me... from this world. If I go after my brother, I'll be walking straight into Caleb's trap.

I return my gaze to Phillip. Nod once. Allow him to lead us back onto the safety of the sidewalk. But...

Michael.

I need to do something. Protect him, somehow.

But how?

I whirl to face the disaster unfolding and focus my concentration of the space at the back of the second floor, Mike's room.

What is so important, it had him dash into a burning building?

Doesn't matter now. *Focus.*

"Elements, I beg that you would hear my request. Send my brother free of this cataclysmic collapse." My words are a whisper, directed at the elements at play within the chaos unfolding in Caleb's home.

Nothing changes.

Everything inside of me is tightening, pushing toward rage. I need my brother out of the burning house now. Right now. I can't stand the waiting.

"Free my brother of this cataclysmic collapse," I yell.

"What are you doing?" At my back, Phillip twitches. Tugs on my arm.

"Fire, be no more!" I lurch forward, straining Phillip's hold upon me.

The wind around us swirls. Sucks into the garage with the power of an inward surging hurricane, eradicating the fire and swallowing all hints of smoke.

My fists squeeze tight. Fly to my chest.

I am magic. I can do magic.

But, where is Mike?

The house groans. Creaks with complaint. And my shoulders drop, my jaw falls slack. My eyes widen, and my throat constricts. Goes desert dry.

The fire is out. The smoke is gone. I spy no signs of Mike. And, the house... the house complains too much of instability.

"Please," I whisper. "Give me a sign that my brother is alright."

A pop. Snap. Kcreeek.

The roof collapses.

CHAPTER TWENTY-NINE

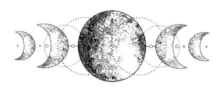

I gasp. My hands fly to my lips. *I did this. Me and my magic.*

Plumes of smoke erupt from every opening. A trillion tiny dust particles that were once pieces of wall and ceiling.

"Mike!" I scream and collapse in on myself. Phillip's arms encircle me, hold me tight.

Belle and Mom are at my side, wailing. Yelling for my brother. Lookie-loos gather, swarm the sidewalk and street, and in the distance, moving ever closer, the sounds of sirens. I struggle free of Phillip and stumble toward the fallen home. An unnatural blueish glow escapes through the crevices in the rubble.

Could it be Mike?

I push through the opening of the garage, lift a large piece of wood and plaster and toss it to the sidewalk beyond. I gaze upward at the gaping hole allowing a clear view of the night sky. Everything we had in this place of Caleb's is now gone. Turned to ash and ruin.

With my chest as hard as stone, I set my resolve. Piece, by

broken piece of old house, I clear a small gap in the pile of debris. I will find Mike.

He's going to be alright; I assure myself. *My brother cannot die. Not by my doing.*

Phillip settles beside me and helps. As do Belle and Mom. The sirens shift to strong horn blasts, igniting the crowd into motion. They clear the street, allowing the fire truck passage. A large engine comes to a stop in front of the home. Before the vehicle even rolls to a complete stop, men are jumping free. A couple of them run straight for us in the demolished garage.

"What are you doing?" one of the men yells. "This area is not safe."

Two of the men grab Belle and Mom, direct them toward the safety of the street.

"My son is in there," Mom says, struggling against their removal.

The pile in front of me stirs. My excavation of the wreckage quickens.

"Here," Phillip yells and shoves his arm into the collection of wood and plaster and brick. Connecting with something hidden beneath, he yanks. A fireman appears at Phillip's side and helps steady him and pull him back. The fire-damaged heap burst to life, thrusting and flying to all sides. From the wreckage, Mike straightens, one hand pressed to the side of his face. A mild glow dissipates from around him.

"Man!" Phillip exclaims. "Damn lucky. Are you alright?"

"I will be. Thanks for the assist." Mike drops his hand from his face and offers it to Phillip. Phillip's jaw drops, but he clasps my brother's hand and adds support to Mike's climb clear of the destruction. The fireman nudges Phillip back and steps in, helping Mike get free.

I stare, unblinking, at the large cut and burn marring the left side of my brother's face.

You did this, a tiny voice whispers in my head. *You and your attempt to save the day with magic.*

When Mike steps free of the broken bits of house, I throw my arms around him. I can't hold him close enough, nor tight enough. I fight the sobs seeking release. "I'm so sorry. So, so sorry."

"For what?" Mike's voice pinches a high note.

"Come on." A fireman ushers us from the remains of the garage. "We need you to move outside."

We're directed toward the side of the firetruck, and the fireman asks a multitude of questions in the process. Most of them directed at Mike. Do you feel lightheaded? Are you having any trouble breathing? Any burning or freezing sensations?

We join Mom and Belle beside the truck and Mom grabs Mike, pats his face and arms, as if needing physical proof of his existence.

"I'm fine, Mom." He presses her arms to her side, settling her fussing.

"It's pretty amazing how you survived that. The house collapsing in on you the way it did," Phillip says.

"Yeah, well." Mike tilts his head. "I have the magic of a positive attitude on my side." He smirks, and the skin on the left side of his face crinkles. He winces and his hand flies to the burn and cut.

"You need to have that looked at immediately," the fireman says.

As if on cue, the two-toned warning bell announces the arrival of the paramedics. They pull to a stop behind the firetruck.

"I'll be fine," Mike says, brushing the fireman off.

"I'll have to insist." He steps away and greets the arriving paramedics when they step free of the vehicle.

I tug at Mike's arm, yank him close. "How did you manage to survive the house collapsing on top of you?' I whisper.

"I have magic on my side." He smirks.

I touch my fingertips to the left side of my cheek and fix my stare upon his scared face. If I am responsible for the events that led to his injury, I may never forgive myself. He frowns and his expression seems to say he senses my guilt.

"You are not to blame for any of this, Miri," he says.

"But I used magic. For the first time! And then this happened," I blurt.

"Not your fault."

The fireman turns toward us, drags the paramedics in our direction.

"I'm sorry," Mike whispers. "But I can't be seen by conventional medical practitioners right now. I gotta jet." He pats my shoulder, turns, and dashes into the crowd of lookie-loos.

Conventional practitioners? I call his name and stare after him, but he is quick to disappear into the mass of locals and tourists.

"Hey. Hey, wait." The fireman and paramedic dash after my brother, but they are not fast enough. They return empty handed.

"Where is he going?" Belle steps up beside me.

"I truly have no idea." I bite my lip and turn toward my sister, my gaze resting but a moment before snapping to Phillip. "If you hadn't shown up when you did, I might have been able to get to him. Save him before the house caved in. Saved him from getting that ugly injury."

"Is that what you think?" Philip replies. "Because I think you would have ended up beneath the pile of rubble beside your brother. Who's to say you would have fared as well."

I drop my head forward. He's right, of course. I know he is, and I tell him as such. Hug him. Thank him for being here and saving me.

I snuggle into his chest, then look up at him. "Why are you here?" I ask.

"Do you not want me here?" he asks.

"No. That's not what I meant." I pull back to better see him. "What I meant was... how did you know to come when you did?"

"Easy," he says. "I called and your sister answered, yelled for me to call the fire department and hung up. I took that as a sure sign that things were in a bad way. I called 911, reported the fire, and then raced over here. Found you with your mom and sister standing on the sidewalk."

A tight, hardly bent smile cuts across my lips.

I blink and shift my gaze to Belle. She is staring at the demolished house. My gaze shifts right and then left.

Where's Mom?

I visually scan our surroundings, taking in everything from the destroyed house, the emergency vehicles and responders, and the pressing horde of curious on-lookers. I spot Mom and suck back a breath. It lodges in my throat. Pressed to her side and holding her arm, as if to hold her in place, is Caleb. His back is to me, but I know it is him... the man who just tried to kill me and my family.

Why is Mom talking to him? Why isn't she screaming for help?

She may harbor some soft spot for the man, given that she is listening to whatever words he is using to transfix her, but I have none. Zero soft spots for him. I will never have an interest in anything that is Caleb beyond seeing him pay for what he attempted to do.

I search out a fireman to send after Caleb, but there are none. They are all attending to the wreckage, moving hurriedly about. Down the street I catch sight of a police cruiser. It's parked and the officers are not inside. Though, the presence of the car suggests there are officers on the scene... somewhere.

"Did you see what happened here?" The question comes from behind me. I spin around and come face to face with a policeman. He's questioning my sister and Phillip.

I recall Mike's warning regarding the police. Is the officer present trustworthy? My brow pinches tight. *I may have to chance it.*

"The fire was already going when I showed up," Phillip says.

I step forward. "That man across the street there." I attempt to discreetly point. "He set the fire, somehow using the car. He did so knowing full well that my family was in the house. He was trying to kill us."

"You know this to be true?" he asks.

"Completely and without waiver," I reply. "I have no doubt an investigation will turn up proof of arson."

"Which man?" He steps closer and I identify Caleb. He still stands with his back to us. Maybe he thinks we won't recognize him if he doesn't show his face, but he is wrong. So terribly wrong. My gut constraints.

"Don't go anywhere. I have more questions for you." The officer crosses the street and approaches Caleb.

Caleb, taking notice, pushes my mom into the officer's path and dashes into the crowd, down the street. The officer pursues.

"Come on," I say to Belle and Phillip, and head for my mom.

Her fingertips tap, tap, tap, against her lips. Her eyes are glazed, and her focus is dust.

"Mom." I brush her arm. She blinks to me. "What's wrong with you?"

"I'm fine. I'm fine," she blurts. "Caleb just said…"

"After all that just happened, you would listen to Caleb?" I jerk straight.

"He…" she stammers. "He's family. Family is everything."

"Family has your back. Has your best interests at heart. *He* is an attempted killer," I blurt, thrust my fist into my hips, and leer at her.

"He was trying to look out for me." She rubs her arms. "Save me for the evil lurking within our home and our blood."

"You mean to say…" I cross my arms. "Save you from your children… your family… and your life." My voice raises in pitch.

"Hey, Miri, come on." Phillip pulls me into his side. "Your mom may be in shock. Now may not be the best time," he whispers at my ear.

My gut ties in a knot and I study her posture. Her behavior. There is something not-right about Mom. Did Caleb brainwash her?

The firemen make sure no embers continue to burn and the policemen question us, gathering any information we are willing to share. An elder officer hands my mom his card and asks us to come into the precinct tomorrow to each give an official statement regarding the crime… or as they call it… possible crime.

Mom pockets the officer's card, and I ask him for another. In my mother's dazed state, I'd rather not depend on her organization skills to manage this situation. If she's been voodooed by Caleb, then she can't be trusted.

I shove my hands into my pockets and lean into Phillip's side. The tragedy is extra eerie in the moonlight, lit by dim streetlights and emergency flood lights. The house is a goner, but thankfully the adjoining residences appeared to be spared. Although, I expect everything in the vicinity to reek for weeks of soot and ash, charred wood, metal, and rubber.

"All my best clothing was in there," Belle says with a reverent tone.

"Mine, too," I say. "Hella bummer." I turn to face Mom. "Where will we sleep tonight?"

"We'll get a hotel room," she replies. People moving by bump into her shoulder, knocking her forward a step.

"Watch it," Belle says, spinning toward them.

"Why not Grandma's? She would welcome us, no questions asked."

She shakes her head. "No. Not there. That house cannot be trusted."

"The house?" I balk. "It's a house. What's not to trust?" I recall grandma's story about the protective wards built into the home. But that can't be what is bothering Mom because she lived there for years without issue.

"Not there," Mom repeats. "I won't go back there."

My gaze narrows, and I think back to the many times Caleb came to visit. Never once did he actually step inside the house. He always waited outside for Mom or us. Could it be because of the protections set in place? Could his influence upon Mom now make that an issue for her, as well?

Belle's lips are tight and her eyes wide, her gaze darting between me and Mom.

"Fine." I square my shoulders. "You do what you want, but I'm not gonna stay in some cheap hotel. I'm going to Grandma's." I turn to face Phillip. "Will you take me there? Us there?" I spin toward Belle. "You'll come, too, won't you?"

"Of course. If that's what you really want to do." Phillip rubs his hands up and down my arms. I nod that I do, then look to my sister.

Belle's mouth pops open and she stares at me, then turns her attention to Mom. Glances over her. Frowns.

"I think I should stay with Mom. One of us should. Mike's

clearly not an option, and since you insist on going to Grandma's, that leaves only me." She sighs. "I don't think Mom should be alone. At least, for now."

My gaze shifts back and forth between my Mom and Belle. "I understand where you are coming from, I really do. Mom is clearly not well."

"I don't appreciate the two of you talking this way about me. Especially when I am right here," Mom says. "I am quite fine, I assure you, and it would do you well to listen to me. Keep our family together as a strong, solid unit."

"That's part of the problem, Mom." I stand straight. "We haven't been very solid or strong since you moved us out of Grandma's house. We've been drifting apart. Ripping at the seams."

"All the more reason for us to stick together." She drops her hands on her hips.

"I disagree." I shake my head, look away for the briefest of seconds. "You do what you need to do. Although, I would advise against listening to any words Caleb has to share," I say. "Just know, I am done following you blindly. From now on, I am making my own life choices. And my first decision is to go back to Grandma's, not follow you to some cheap motel."

"Hotel," Belle corrects.

I shoot her a bewildered stare. Why is she defending Mom?

Phillip shifts awkwardly at my side.

Mom's brow furrows, and she crosses her arms.

"Look Mom." I extend a pleading hand in hopes of striking a balance between us. "I love you. Always have. Always will. But I can't live with you until you pull yourself together. And I don't think Belle should live with you either. She should come with me."

Mom's gaze shifts to the ground between us. Her shoulders and neck are tense, and her jaw is twitching.

"Maybe the time alone will give you the chance to clear your mind. Help you understand how your need to force us into a two-parent family unit, with an unqualified and undeserving man in the father position, brought us to this mess. A broken place lacking in trust."

"A bit harsh, don't you think?" Belle says.

I shrug, but frown. A nauseating burn churns through my inner workings.

"I'm sorry Mom." I drop my head and shake. "I just can't do this anymore. Not right now, anyway."

"You do what you need to do," Mom says, her voice quiet, yet calm and decisive.

"But I'm not joining you," Belle adds. "Not right now. Maybe later. Hard to say."

My head snaps up. "You have to come." I reach for her hand. "It's not safe anywhere Caleb might still have some control." I glance at my mom, making it clear I suspect Caleb still has far too much influence over her.

"Maybe," Belle says with a shrug. "But I don't think he sees me or my kitchen magic as a threat. I think he'll let me be."

"How can you be sure?" I tighten my grasp upon her wrist.

"It's just a feeling I have, here and here." She points to her head and then her heart. "I think I might be able to do Mom some good, but you should go be with Grandma. Because, yeah, I think he does take issue with you and Michael for some reason, and that isn't healthy or safe."

"You think so?"

"I'd bet my broom on it." She smirks and cocks her head. "And if for any reason, he tries something with me, I'll give him a spice-inflicted sneeze attack so severe he'll be completely disabled and fear sneezing his brain into his hands." She grabs a handful of spices from one of the apron pockets and tosses it up into the air. The spices swirl, spin, and drop to the ground.

My eyes widen, and my tongue is tied. When did my little sister become so fierce?

"That was some crazy wind that captured those spices the way it did but didn't toss anyone's hair," Phillip says.

Belle and I glance at Phillip. We both giggle, snort, shake our heads. I release Belle's wrist and pull Phillip into my side. "Crazy wind, indeed," I whisper at his ear.

I turn back to Belle and Mom. "Are you sure you guys won't come to Grandma's with me?"

"I'm sorry. I cannot go back to that house. Not like this." Mom raises her chin high.

"I've got this," Belle says. "Don't worry about us. You should focus on yourself and that new journey of self-discovery you started with Grandma."

A heavy weight drops over me. It's a mixture of emotions that will take time to work through and resolve. Concern and fear for my family. A sense of selfishness and betrayal on my part. Even if I am doing the right thing for me, I feel like I should be doing something more for everyone else. But what? I'm not a powerful witch. Not yet. And I'm only sixteen.

My lips curve with a combination of sadness and acceptance. "If that's what you want, I will honor your decision. But you call or come find me should anything funny arise." I narrow my gaze and pray she understands my meaning of *funny*. Caleb appearances. Caleb influences. Basically, anything Caleb related. She nods and I shift my attention back to my mom. "How are you going to pay for a hotel, even a cheap one? Wasn't your purse in that mess?" I toss a weak point toward the demolished house.

"Don't you worry." She pats her pockets. "I have it covered. And after all we've been through, I could really do with a long shower." She gazes past me to the fire damage.

A shower does sound nice. I agree, hug Belle, chat for a tab bit longer, and then say our goodbyes... for now. Phillip walks with me to the trolley and rides with me to my grandmother's. Our travel is awkwardly absent of words, but I haven't anything I wish to say. Nothing good, anyway.

When Phillip and I arrive in the Garden District, Grandma is standing on the porch, waiting. I rush up the steps and into her arms. Within her embrace, my body warms and calms. Her presence brings me comfort and a sense for a safer future.

CHAPTER THIRTY

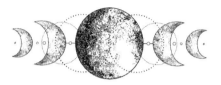

fter Phillip leaves, I take a too-long shower and then toss and turn my way to sleep. Sleep until I'm awakened by a pre-school call from Phillip. I'm still tired and I keep the call short. I tell him that even though it's the final day before winter break, I have decided to skip school. After the events of last night, I can't find it within myself to sit through hours of topics completely irrelevant to my current situation. So, we make plans to meet afterwards.

I doze for an additional hour past my normal school-day wakeup time. When I finally do rise, I savor a large mug of tea with Grandma and check in at the police precinct, give my statement. Tell the officer all about Caleb and the things I heard him say or saw him do.

My body and mind are a whirlwind of sensations... emotions. My heart jittery, my blood rushing, my skin perspiring.

I am a witch. A bloodline witch. Possibly, a powerful one, at that. Powerful enough that my ancestor wants control of my body, which I refuse to allow. Threatening enough that my mom's boyfriend tried to kill me. And reckless enough that I scarred my brother... dropped a house on him.

All my years, with my abilities suppressed, not learning how to use what I have... has it made me dangerous?

When I leave the police precinct, my mom and Belle are on their way in to give their own statements. I give Belle a warm hug... it appears I'm not the only one who decided to skip school... or work. I spare my mom a glance but say little to her. From the precinct, I cross the street and head toward the cemetery, feeling oddly drawn to the space. From the front entrance, I glance back and spy Mom watching me. I frown. Turn away. Step inside.

My steps take me through the cemetery maze as if I am in a haze, moving on automatic pilot. Maybe I am, maneuvering with a sense that isn't fully my own, but something hereditary, something magical.

The voice of a long-dead relative whispers in my ear. She may whisper to me from the many graves of those she has possessed over the years, graves located in various cemeteries, but the call at this location is the strongest. The hardest pull to ignore.

I wander deep into the city of the dead. Find myself taken to a collection of decrepit crypts. Some of the oldest existing within the boneyard. Names are gone. Any defined structure, crumbled.

Perched on top of the disintegrating grave is a black cat. The black cat I've seen in multiple locations. I'd all but swear that it is.

"Come here," I say to the kitty and scratch his chin. "Why are you following me?"

He purrs and rubs against my wrist.

"Is there a reason you keep showing up everywhere?" I pat his head and he meows. "If you insist on following me everywhere, I'll be forced to give you a name. How do you feel about that?" He meows again and pushes against my hand. "Alright then. I shall call you..." I tap my cheek. Names race through my mind, until they are all shoved away, aside from one. "Bastian," I say. He agrees with a purr.

"You are here. You could not help but come." The voice is strong at my ear. I jerk and spin. No one is there. "You have unpacked your power." Breath brushes the back of my neck. I whirl again. "The energy swells within you, and together we shall be quite formidable."

Together, she says. There will be no *together* that involves her and me.

Bastian hisses. Does he hear what I hear? Or can he see what I cannot? My nasty, pushy ancestor.

Even with my inherited gift unbound, she wants to control me. Maybe I can hold her off, but can I stop her from harassing me? I do not want to spend the rest of my days listening to her urging me, pushing me, endlessly nagging me.

My muscles tighten to an ache. I shiver and throw my hands up at my side. "You can't have me. You can't have any part of me... ever."

Lightning cracks through my skull, and all I see is dark purple with flashes of red. Intense prickles stab at my temples and a beefy thrust pushes against my forehead. My body wobbles and my senses tense.

My mind and soul struggle to maintain control against my dead ancestor. My systems shut down, and I am locked in an internal battle for my life. Where I am and how long I am there, slips from my consciousness.

The struggle unfolds with the sense of a passing lifetime.

"Miri?"

I jolt. Then shake. "No," I yelp, and my eyes pop open. I

spin toward the call of my name, my hands flaring firm before me.

Bricks explode from the tomb at my side. Fly into the walkway around me. Belle squeals and Mom shrieks. I blink the muddle in my head clear and grasp a firm hold on an in-the-now awareness.

"Oh my gosh! Are you alright?" I lurch forward, grab my mom. Her hand is clasped over a gash in her upper arm. "I don't know what happened," I say. "I'm so sorry."

"This is why you were bound," she says with a sneer. "You are dangerous. You have always been dangerous."

I step back from my mom, dropping my arms. My gaze swings to Belle. She sits on the ground, rubbing her head.

"Oh no! Did I hurt you?" I rush to her side.

"I'll be alright. Impressive display of power." Her face widens, and she nods toward the tomb.

"Yes, well..." I offer her my hand, and I help her to a stand. "The magic in my blood appears to be a bit of a wildcard."

"That's not always a bad thing." She gazes at her open palm, likely checking for blood. Thankfully, there is none.

"You are a danger to all those around you," Mom blurts. "You were unwise to unleash your nature."

I exchange a glance with Belle. She frowns and shakes her head. "I'm sorry," she whispers.

"Was there a reason you followed me over here?" I turn toward Mom.

"I..." Her gaze drifts from me, to the grave at my back, to Belle, and back to me. "I needed to know."

"What did you need to know?" I push.

"She wants to stifle your potential," the ancestral voice whispers. "She wants to prevent you from being who you are meant to be."

My shoulder tightens. "You have no power over me," I say.

252

Mom narrows her stare upon me. "What you have is evil and dangerous."

"You know what," I say and glance at Belle, dip my chin. "I'm sorry you think I'm evil. There isn't anything I can do about that. I am who I am, which is your daughter. I can't ever change that. But, until you are able to accept me for who and what I am, I think I'll stay with Grandma." I shift my gaze to Belle, press my lips tight, then turn and walk away.

I walk out of the cemetery and down the street. Bastian the cat follows me. We keep walking until we're climbing Grandma's porch and moving into the house. I introduce Bastian to Grandma and his new home. She welcomes him into the home as if he were an old familiar and she had been expecting him. We take a seat at the table, Bastian included, and discuss my future plans. Grandma scribbles a name, address, and phone number and hands it to me. Shortly after school lets out, Phillip calls, and we talk for several minutes. According to his father, Caleb is in custody, and the word is the new chief wants to make an example of him.

I seriously hope so.

I prepare for Phillip's arrival and update Grandma of my plans. Then I sit at the window and wait. Think of all the things... all the horrible things. I thought I wanted to experience the power that had been stifled deep within me, but that power unbound has only brought pain to those close to me. My magic scarred my brother. Buried him under a heap of a broken house. My unchecked ability threw bricks at my mom and cut her. Knocked my sister on her butt and gave her a large lump on her head. And then there is the voice, no longer confined to my nightmares.

Bastian curls up beside me and also watches the view beyond the window.

Phillip pulls up in front of the house on his motorcycle and waves to me through the window. I grab my bag from the chair at my side, rub Bastian, and spin toward the front door... and my grandma.

"I hope you understand," I say, throwing my arms around her, and hugging her tightly. "I just need to get away, if only for a couple of days." I step back. "Too much has happened. There's been too much bad mojo this last month that I need to come to terms with."

"I understand, dear. This is your journey, and you must see it through. I'll be here if you need me." She kisses my forehead. "I assume you are leaving me in charge of the cat's care until you return?"

"Please." I smile wide and squeeze my hands together.

She returns my smile and walks me to the door. A final goodbye to my grandma, and I dash down the front steps to meet Phillip. He hands me a helmet, and I climb onto the back of his bike.

"You ready? Just you, me, and the road?" he asks.

"Anywhere you want to go." I slip on my helmet and wrap my arms around him. "I only have one request."

"Request away," He says and starts the bike.

"I'd like to see a man about a little medicinal help." I say the word *help* with emphasis.

"You had better not be talking drugs, because I can't be down with that," he says.

"It's not drugs," I vow. How do I tell him the world of magic is real, and I'm seeped deep in it? I'm in need of a fix that holds my magic in check, as well as keeps the ancestral voice at bay?

Phillip revs the engine. "Okay then. I'm trusting you. Tell me where, and we are on our way there." I give him the slip of paper with the address my grandma wrote down.

We wave at my grandma, and he pulls away from the curb. Sets us on route for the next stage of my life. One without

Caleb and possibly without my mom. One with my magic not bound, but kept firmly in check, always. An escape with Phillip to clear the debris my mom has crammed in my head.

Today is the start of a new me. The power—my inherited witch abilities—thrums heartily in my blood, and I am not going to tap into it. I'm going to relinquish it for something better, something stronger. I shall be true to the soul relationships built on trust and love.

The End

Continue following the adventures of Miri and Belle in
Bewitching Belle
https://amzn.to/2QhpV7N

GIFTED GIRLS SERIES

To secure your Gifted Girls extras, various story peeks, and ensure notification when new stories are released, sign up for Debra Kristi's newsletter.
https://www.debrakristi.com/claim-your-free-gift/

Oh! And...
Follow *The Gifted Girls Series* on Facebook for witchy-inspired humor and spell-tip posts, as well as series shares and extras:
https://www.facebook.com/GiftedGirlsBookSeries /

FROM THE AUTHOR

Dear Reader,

I hope you enjoyed reading Magical Miri. This particular story flowed, rather quickly, onto the page with ease. The overarching story of the family will weave through five books, each of which will be told from the point of view of a different family member. All of which will release within the same year. I do so hope you follow along and enjoy the journey.

Also, I'd really, really love it if you would consider leaving a review. Not only do I love receiving feedback but reviews also help other readers find what they are looking for. It's the readers and reviewers who make up the foundation of our author world, and we love you madly for all you do!

Thanks! Until next time, keep the magic real.

~ Debra Kristi

MEET THE AUTHOR

Debra Kristi was born and raised a Southern California girl. She still resides in the sunny state with her husband, two kids, and several schizophrenic cats. Unlike many of the characters in the stories she writes, Debra is not immortal, and her only superpower is letting the dishes and laundry pile up.

When not busy drumming away at the keyboard, spinning new tales, Debra is hanging out, creating priceless memories with her family, geeking out to science fiction and fantasy television, and tossing around movie quotes.

Find me online and connect!
Discover more about me and my books on my website:
http://www.debrakristi.com/
And join me on my Facebook author page for updates, news, discussions, and more:
https://www.facebook.com/DebraKristi.writer/

ACKNOWLEDGMENTS

Thank you seems like too small of a word to sum up how everyone's contribution to this end product has been. Everyone listed, and so many more, have been instrumental in sustaining my sanity, increasing my productivity, or bettering my final product. Hugs to each of you. I couldn't have done it without you. If you are not listed here, it does not mean you are not appreciated. So many people touch my life each and every day, and every one of them is cherished more than a flying broom. This world, and the people in it, are constantly teaching me so very much!

Now for the roll call...

Eden Plantz, editor and friend. Thank you for believing in Nowhere Nara, and from that, helping me bring Magical Miri to life. Your faith in me and my work means more than you will ever know. Plus, I really dig your grammar fixes.

Ljiljana Romanovic (Moonchildljilja) for bringing the series to life with your magical artistic talent. And to think, it started with Nowhere Nara two years ago for a boxed set.

Finally, the time is here when all your work for this series will hit the bookshelves.

Rebecca Hamilton, not only for believing in me and my ability to tell a story but for giving of your time and talent to help me understand and learn the other side to the author business.

Leandra Savage who added some of Miri's wild adventures, through adventures of her own.

J.A. Culican for her help and guidance in launching the Gifted Girl series.

Lloyd Thompson-Taylor with Dragon Realm Press for the final proofread. Sorry I didn't keep all your recommendations. Though, technically correct, some of the requests were left unaltered for the sake of "author voice."

My extended family and friends, for all the amazing things you do. Street team peeps, you fall in this category.

It's been two years now, and I lost my records, but thank you, special team member (newsletter or street team) who named our pretty black cat. He shall be immortalized in the Gifted Girl Series.

Mom. Always my number one fan willing to share all my bookish posts. Love you!

Scott, for never swaying in his faith or pride in me. You are my forever mate.

My kids for putting up with my frustrations and lack of grocery runs. And for, also, stepping up and helping around the house so that I have a bit more time to play in my imaginary worlds.

My sister and father, watching me from above.

Made in the USA
Columbia, SC
06 March 2020

88811694R00167